NEW BEGINNINGS ON WHISLING ISLAND

JULIA CLEMENS

PICKLED PLUM PUBLISHING

CHAPTER ONE

GEN STOOD in the doorway of what used to be their guest room and leaned against the doorframe as she gazed over the room. It had been overrun by the color pink, and Gen wouldn't have it any other way.

There had been a day, once upon a time, when Gen had imagined this room would be the perfect space for her future son or daughter, and now it would be. This room was going to the sweet baby girl who would be coming home with her husband, Levi, in just a couple of hours. Although the baby girl was not biologically hers, that did nothing to tamp down the feelings of excitement in Gen's stomach.

She never would've expected that she could warm up to, and even excitedly anticipate, the idea of Maddie, the daughter of Levi and the woman he'd betrayed Gen with, moving into their home. But nothing about this experience had gone according to expectations, including the fact that after years of hard work and forgiveness, her marriage was now better than ever.

Sweet Maddie had just lost her mother in a battle with cancer, not something any two-year-old should have to endure.

Mal, Maddie's mother, had had to leave behind her greatest joy. Gen had no doubt Mal was in heaven now, watching over her precious daughter. But she also knew it couldn't have been easy for Mal to leave her heart behind. And Mal had left her heart with Gen.

After the week Mal and Maddie had spent in Gen and Levi's home, allowing Maddie to get to know the father she'd never met, Gen had visited Mal a few times. The first couple of visits were in Mal's home, which she'd shared with her parents, and that last one was rough. Mal was admitted to the hospital and knew she wouldn't be coming back out. The doctors hoped to be able to get her back home to spend her final moments with the ones she loved most, but Mal knew she wouldn't make it. It was something she'd confided in Gen.

Gen had held Mal's hand as she promised that she would love Maddie like her own. Mal never asked Gen to make sure Maddie remembered her. She only expressed her wishes that Maddie feel completely loved, not the hole that losing her mother could leave in her heart. Gen couldn't promise that she would fill that hole because she wasn't going to let a day go by without Maddie knowing how much her birth mother loved her, but Gen would love Mal's adorable little girl with all of her heart. It was impossible not to.

Maddie had taken residence in that vital love organ of Gen's the moment they'd first met. Gen had been wary of meeting the baby who was the product of a one-night affair between a drunk and heartbroken Levi and Mal, especially since Gen's own womb hadn't yielded her her own sweet baby. But Maddie hadn't allowed the wariness to stay. She opened her arms and heart to Gen immediately, and Gen couldn't help but do the same.

Maddie's origin no longer posed an issue when Gen felt the love that she did. Not to mention the fact that with getting to know Mal during her last days, any vestiges of anger Gen had felt toward the other woman were long gone. With Mal no longer the enemy, Gen had a peace and calm in her heart that hadn't been there in years.

And it was because of that peace and calm that she could stand in the doorway of that room and anticipate Maddie's arrival with only pleasure.

Gen knew it was going to be hard on the little girl whom she'd already come to think of as her own. Maddie had lived with her mother and grandparents her entire life because Mal didn't want to upset Levi's world by telling him he had a daughter. She knew Gen and Levi had worked through the marital issues that had been at the root of why Levi had strayed.

Gen and Levi had been somewhat separated at the time of the affair—a distraught Gen, who had just lost her second invitro pregnancy, had kicked Levi out of their home, saying she wanted a divorce. He'd tried to come back every night for two weeks, but each time she'd told him to never come back. So he'd gone to a bar, gotten drunk, and gone home with a woman he'd met that night.

Gen eventually asked Levi to come home, and as soon as she would listen, Levi came clean. Although the couple had been in a gray area, Levi's actions were still infidelity and betrayal, so they'd had to work through that. And they had.

Mal hadn't wanted to disrupt that happiness, but when she found out about her illness, she felt she needed to alert Levi of the truth. She didn't feel right leaving her daughter parentless when there was a man who would be an amazing dad if just given the chance.

And boy was Levi an excellent father. Gen had dreamed of the day Levi would take their child into his arms and throw a little girl or boy in the air. The child would scream and giggle with delight, asking Levi not to stop. And Maddie had done just that. Many times. Gen waited for an ache to fill her chest that it wasn't her child being flung in the air by Levi, but it never came. And that was when Gen knew; Maddie was hers. And she would be forever.

Gen's phone buzzed, and she looked down to see a text from Levi. *On our way home.*

Home. This was to be Maddie's home now that her mother was no longer on this earth. The last week had been a heavy one with the passing of a woman whom Gen had come to admire and her subsequent funeral. Gen sat in the back row, allowing Levi to be the only one to support their Maddie in the front row with Mal's parents. To Gen, it only seemed right, even though all involved had asked her to join them. But that day was for Maddie and Mal's parents to mourn. It didn't seem right for Gen to join them in their grieving. She, a woman who had hated Mal for so long, even if those feelings of malice were no longer in her heart. Levi insisted that Maddie stay with Mal's parents on the night after the funeral, but it was now the next day, and it was time for Maddie to come home.

Gen pressed a hand to her queasy stomach. The dang thing had been upset for over a month now. At first, Gen had blamed it on the grief of knowing her husband had had a child with another woman. But Gen had worked through that grief, and still, the turning in her stomach remained. Maybe today's queasiness could be blamed on anxiety that Maddie was coming to live with them for good. Even though Gen was thrilled at the prospect, it didn't stop her from wondering if Mal had made the right call. Gen had never been a mom. Would she be able to step up to the plate? Be enough for a girl who had already been through so much? Gen didn't know. But she was sure as heck going to give it all she had.

Gen stepped into the room and brushed imaginary wrinkles out of the pink bedspread she'd chosen with her friend, Olivia.

Olivia had two little girls, and Gen could think of no one better to lead her into the world of raising Maddie. Olivia had basically raised Rachel and Pearl on her own since her ex-husband hadn't been a present father. Gen was grateful that even if she lacked in the mom department, she would have Levi by her side every step of the way.

As Gen sat in the white rocker she'd placed in the corner of the room next to a pink bookshelf full of her own childhood favorites, she thought about how far she and Levi had come in such a short time.

She remembered the moment he'd come into her office that morning, and before he'd said a word, she'd known something was wrong. But she'd vowed then and there to stand by the man she loved. The man who loved her. With all of his heart. Through all of this mess, Gen had never doubted that. Levi had made a terrible drunken mistake that he couldn't ever take back, but Gen had to own that she'd pushed him away. And although he was fully to blame for the extent of his actions, Gen wanted to forgive him. It was because of his pain that he'd gotten so drunk that night. He'd handled it all wrong, but she knew he still loved her. Crazy as that may seem. And she still loved him.

So they'd worked through the pain, man that had been an uphill battle, and they'd dug down to the heart of their problems. Working through it hadn't been easy, but sitting in that rocker, waiting for her husband to bring home their baby girl? Gen had to admit it had been worth it.

Gen's stomach turned again, and this time she had to rush to the nearest bathroom, losing the little bit of breakfast she'd been able to get down that morning. As she sat back up and leaned against the bathroom wall behind her, Gen caught sight of her box of tampons. Since the tampons were in the guest bathroom, Gen hadn't noticed them out. And it wasn't until now that she realized just how long it'd been since she'd needed them. She'd been so overwhelmed by the Maddie, Mal, and Levi situation that, until that moment, she'd forgotten what she'd been thinking before Levi had entered her office on that fateful day. Minutes earlier, she'd realized her period was late. But then Levi had revealed Mal's confession about Maddie, and life had gotten away from her.

But she still hadn't gotten her period. That meant she'd completely missed her period at least once. If she wasn't wrong, she was actually due for a second period soon.

Hope immediately swelled in her chest, a feeling that had happened all too often over the years. How many times had her period been a week or even two late, and Gen had been sure this was finally it? But time after time, the tests had read negative, only to cause Gen's heart to plummet from the stratosphere of hope right back down to earth.

But this wasn't just a week or two late. Gen jumped up and ran to her phone to look at her period tracking app. She hadn't updated the app in over a month; she'd been too busy with all of the Mal and Maddie stuff. But she knew she'd recorded the dates of her last period. Her hands shook as she opened the app and looked at the dates. Sure enough, her last period had been in early May. It was now early July. Gen was nearly two months late.

This was a first, but her lateness could be due to all of the stress on her body, right? In just a short while, she'd learned that her husband had a daughter with another woman, that the mother was terminally ill, and that she and her husband would be raising the baby as their own. She'd also helped her sister, Bess, open her food truck, not to mention she'd continued running her busy hair salon through all of this. Maybe the stress had gotten to her? Or maybe Gen was just getting older. She'd be celebrating her thirty-eighth birthday in less than a month. Could she already be going through menopause?

That thought shot down her balloon of hope in a hurry. If she was in the early stages of menopause, that meant that not only was Gen not pregnant now, it would never happen for her. Maddie had filled Gen's heart to brimming with joy, but she knew she was still holding out a tiny hope that she'd be able to give Maddie a sibling.

However, menopause would kill that dream. Unless they adopted more children? Gen had always been wary of adoption because her heart was already on such a roller coaster with trying to conceive. She'd heard horror stories of mothers being moments from taking their babies into their arms, only to have the birth moms renege on their agreements.

But Gen had also heard several happy stories of families who'd only found completeness after adoption. With conventional ways of growing their family no longer available, would Gen be ready to take on the road to adoption? She wasn't sure. She guessed she should allow herself a moment to grieve her first dream before finding a second one.

What about the vomiting? A little voice reminded her that it wasn't just the lack of a period that had alerted her to the fact that something might be up with her body. What about the queasy stomach? The nearly once-a-day vomiting?

And she had been peeing a whole lot more as well. She'd even had to have some of the other stylists in her salon cover for her during a hair wash or blow dry so that she could run to the bathroom. She'd never had to do that before.

But she wasn't craving any weird food and—Gen stopped. She was going to drive herself insane with all of this back and forth.

Gen pushed off the wall of her guest bathroom, resolved to do all she could do in that moment. She hurried down the hall to the master bedroom and then into the master bathroom. She rummaged through her cabinet under her sink, knowing she still had a couple of pregnancy tests that hadn't been used. She pushed past her hair dryer, curling iron, straightener and several hair products to get to the pink box in the back of the cabinet.

There had been a time when Gen had taken one of these tests daily. She thought about the hundreds, maybe even thousands, of dollars she'd wasted on these tests over the years. It was part of the reason why they were so far back in her cabinet now. About eighteen months before, she'd told herself no more. No more taking a test because she might've felt a twinge of heartburn. No more taking a test because she felt a little sick to her stomach after eating an entire burrito. No more taking a test because it was five days before her period and the test said that was the soonest it could pick up on the pregnancy hormone. No more coordinating her entire life to revolve around a possibility that very well might never happen. And Levi had sweetly supported her as she'd shoved the box back into the hair product abyss with tears rolling down her cheeks. He'd pulled her into a hug and then carried her to the couch, reminding her that he loved her body no matter what and making her feel treasured when she'd felt useless moments before.

Gen checked the expiration date on the box—it wasn't until next month—and then pulled out the pink-wrapped test. She tore the wrapper away to reveal the white stick that had been her nemesis for so many years. She put the box away, not needing directions on how to take the test, and then stared at the stick. What if it was negative? Did that mean Gen would never carry a child? Was this the end of the road?

But what if it wasn't negative?

Gen swallowed, pushing as much emotion aside as she could, and then peed on the stick. She set it on a piece of toilet paper and then looked at the clock in her room. She had three minutes until the test would tell her anything.

Gen paced the small space of the bathroom back and forth

eight times before realizing she would make herself dizzy if she continued to do that for the next three minutes. She moved to her bed and stared across the room at the test.

What if there were two lines? What if there was one? There had been moments in her marriage when she'd wondered if she and Levi would come to their demise as a couple at the same time Gen's chances for having a baby ended. But after years of talking and lots of therapy, Gen truly believed Levi was in this marriage for better and worse. Because those two often happened at once. There was no *or* about it.

So she'd have Levi forever. No matter what the test read. And now she had Maddie. Sweet Maddie who had given her a new lease on her mother heart. The heart that had been slowly dying until Maddie had come into her life. Gen was going to be a mother. She was a mother. She had already vowed to step up to the role. So did this test matter so much?

Maybe not as much as it might've even a couple months before. But it still mattered. Gen couldn't lie to herself and say it didn't. One child was a blessing, a miracle for her. But if she could have two? That would be the greatest blessing of all.

Gen looked up at the clock. How had only one minute passed? She knew she had to stop watching the test.

She got up and walked into her closet where she noticed a pile of clothing on the ground. Gen wasn't the messiest person around, but she also wasn't the neatest. It was a big part of why Levi had constructed a second closet in their master bedroom, one of the many perks of being married to a contractor. Levi was the neatest person Gen knew, and he hated the way she threw her clothing on the ground as she tried to decide what to wear. But how was one to have enough time to try on several outfits and get out the door promptly without leaving everything on the floor? So they'd compromised with Gen getting to leave her floordrobe (wardrobe on the floor) in her closet, while Levi could go on living in his world of neatness.

Gen began to gather up the black dresses and skirts on the floor, hanging each back up. This was the mess left over from the funeral. Time had moved deceptively since she'd met Mal, sometimes going slow and other times too fast. The last two days had moved along at a snail's pace, and Gen couldn't believe the black clothes were from just the day before.

She hung up three dresses, a blouse and two skirts before checking the time again. Thankfully, the large clock in her room had a second hand telling Gen there were just thirty seconds left. She walked slowly out of her closet and past her dusty blue duvet that covered her and Levi's king-sized bed. She pushed her way passed the walnut-finished dresser that matched the nightstands on either side of their bed, as well as the shelves Levi had mounted on their walls that held many of Gen's favorite books along with knickknacks they'd collected over the years.

Gen stopped at the door to her bathroom, looking from the gray carpet of her bedroom to the white subway tile of her bathroom floor. Her gaze lifted past the walnut cabinets to the white travertine countertop that held the white stick.

Thirty seconds and more had passed. It was time for Gen to look at the stick.

She took a few steps forward and stopped when her stomach hit the countertop.

Gen gazed in the mirror and looked at her reflection, not quite able to look at the test. The woman who looked back at her held hope in her big brown eyes. Looking at that test could cause the hope to die. Could Gen do that to herself?

But then again, could she not check?

No. That wasn't realistic.

Gen drew in a deep breath. This didn't have to mean

anything. Just because she wasn't pregnant didn't mean she was going through menopause. This didn't have to be the end. And she would always have Levi and Maddie.

She gulped and then picked up the test before she could chicken out. It had to be done.

Gen covered most of the test with her hand, exposing only one pink line. There was always one line that worked as a control line on every test. It was the second line that would tell her everything. Gen allowed her hand and then her eyes to move. She caught a hint of more pink.

It couldn't be, could it? Gen had taken so many tests, squinted at them just praying she'd see that second line.

But today there was no squinting needed. As Gen's eyes began to fill with tears, she knew what they'd seen. Two very clear pink lines. Gen fell to her knees as she let out a prayer of gratitude.

Gen was pregnant.

CHAPTER TWO

DEB HURRIED up the path to her best friend, Bess's, home, ready to take the next step in her life. Bess had been busy with the opening weeks of her new food truck, but she'd finally decided to hire another cook so that she could have the evenings off. Bess had been on her feet working from at least eight am to nine pm every day for the first few weeks, and even if she hadn't been at the age where some were already thinking about retirement, it would've been a rough schedule. Deb and Olivia, Bess's finance woman, along with Gen, Bess's sister, had staged an intervention and told Bess that she couldn't do it all. Bess had thankfully taken their words to heart and finally closed the food truck for an evening to interview a couple of promising cooks, hiring one on the spot.

Alexis, the new cook, was just out of culinary school and had come home to Whisling Island to find that her laidback style of cooking didn't match with the restaurants on the island. She'd heard about Bess's truck and had begged her mother, one of Bess's high school classmates, to get her an interview. It had taken Bess all of fifteen minutes to figure out Alexis was the perfect addition to the truck, and before the hour was out, Bess was teaching Alexis some of the truck's patrons' favorite recipes.

Bess had been able to cut down her hours from all day to basically six hours between eight am and two pm, depending on the lunch rush. So now Deb was able to have her best friend back. Not that that was the reason she'd helped to persuade Bess to take a step back from her food truck, but it was a nice perk.

Deb opened the door to her friend's home—she'd gotten a key many years before and didn't hesitate to use it—and stopped by Bess's kitchen to find something to munch on before joining Bess in her living room.

Bess sat looking out her window at the cove she loved so much when Deb came into the living room and joined Bess on the couch.

Deb took a bite of the chicken pasta she'd nabbed from the kitchen and moaned.

"How is this so good?" Deb asked.

Bess grinned. "It's the smoked chicken. Alexis's idea," Bess said like a proud mama.

"Well, it's insanely delicious," Deb said, and Bess nodded.

"We're going to try it as the special on the truck tomorrow. I'm pretty sure we'll sell out before closing," Bess said.

This time Deb nodded. That wouldn't surprise her. "Are you enjoying your time off?" Deb asked.

Bess shrugged. "I know it's good for my body and even my mental state to not be running like a chicken with her head cut off all the time, but is it weird that I miss the truck?" Bess asked.

Deb grinned. "No, it's not. But Alexis has it covered," she said.

"I know. She's incredible. I'm lucky to have her."

"Aren't there things you've been putting off that now you can get to? Like calling your kids?" Deb asked.

"I already called them all," Bess said as she turned to Deb.

"Stephen was about to run into another interview, Liz was in the middle of work, and James didn't answer. I know his classes this semester have been pretty demanding."

"Hmm," Deb said, knowing she needed to find a way to keep her friend busy or Bess would run right back to her truck. And Bess needed this daily break.

"I already closed the truck on Mondays, so I was able to use that day to get everything done in my personal life that I needed to. There isn't much left for me to do around here ..." Bess said as she gazed around the spotless room. "Even though dinner isn't as busy as lunch, I'm sure Alexis could use my help." Bess shifted in her seat, and Deb knew where this was going.

"You've worked out a great schedule, Bess. And if you go back to the truck now, it will look like you don't trust Alexis," Deb said, knowing it was a little bit of a low blow to bring Alexis's feelings into this. But Bess needed the break. She'd been running herself ragged, keeping too busy, especially since she'd finally signed her divorce papers.

Deb, Olivia, and Gen had known Bess could only run at that pace for so long. Sure it felt fulfilling in the moment ... until she broke.

Deb wouldn't let her friend break, especially after the year they'd both had. Deb's husband, Rich, had left her for his mistress in London, and although Bess's cheating husband, Jon, hadn't had nearly the secrets Deb's ex had, Jon wasn't much better. He'd cheated on Bess with his student aide and had almost lost his job on top of losing his wife of thirty years. Bess had picked up the pieces of her life one by one and even built this food truck from the ground up. Bess was as strong as women came, but even the strongest could break.

"I know," Bess groaned, leaning back into her couch. "But I'm bored, Deb."

Deb laughed at her friend's admission.

"Well, you won't be for long. Because I've made a decision," Deb said, sitting up and setting her now empty plate on Bess's coffee table.

"Oh yeah?" Bess said, looking over at Deb with piqued interest.

"Yup. I'm going to get back in the saddle," Deb said.

Bess raised an eyebrow in confusion and then let it drop. "Wait, you mean you're going to date?" Bess asked, her eyes going wide.

"Better than that. I'm going to set up an online dating profile," Deb said.

Bess shook her head. "No," she groaned as she stood, taking Deb's plate into the kitchen with her. "That can't be smart for women our age, can it?"

Bess turned back to Deb who had followed her into the homey room which boasted blue and white wallpaper and a kitchen table that could seat twelve. Bess had decorated her home with entertaining in mind—she loved having her home full of the people she loved—and her kitchen reflected that well. The island that sat in the middle of her kitchen allowed seating for eight more, and the brightness of the white and tan marbled countertops along with the large window above her sink let in lots of light and warmth, even on the coldest days.

"I'm not going to start swiping left or right or anything like that," Deb said, mentioning the action of one of the dating sites her son was on. She would never join a site that could possibly host her college-aged children. But there were other sites. Sites more appropriate for someone her age. "But if I wait to date the real-life way, I may never get another date again. Do you know how many eligible bachelors are on the island?" Deb asked, and Bess shook her head.

It didn't surprise Deb that Bess had yet to appraise her *new man* possibilities. Bess hadn't moved on as much as Deb had, although Bess had discovered her husband's cheating before Deb had found out the man she'd shared her life with was also a scoundrel.

"Two. There are two eligible bachelors. And I don't know how eligible they are considering you're related to one of them—"

"Who?" Bess interrupted.

"Your cousin, Daly," Deb said as Bess burst out laughing.

"Daly is considered eligible?" Bess asked about her cousin who'd had an interesting relationship with the law his entire adult life.

"I told you the pickings are slim," Deb reiterated.

Bess nodded. "Evidently. Wait, you wouldn't date Daly would you?" Bess asked, pulling her head back in disbelief.

"No," Deb said with a roll of her eyes. "I was making a point that I have to stretch my borders if I want to date again."

"Thus this online stuff," Bess said.

Deb nodded. "I don't want to be alone forever. Do you?" she asked Bess.

Bess sat watching Deb for a moment too long. "Well, I'm not alone. I have you, my kids, Gen, Olivia, and now Alexis."

"Yes," Deb said slowly. "But don't you want more?"

Deb knew that she did. She had imagined forever with Rich and now ... well, Rich wasn't even close to being an option for her, so she had to move on. Maybe that was Bess's issue. Maybe she still held out hope that Jon would end up back in her life? Wait, Bess didn't want Jon back, did she? Deb thought they'd moved beyond that since Bess finally pulled the trigger on her divorce.

"I don't know," Bess said. Deb knew Bess was answering her questions vulnerably and honestly, so she wasn't going to jump into that slight opening to push Bess into joining an online dating site with her. But hopefully Bess would be ready to move on one day. She deserved a love that lasted a lifetime.

"Are you still holding out hope for Jon?" Deb asked in the most nonjudgmental voice she could muster. She knew she usually erred on the side of being too brash, but her friend needed her to be a little more sensitive right now. Deb could manage that for Bess.

"No. I don't think so," Bess amended. "I divorced him."

Deb nodded.

"But ..." Bess let that one word hang out there, and Deb had to say one last piece on the subject before moving on.

"Bess," Deb said. She could already see her friend hunching her shoulders and going into the defensive, the last thing Deb wanted. "I know I've been very vocal about this."

Bess spit out a laugh.

"But if you're happy, I'm happy. I promise."

Bess's shoulders relaxed.

"I need a promise from you, though," Deb said, and Bess eyed her hesitantly.

"Just promise me that whatever decision you make for yourself, it's because it's what *you* want. Not because you are worried about Jon's needs or because life will be easier for your kids if their parents are back together. Or worse yet, because you're afraid dating someone new would disrupt the lives of those you love. Bess, you deserve every happiness, including fulfilling your dream of having a man to share it all with. I know that's what you've always wanted. Jon filled that place in your dream for a long time, but just because plan A didn't work out the way you imagined doesn't mean plan B can't be everything you wished and more. Don't settle before you give plan B a chance."

Bess's eyes glistened with unshed tears. "That may have been the sweetest thing you've ever said to me."

"And I meant every word," Deb said brusquely, uncomfortable with so much emotion. "Now let's get back to the reason I'm here."

"Your online dating profile," Bess said as she pulled her laptop closer which had been at the other end of the couch.

"Yup," Deb said popping her *p*. She was grateful she'd said what she needed to, but now she was ready to find herself a date ... or seven.

Bess opened her laptop, setting it on the coffee table in front of her. "So which site?" Bess asked, staring at her home screen.

Deb rattled off the name of the one Doug had suggested to her. It might seem like a weird recommendation to get from one's divorce attorney, but Deb figured if anyone had experience with newly single people, it was Doug. Besides, since they'd dated many, many years before, Deb trusted Doug in a way that she didn't trust most.

Bess typed in the URL, and the page that came up on her computer showed a picture of happy couples who looked to be in their late thirties to late sixties. This was exactly the kind of place Deb needed.

Deb grinned as she stole the computer away from Bess and began scrolling through what she could. She stopped at the page that showed the cost of membership.

"Eighty dollars?" Bess exclaimed, leaning in to read the fine print. "A month?!"

Deb laughed. "Can you really put a price on true love?" she asked, even though the last thing she was looking for in that moment was true love. She hoped to find it down the road, but as long as she got a few dates with attractive men who found her equally attractive, she'd be pleased. She wasn't about to lie to herself and say that losing her husband to a younger, beautiful flight attendant hadn't done a number on her ego. She needed to pump that thing back up.

"Yes. Apparently it costs eighty dollars. A month," Bess said, and Deb had to once again laugh at the incredulous look on her friend's face.

She only stopped to begin filling in the personal information on the site. Her name, age, hair and eye color. Were all of these questions going to be about her physical appearance? But just as Deb thought the concern, the questions on the page changed to asking about her political affiliation, her religion, and what she found important in relationships.

"Wowie gazowie that's a whole lot of questions," Bess said as Deb continued to scroll.

Deb nodded as she kept her concentration on the page. She wanted to get these just right. She wasn't going to pay eighty bucks a month to have a website give her the wrong match.

Bess stood, but Deb was too into her questionnaire to even notice that her friend had gone.

When Deb felt the couch beside her move upon Bess's return, she looked over to see that Bess had a plate of cookies.

"Sustenance. Good idea," Deb said as she swiped a cookie and went back to typing.

Bess leaned in to read over Deb's shoulder as she bit into a warm chocolate chip cookie of her own.

"You do not like baseball," Bess said as she pointed to the question Deb had answered about her favorite American pastime.

"I do," Deb said defensively. "Besides, how many other American pastimes are there?"

"It is a weird question for a dating profile, but picnics, fireworks, and swimming in lakes come to mind," Bess offered.

Deb shook her head. "You just named things that one could do on the Fourth of July," Deb said.

"Yes, American pastimes," Bess said.

"Every Regency novel I've read has included a picnic," Deb

said as she typed the answer to how she felt about furry animals. *Love them.*

"And?" Bess asked, obviously missing Deb's point.

"So picnics are clearly more than American," Deb said. "And have you watched Pride and Prejudice? Mr. Darcy definitely did *swimming in lakes* justice as well. While fireworks originated in China. None of those are American pastimes."

"Baseball is played in other countries," Bess said.

"But it started here, didn't it?" Deb asked.

Bess shrugged. "I have no idea. Jon and Stephen are the baseball lovers, not me," Bess said about her ex and first born.

"Well, it doesn't matter. I want a guy who will match with me when I say baseball. That was the answer my gut told me, so I have to go with it," Deb said as she reread the question in front of her. Were they really asking her if she had a fear of snakes?

"Even if you hate baseball?" Bess asked.

"I don't hate baseball," Deb said.

"I am going to quote you from last summer when you came over during the World Series. *I hate baseball,*" Bess said, and Deb chuckled.

"I just said that to get a rise out of Jon," Deb said with a grin.

"Well, it worked."

"I know." Deb beamed as she went for another cookie. "Besides, Rich hates baseball."

Bess was quiet for too long, so Deb paused her question answering to look at her friend.

"What?" Deb asked when it was obvious Bess was waiting to say more.

"Are you answering the questions the way you want to? Or are you making sure you don't get a Rich?" Bess asked.

Deb looked back at Bess's computer. "Both," she said matter of factly. "I want to answer the questions in a way that will keep me from getting a Rich."

With Bess's calm, zen way of approaching life, there was no way she could understand the anger Deb felt for Rich every day. Deb wanted to be rid of it but wasn't sure how. The man had not only cheated on her and then lied about it, he'd started a new home with a new woman while Deb had been waiting for him. He'd made a fool of her while shredding their vows and her trust to pieces. She hated that man, which wasn't good considering he was still the father of her children. So Deb hoped that moving on would help to temper some of the boiling anger she woke up with every morning. She hoped she could one day think about the father of her children without wanting to kill him.

"Deb ..." Bess said in her tone that told Deb she expected her to be more mature than petty. But this wasn't petty. This was saving herself from future headaches and, if she really let herself be honest, heartbreak.

"Bess, I've got this under control," Deb said as she scrolled through her pictures that she'd emailed herself. "Well, not this part though. Which pictures do I choose?"

Bess looked at the screen and easily pointed out three. One of Deb at her most recent art show, another of Deb on the beach, and one with Deb and her kids.

"I don't know that I want the kids' faces on a dating site," Deb said as she evaluated the pictures. Bess had chosen ones where Deb was doing what she loved while looking pretty dang great, if she did say so herself.

"Blur their faces, but these guys need to know you're a package deal," Bess said, and Deb knew her friend was right.

Deb went to upload the photos and then waited for the process to finish, leaning back on the couch and feeling better about her future than she had in a long time. She wasn't foolish enough to think that she'd find her dream guy immediately, but

Deb was on the road to getting Rich and his memory out of her home, heart, and life.

"As easy as that?" Bess asked when the screen changed to half a dozen photos of men. "Wait, he's handsome." Bess pointed at the last photo, and Deb smiled. He was handsome.

"As easy as that," Deb said, clicking on Mr. Handsome. She was about to make a match with someone new.

CHAPTER THREE

OLIVIA UNFOLDED the flaps on the final box in her bedroom. She'd finished unpacking the girls first and then moved on to the combined spaces like the living room, kitchen, and bathroom. It was a little strange that she was sharing a single bathroom with both of her girls *and* any guests that came over. But Olivia couldn't afford more than a two bedroom, one bathroom place on the island of Whisling. Real estate prices were through the roof, and she knew she was lucky to even secure this kind of space. Lucky, and she had the kindest landlord on the island.

After Olivia's divorce had been finalized, she'd had a few choices for what she could do next, as far as housing. Her parents had been marvelous, but Olivia had mooched off them for more than long enough. She needed to move out on her own. Thanks to her attorney, Olivia had gotten an amazing settlement along with monthly child support and alimony. The latter two, along with Olivia's job working for Bess doing her bookkeeping for her food truck, were enough to cover the daily cost of living on Whisling along with rent for their new beach bungalow.

Olivia could've dug into her settlement and spent more day to day, but she knew it was smart to invest that chunk of money and live well within her means for the time being. She knew she wanted to buy a home for her girls eventually but decided it was best to make a little more and have a bigger nest egg before taking the leap into homeownership.

"You're so stupid!" Rachel shouted, and Olivia knew her box would have to wait.

She hurried into the living room to see Rachel standing with the remote control for the TV high above her head and Pearl jumping to get at it. The latter got smart and hopped up onto the couch, yanking the remote away.

"I'm not stupid. You're stupid!" Pearl retaliated as she held out the remote like a trophy.

Olivia shook her head.

Part of her wanted to crawl back into her room and hope that her girls figured this out on their own. Her daughters had always fought, but their fighting had only intensified since leaving Olivia's parents' home. It had been her and the girls' refuge after leaving her husband, Bart, six months before. Olivia knew the girls were having a tough time coming to terms with their new living arrangement. They'd gone from living in a mansion on one end of the island to a smaller home on the other, but they'd been blessed with immense love from their grandparents.

Now, even though they'd landed on the same street as Olivia's parents, they were away from both places of security, and Olivia couldn't blame her girls for acting out because of their fears. But couldn't they learn to work together? Didn't they get that few bonds were stronger than that of sisters?

"Girls!" Olivia finally got up the energy to intervene. It felt like she was refereeing fights all day and night. The only reprieve she got was while she was at work or the girls were at school.

"Yes, Mama?" Rachel turned her attention to their mother with a sweet look on her face that was nothing like the scrunched-up resentment she'd been wearing moments before.

Pearl, unlike her sister, was unable to hide her fury, and when she turned to Olivia, she still wore the same wrath she'd been throwing at her sister. Pearl's lips were pursed tightly and her eyes were narrowed, nothing like the big blue eyes and bright smile Rachel was shining at their mother. It wasn't a wonder it was hard for them to get along. They were yin and yang at its best ... and worst.

"What did I say about the word *stupid*?" Olivia asked, and Pearl somehow narrowed her eyes further as Rachel shrugged her shoulders.

"Rachel?" Olivia said, expecting an answer. She'd warned about the phrase enough times to know both girls could repeat the way she felt, word for word.

"It's not something we say to someone we love," Rachel said, now pouting alongside Pearl.

"So why did you say it?" This time Olivia turned to Pearl.

"She said it first!" Pearl pointed an accusing finger at her sister.

"You said it second!" Rachel turned to yell at her sister.

Olivia drew in a deep breath. This was going nowhere.

"What happened?" Olivia figured she could maybe get a little backstory and begin to work things out from there.

"I wanted to watch TV, and when I was about to grab the remote, Rachel took it and wouldn't let me have it," Pearl said.

"Rachel?" Olivia said after hearing Pearl's side of the story.

"She wants to visit Dad," Rachel said, and Olivia nearly fell back at the words. That, she had not been expecting.

"What?" Olivia asked. She knew she'd have to come up with

something better to say soon, but she was still reeling. Besides, what did one thing have to do with the other?

"Pearl said she misses Dad and wants to see him. I told her that was dumb because Dad doesn't love us anymore. He loves his new baby. Pearl said he still loves us, and then she said she wanted to watch TV," Rachel said.

Olivia could see her daughter was on the verge of tears. "Your father loves both of you so much," Olivia said, needing her girls to know that. Even if Bart did a crap job of showing it, Olivia knew somewhere deep down he loved his girls.

"Then why don't we see him?" Rachel asked. "He divorced us."

Olivia swallowed hard. How had she missed how much her girls were picking up on? She'd assumed because they hadn't asked for their dad, they hadn't really noticed his absence in their lives. But just because he hadn't been around much while Bart and Olivia were married didn't mean they wouldn't miss him at all. Olivia had been such a fool.

"He divorced me, Rachel. Not you and your sister. You both will always be your daddy's girls," Olivia said, smoothing things over the way she'd tried to the whole time she'd been married. How many times had Bart not come home for a weekend and Olivia had had to tell her girls their dad had to work but still loved them? It had been a long time since it had seemed like they cared where Bart was or what he was doing. But of course they cared. He was their father.

Rachel shook her head in disbelief. Her daughter knew and saw too much to take Olivia's words at face value anymore. When had her little girl become this big girl who understood so much?

"I know. And I think he misses us. We should go see him," Pearl said, seeming to be completely unaffected by the emotions overtaking Rachel. How could both girls come from the same womb, be raised in the same home, and be so different?

"He doesn't miss us, Pearl!" Rachel said too loudly.

"Yes, he does. He wants to see us!" Pearl turned to shout at her sister, Olivia long forgotten.

Olivia longed to agree with Pearl and put her girls' minds at ease, but Olivia hadn't talked to Bart since their divorce. She had no idea what he wanted because she felt like she no longer had to care since they were no longer married. But for her girls, she needed to get to the bottom of this. Bart had given up full custody easily, but he hadn't meant to sever his relationship with his daughters, had he? Olivia hoped not.

She'd kept her girls away from him for the time being because she figured it was best for them. A new type of relationship with their father along with all of the other changes in life would've been confusing. But why had Olivia thought no relationship would work? Maybe it was because that was what she wanted so badly. But both of her girls were hurting. And it was Olivia's fault.

"Mom, tell her," Rachel demanded, and Olivia knew she had to ease tensions along with not promising too much. Bart was the most selfish man she knew, and he could possibly not care to see his daughters again. She hoped in her heart that that wasn't the truth, but she just couldn't know. If there wasn't something in it for Bart, he hardly ever stepped up to the plate. It made him an excellent businessman but a worthless husband. However, Olivia needed to put her feelings aside and figure a way to work this out for the sake of her daughters.

"I'm going to be honest with you, girls. I don't know what your father wants. I know he loves you." Olivia still felt like she could be honest in saying that. Bart did love his girls. Just not in the way a normal man would. He was happy to send them the money they needed; she knew he had set aside a trust fund for each of them. But just because he loved them didn't mean he would want to carve time out of his day for them, especially if it meant added parenting work for him. Bart was a complicated man, and Olivia, with her choice in marrying Bart, had created a complicated life for her girls. It wasn't fair. "But we all know how busy he is."

"Too busy for us," Rachel said.

"I didn't say that," Olivia responded, making eye contact with her eldest.

Rachel bit her lip as she waited for her mom to say more. Pearl watched Olivia with wary eyes. Olivia needed to say the right thing.

"I'm going to call him and see what his schedule looks like. We'll do our best to find some time for you to spend with him," Olivia said.

"Can we go this weekend?" Pearl asked. Confidence that her question would be answered in the affirmative shone bright in her eyes.

"Um," Olivia hesitated to promise anything.

"Lacey's mom and dad are divorce," Pearl said.

"Divorced," Rachel corrected harshly, and Pearl shot her an evil eye.

"Divorced," Pearl said smiling because she knew she'd gotten the word right. "And Lacey sleeps at her mom's house on Monday, Tuesday, Wednesday, and Thursday, and then she goes to her dad's house the other days. We could do that," Pearl said happily, sure she'd found a solution to their problem.

If only it were that easy. If only Bart were like Lacey's dad.

"But I would miss you so much if you were gone all of those days," Olivia said, pulling both of her girls into a hug. Why had she done this to them?

No, Bart was doing this. Olivia would love for the man to want a real relationship with his daughters. Olivia may not have advocated for it, but that was because he'd made it obvious during their marriage that he didn't need one. So Olivia hadn't pushed when it seemed like her girls were happy without it too. Olivia had been trying to do what was best. Olivia often let her guilt be her first guide, but that helped no one, as her therapist had pointed out time and time again.

"Then we could go on just Saturday," Pearl offered from within the hug.

"I'll talk do your dad. We'll figure something out." Olivia said what she could promise.

Rachel pulled away from the hug. "He didn't even come home on weekends to see us when we lived with him, Mom." Olivia swore the girl was ten going on twenty. How did she remember and notice so much?

"I'm sure he misses you, Rach." Okay, that may have been a bit of a lie. Olivia wasn't exactly sure of that, but she really did hope so.

"Tell him what Lacey's mom and dad does," Pearl suggested.

"He won't care, Pearl," Rachel said, but Olivia shook her head at Rachel.

"I will tell him, Pearl," Olivia said, and Pearl nodded happily.

"I don't want to see him," Rachel said.

Olivia closed her eyes before responding to her daughter. Now what was she going to do? It wasn't fair to push Rachel into this if she wasn't ready. Olivia needed to be patient with her girls' needs.

"You don't?" Olivia asked. Rachel deserved to have a say in this.

Rachel shook her head.

"Are you sure? Or are you just mad at him right now? Maybe by the time we arrange a time for you to see him—?"

Rachel shook her head again, the gleam in her eyes telling Olivia she was adamant.

"I'll talk to your dad. We'll see what he says. And then you can make your decision. I promise not to force you to see him, but you have to promise me you'll really think about it," Olivia said.

Rachel glared at Olivia, but Olivia didn't back down. "Fine," Rachel said as she fell back onto the couch with her arms folded.

"You'll want to see Dad. It'll be fun," Pearl said as she scrambled onto the couch and nestled in beside her sister.

Olivia breathed a sigh of relief when Rachel didn't push Pearl away. She wanted to leave things there but knew she had to address the *stupid* situation.

"And can we both agree not to use the word *stupid*?" Olivia asked.

Rachel shrugged as Pearl nodded.

"I'm sorry I said *stupid*," Pearl said sweetly, and Rachel grunted.

"Rachel?" Olivia said.

"I'm sorry too," Rachel said unhappily, but she said it.

"Great. Now I'm giving this to Pearl." Olivia handed the remote to Pearl. "But you need to both agree on what you watch or no more TV."

Pearl took the remote with a grin, and even Rachel showed the barest hint of a smile.

Olivia sighed as she went back to her room and her last box. She had a feeling this would get a whole lot harder before it got easier.

She lifted the flaps on the box once again before realizing she should probably call Bart immediately. She'd promised her girls, and Olivia knew there would never be a time she'd look forward to that call. Better to get it over with.

Olivia dialed the office number she knew by heart and

waited for Bart's secretary, Annie, to answer. Annie had been working for Bart since the beginning, but she was one of the few women Olivia had trusted around her husband. Annie wasn't stupid enough to fall for Bart's charms. Maybe Olivia needed to stop using the word she'd banned her children from using.

"Hello, Bart Birmingham's office," Annie answered the phone. Most people had to call the main operator and be directed to Bart's office. Although years of being married to Bart hadn't yielded Olivia much, she had gotten his direct office phone number.

"Hi, Annie," Olivia said, feeling her heartbeat in her throat, she was so nervous. She knew Annie would be kind, but she also knew Annie wouldn't send her call through to Bart if Bart didn't want to speak to Olivia.

"Olivia," Annie said pleasantly, and Olivia hoped that was a good sign.

"I was wondering if Bart was in this evening?" Olivia asked, knowing there would be little chance that her ex was already out of the office for the day. Bart rarely left work before eight pm. It was why he had insisted on living in Seattle during the work week.

So if he wasn't able to answer her phone call, it either meant he was in a meeting, out with a client, or he didn't want to speak to Olivia. Olivia was ready for any of those three possibilities.

"He is," Annie said slowly before adding, "but I need to see if he's taking calls."

Olivia heard the apology in Annie's voice as she said the last words. Olivia knew what that meant. Bart was in and wasn't busy, but Annie wasn't sure that Olivia's ex wanted to hear from her. But Olivia hadn't expected a red-carpet welcome, so she wasn't discouraged.

Olivia began to tap her fingers against the brown cardboard box as she waited. She suddenly realized her bedroom door was still open, and she stretched forward to close the door just in case her children shouldn't be hearing whatever happened during Olivia's conversation, or lack of conversation, with their father.

Part of her loved that Pearl had stuck up for her dad and her need for a relationship with him. The other part of her agreed with Rachel that Bart wasn't worth risking their hearts for. Olivia hoped with all of her that Bart wanted a relationship with his daughters, but she just didn't know what to expect when it came to this. Bart was so selfish, it was hard to predict what he would do when it came to his own flesh and blood. Could he do what they needed without requiring anything in return? Olivia knew it hadn't been possible for Bart to do that for her. But maybe for his daughters? Then again, he had given up full custody with very little fight. Olivia banished the urge to hang up and hide in her bed covers. She was stronger than that. She had to be.

"Olivia?" Annie's voice said again, and Olivia felt her heart drop. Bart wouldn't even speak to her.

She guessed she could try his cell, but if he was screening his calls through his secretary, what would compel him to answer when Olivia's phone number appeared on his phone screen? Did she have the courage to show up at Bart's home on a Saturday when he should be back on the island? Olivia knew she'd do anything for her girls.

"Yes," Olivia finally responded to Annie.

"I'll put you through to Bart," Annie said, and Olivia almost dropped the phone.

Wait, Bart was willing to take her call?

"It was good to hear from you, Olivia. Have a great day," Annie said, and Olivia felt herself smile even as she tried to scramble for what she was going to say now that Bart was willing to take her call.

She realized that she'd been sure Bart was going to avoid her. They hadn't spoken since the day Olivia had left Bart's home for the last time. Sure, they'd seen one another in court, but that hadn't been the right place for a conversation, and there had been no need for them to communicate. Their lawyers had done all of it for them. Until now. Maybe Bart had matured in these last few months?

"Olivia." Bart said her name the way he always did. Sure and as a statement. Of course she was the one calling him.

"Hello, Bart," Olivia said, and then she drew in a deep breath to gather her courage. Olivia had grown in spades since leaving Bart and their home, but hearing his voice did something she didn't like. She felt smaller than she had in months.

"Did you call for a reason?" Bart asked. He did nothing to hide the irritation in his tone. So much for wondering if he'd changed since she'd left. The man was exactly the same, and Olivia needed to step up to the plate. For her girls and herself.

"I did. Our daughters," Olivia said, and she heard Bart sigh in return.

Olivia bit back the curse that she wanted to use hearing that sigh and focused on her reason.

"They miss their dad," Olivia said.

Bart grunted. "Maybe you shouldn't have taken full custody," he said.

Olivia shook her head. Were they going to go back to this? Bart had been the one to offer Olivia full custody from the get-go. But when Bart had heard Olivia wouldn't take the initial deal his lawyer had offered, one that gave her full custody of the girls but a pittance of their financial earnings, Bart only then rescinded his offer of giving Olivia full custody. Olivia would've been happy to give her ex partial custody if she'd known he wanted the girls as more than a bargaining tool. But he didn't care about custody. He just wanted more money. And he knew

Olivia would fork over loads of it to keep time with her girls. That kind of manipulation was what made Bart tick. So Olivia had fought tooth and nail for her girls, but that didn't mean she didn't want their father in their lives. She just wanted to be in full control of the time they spent together. She knew, sadly, that she was the only one of their two parents who would put the girls' needs before her own.

But the custody arrangement and Bart's manipulation didn't matter in this moment, only their girls and their needs. Bart was the man she'd decided to start a family with, so now this was the only father her children would ever know. Thanks to Olivia. If she had to bite back her pride and even grovel a bit for Bart to do what he should want to do, Olivia would do it.

"Bart, we aren't going back there," Olivia said in a way she wouldn't have dared to half a year before. But things were different now. Bart didn't rule her every movement. He didn't have power over her thoughts.

Olivia could imagine Bart biting his lip as he worked over what he wanted to do and say next, how he wanted to use Olivia. Was this the right move? Allowing her girls to spend time with a man like Bart?

But they wanted to see him. At least Pearl did. And he'd always been less manipulative with the girls than he'd been with Olivia. It was more that he just hadn't had time for them. But now Olivia was going to make him have time. Or at least everything she could to make it happen. Because her daughters deserved that.

"Fine, Olivia," Bart said. "So what do you propose?"

Okay. Olivia had not been ready for that. This was not a typical Bart play. Giving Olivia a say? Was this a trick? This had to be a trick. But Olivia had to say something, although she would be sure to tread carefully.

"Are you coming home this weekend or next? Maybe you

could take the girls to the beach for a couple of hours?" Olivia offered the one activity Bart had seemed to enjoy with his girls in years past. And it was something just fun enough that hopefully Rachel would be tempted to join.

"I'll be home this weekend," Bart said. Then he added, "I come home every weekend now."

Olivia knew that was meant to be a dig at her. He was telling her that he hadn't come home so many weekends with her because who he was coming home to wasn't enough. His new girlfriend and their soon-to-be child were enough.

But Olivia chose to ignore the dig. Bart only had power over her emotions and thoughts if she gave it to him. And today he wasn't going to get it.

"That's fantastic," Olivia said with genuine pleasure when she focused on the opportunity Bart coming home was for her girls. "Would Saturday afternoon work? I could drop them off at your place around one and pick them up by four?"

Bart's home was mere steps away from his favorite beach on the island. She figured three hours when they would just be taking a jaunt into his backyard should be more than sufficient time for their activity but not so much that Bart would get annoyed or resent his time with the girls. She wanted to protect her daughters from their father's sometimes unfeeling and callous ways if she could.

"Make that noon to three," Bart said.

Of course he had to make a few changes just to feel like this was more his idea than Olivia's. But whatever. He was going to spend time with his daughters. Olivia would take any win when it came to Bart.

"Perfect. I'll drop Pearl off and hopefully Rachel," Olivia said, not wanting to promise her older daughter's involvement unless she wanted to go.

"That won't work," Bart said, and Olivia could almost hear

the smile in his voice. This was what she'd been waiting for. But what had he found to complain about? Olivia had thought her plan was solid.

"What won't work?" Olivia asked, trying to keep her voice light.

"Both girls need to come," Bart said.

Olivia fought the urge to grit her teeth and scream *why?*

"I'm not sure Rachel is ready for this kind of outing yet," Olivia said cautiously. If she said anything about Bart's involvement in Rachel's wariness, she could see Bart cutting all ties. Poor Pearl didn't deserve that. Olivia had to make it seem as if the indecision lay with her daughter, as much as she hated it. This was all Bart's fault, but pointing that out helped no one.

"Going to the beach?" Bart asked, and Olivia pulled the phone away from her mouth so that she could grit her teeth, the frustration nearly overwhelming her.

"She's feeling a little cautious," Olivia said.

Bart let out a single, unamused bark of laughter. "I can only imagine why. You've kept the girls from me for half a year. Of course she's feeling trepidation," Bart accused.

Olivia wanted to fling the accusations right back. She'd kept them away for so long because of him! He was the one who didn't have time for them. Even now he would only see them on his terms.

"Both girls or this doesn't happen. See you at noon, Olivia," Bart said, and then a dial tone greeted her ears.

Insufferable man! Olivia wanted to scream and shout but only refrained from doing so for the sake of her daughters in the next room. That was one thing she missed about the enormous space in Bart's home. She could scream on one side of the house and they'd be none the wiser.

Why did it have to be both or nothing? Just so that he could have the upper hand? And of course he would say *see you at noon*. He was so sure Olivia would make this work for him in just the way he wanted. Ugh!

Olivia dropped her phone before she gave in to the urge to throw it, then leaned back against the foot of her bed. Being angry at Bart would pass, and then what would she do? Pearl needed to see her dad, but she couldn't force Rachel to do so if she really didn't want to see him.

Why did I marry Bart? Olivia asked herself for the hundred thousandth time. But it always came back to the fact that she couldn't regret her decision. She had Rachel and Pearl, thanks to that marriage.

But now her poor girls were going to suffer because of whatever game Bart had decided to play now. Olivia realized that if Bart couldn't get anything out of this arrangement with her girls, he'd at least make the situation entertaining for him. And knowing the kind of agonizing decisions Olivia faced would entertain a man like Bart. Maybe it would be right to keep Pearl away?

Olivia looked at the time and saw that it was nearing the dinner hour. She had about thirty minutes to get something on the table or she'd have an adorable mutiny on her hands. She stood up and walked away from the box—it would have to wait until tomorrow to be unpacked—as well as away from her thoughts about what to do this weekend. At least Saturday was still four days away. She had some time to think. To make this work for both of her girls. But she wouldn't agonize in front of them. They'd dealt with a distracted mom, thanks to her divorce, long enough. One of Olivia's resolutions when she'd finally come out of the fog that was her divorce was that she would shelter her girls from as much of the bad that came to their little family due to Olivia's choice of a husband as possible. And this was one of those cases where she would have to do that. Put on a happy face and freak out later.

But that didn't mean she was going to make dinner. Bess's food truck would save her once again.

"Who's up for some pasta?" Olivia offered, and both girls yelled, "Me!" in return.

Dinner, bedtime, and then freak out. Olivia could do that.

OLIVIA SAT on her small front porch with the dessert Bess had snuck into their to-go bag from dinner. Of all the eating establishments on the island, her girls almost always chose Scratch Made by Bess, which made Olivia smile. She knew part of her daughters' love for the food truck was because they were proud their Mama had a hand in the truck's operations. The other part was just that the food was dang delicious.

"No walk along the beach tonight?" Olivia's stomach tumbled at the sound of her almost too attractive neighbor and landlord.

His brown hair looked tousled, and since Dean was coming from the direction of the beach behind their homes, Olivia was going to guess the wind was the culprit for that one. Even in the yellow light of Olivia's front porch, it was easy to see the tender gaze Dean shot her way.

Olivia willed herself not to get lost in his forest green eyes or notice the way the wind tugged against his blue button up shirt, allowing Olivia a great view of what she knew to be a pretty incredible set of abs, thanks to the times Dean had run shirtless along the beach. Not that Olivia had been watching or anything. Okay, maybe she had been. A little.

But tonight was about figuring out a solution for her girls and keeping things platonic with her incredibly hot neighbor. Soon after he'd moved back to the island some months ago, Dean had revealed he'd had a crush on Olivia back when they were in high school. She could've sworn he was going to ask her out a few weeks later, but then nothing. Other than Dean being an amazing friend and just what Olivia needed.

And as much as she wished things could be different—her attraction to Dean was off the charts—she knew things were just the way they should be. She was in no place to think about adding another man to her life, to the lives of her girls. Besides, what did she have to offer a guy like Dean? Not much. And even if his old feelings fooled him into thinking he wanted to date present-day Olivia, after a few dates he'd see Olivia for what she was. An almost middle-aged woman with two kids who had no idea how to keep things together every day. Who had no idea how to make a man love her and only her. If Bart's numerous affairs had taught her anything, that was it.

"I didn't want to be far in case the girls woke up. The only negative to having my own place. No more built-in babysitters," Olivia said, referring to her parents' home.

Olivia didn't have to go far for babysitters since she still lived on their same street, but they weren't in the same home, so she couldn't sneak off to the beach the way she had in the past.

"If you need a walk, just let me know. I'd be happy to sit here and listen for the girls," Dean said with a grin as he took the seat next to Olivia on the porch swing that had been installed years before. The swing creaked in accusation as Dean sat down.

"Is this thing safe?" Dean asked as he looked behind him to check the ropes that held the swing to the roof of the porch.

"I don't know. Ask my landlord," Olivia teased, and Dean chuckled.

"The Arnolds installed this thing about twenty years ago, and according to them, it's still going strong," Dean said about the previous owners of the house. Dean was a recent transplant to Letman's Cove, the small neighborhood with eight homes that sat right on its small beach. But he'd grown up on the island. He'd spent the years after college in Portland but had felt the call to come home. Which Olivia was immensely grateful for. She now had a home because of him, and the view of his abs as he ran along the beach was also a plus.

"I guess I trust the Arnolds," Olivia said in a nervous tone as she looked up at the ropes. "Wait, is it fraying right there?" she asked and then began laughing at the sight of alarm on Dean's face, no longer able to keep up the charade.

Dean chuckled along with Olivia's laughter, proving he was not only oh so good looking, he was also a great sport.

"The girls and I sit out here all the time. This swing is more than adequate," Olivia said.

Dean grinned as he swiped a hand against his forehead in an exaggerated manner. "You seem like you're in a good mood," he said.

Did she? She hadn't been until Dean had come up, but she couldn't tell him that.

"I have dessert from Bess. How could I be in a bad mood?" *When in doubt, blame all happiness on food* was a motto Olivia was beginning to wonder if she should live by.

"Tiramisu?" Dean asked, and Olivia nodded.

"I have an extra fork," Olivia offered as she took another fork out of the bag Bess had given her.

Dean shook his head. "I couldn't," he said as his eyes longingly took in the dessert.

"You would leave me with this huge piece of tiramisu? All to myself?" Olivia asked.

Dean smiled. "Really? I don't want to intrude on your porch time."

Olivia looked pointedly at where he was now seated.

"I was just about to leave," Dean said, his eyes large and full of mischief. Olivia knew that Dean would never leave without at least a taste of the tiramisu. He had quite the sweet tooth, and Bess's desserts were his favorite.

Olivia offered him the fork again, and this time Dean took it.

Olivia took the first bite because she knew Dean would insist and then passed the plastic container to Dean.

"So good," Olivia moaned as she swallowed her bite. She'd been eating Bess's food nonstop thanks to her job as Bess's book-keeper, but she still enjoyed every meal. She didn't know what Bess did to her food; Olivia could only guess it was magic. She knew nothing that came out of her own kitchen was near Bess's quality.

Dean nodded as he savored his bite and then turned to Olivia. "So were you just out here to get some fresh air?" he asked, somehow knowing Olivia needed to bounce her ideas and emotions off of someone. Dean had been there for her during some hard conversations she'd had with herself in the past few months, and he'd been the perfect sounding board. His intuition that she needed him again was spot on.

Olivia took another bite before setting her fork in the container and leaving it for Dean. She'd already had Bolognese and garlic bread for dinner. A few bites of dessert more than sufficed.

"Pearl wants to spend time with her dad," Olivia said.

Dean leaned back in the swing as he watched Olivia and waited for her to say more.

"But Rachel doesn't."

"Oh," Dean said softly, and Olivia nodded as she turned her body to him.

Dean took another bite, never taking his eyes off of Olivia. He somehow made her feel supported but not pushed. He was there for her as much as she needed.

"So when I talked to Bart, he said he's happy to spend time

with the girls. But both girls. It's either both or nothing," Olivia said, shaking her head.

"I want to give him nothing," Olivia added, and then she pursed her lips.

"But that isn't fair to Pearl," Dean said.

Olivia nodded.

"But making Rachel go isn't fair to Rachel," Dean said.

Olivia nodded again. Of course he understood.

Olivia heard the sound of nails scraping against her wooden porch and looked up to see Buster, Dean's dog, headed their way. He slid to a stop in front of Dean, causing Olivia to giggle at the forlorn expression on Buster's face. He wanted some of that tiramisu.

Buster was the reason that her girls had agreed to move into the small cottage on Dean's property, even though it meant leaving their beloved grandparents' home. The girls loved dogs, and they especially loved Buster after a chance encounter at the park. Her daughters had gone over to Dean's a few times before they moved, begging for time with his dog. So now that they shared a yard with Buster, they were in heaven. Olivia thought about the way Dean had joined in the games with her girls and Buster over the past couple of weeks, in a way Bart never would've. Dean understood the situation with her girls, not only because he was smart but also because he knew her girls.

"Sorry, boy," Dean said as he nudged the dog away with his knee. "Not your kind of dessert."

Buster seemed to look even more pathetic after Dean's denial, and Olivia bent over to give the poor dog a hug.

"How can you say *no* to this face?" Olivia asked as she pulled Buster's face into her hands and faced him to Dean.

"Coffee," Dean said matter of factly.

"Oh right," Olivia said. "I guess this is why I'm a human parent and not a dog mom."

Olivia felt a little ridiculous that she'd forgotten coffee could be poisonous to dogs. Fortunately, she wouldn't have fed Buster even if she had been alone, but she guessed living in his yard, she needed to read up on her dog facts. She was beginning to love Buster as much as her girls did.

Dean set the dessert down and took over hugging and cuddling his dog for a minute before sitting back up.

"Go to bed, Buster," Dean said in a commanding tone, and Buster gave one last longing look toward the tiramisu before scurrying away from Olivia's porch.

"He's a good dog," Olivia said.

"The best," Dean responded, staring after the sweet animal. "He's been with me through a lot."

Olivia knew Dean had endured his own divorce recently. Another reason why she needed to stay just friends with him.

"Back to your situation," Dean said, turning his attention to Olivia.

"Yeah. Have you come up with a solution in the past two minutes?" Olivia asked, trying to give Dean a smile. She hoped her ridiculous question would lighten the mood. She felt like she was always a downer when Dean was around.

"Not yet." Dean returned her smile as he went back to the dessert. "Are you sure you don't want more?"

She shook her head, and Dean dug back in.

"Did Bart tell you why he wanted both girls instead of just Pearl?"

Olivia shook her head. "I figured he was just trying to be difficult. Besides, Bart hates when I question him."

Dean shook his head slowly, his disgruntled frown hard to miss. Olivia figured that meant he was keeping one of his many unpleasant thoughts about Bart to himself.

"You endured a lot, didn't you?" Dean said softly.

Olivia wasn't sure how to respond.

"You're amazing. You know that, right?" Dean asked.

Olivia shook her head, causing her red hair to brush her shoulders. Olivia had been blonde from high school until recently, when she'd dyed her hair a dark red that was close to her original hair color. When she caught her reflection, it still sometimes surprised her. But she loved it. Not only because Bart loved blondes and had made her keep her hair that color for all of their marriage, but because the red hair helped Olivia to feel more like herself than she had in years.

"I managed," Olivia muttered.

"You survived and got out. Got your girls out," Dean said.

"But that doesn't shelter them from this new situation," Olivia said as she leaned back against the armrest of the swing behind her. "I sometimes hate myself for doing this to them."

And that was the crux of every issue when it came to Bart. Olivia's anger toward her ex would only take her so far because it would always come back to Olivia. Olivia had chosen Bart. And now they all had to deal with the consequences.

Olivia tucked her legs under her as she waited for some kind of inspiration to hit her. She didn't see how this could work and be fair to both of her girls.

"Have you talked to them?" Dean asked as he set the now empty container that had been holding their dessert on the ground beside the swing and then sat back up.

"The girls?" Olivia asked, and Dean nodded.

Olivia shook her head. "It doesn't seem fair to involve them either. They're only ten and seven. They shouldn't have to think of solutions to parental disputes."

"They shouldn't," Dean agreed quickly. Then he added, "But sometimes life isn't fair, Olivia. And I know I'm not a parent, so maybe I have no room having an opinion. But isn't that something you want your girls to learn?" Dean asked softly.

Of course Dean had every right to his opinion. She was

coming to him with her issues, and he was not only being kind enough to let her vent but was honestly trying to help her come to a conclusion. What kind of man did that? The good kind.

Olivia mulled over what Dean had said and then tried to figure out how she wanted to respond. "I do want them to learn that. It's an important part of life. But I don't want them to learn it like this, I guess?" Olivia said, her voice getting higher with her last sentence because she wasn't sure what she felt.

"Maybe we are looking at this the wrong way. Bart has made a terrible situation for you and your girls. I'm not going to deny that. And my first inclination is to want to drive down to that little mansion of his and knock some sense into him," Dean said, the look on his face a cross between anger and helplessness. But then he let out a pent-up breath along with a sound that was kind of like a laugh. Olivia loved that Dean let his anger go so easily.

Olivia chuckled as she shook her head. She knew Dean well enough to know he would only go to violence as a last resort, but she felt safe and comforted to know he had her back. She hadn't had someone of the male variety who wasn't related to her have her back in a long, long time. And it felt nice.

"It's a very typical mansion. Not little at all," Olivia tried to joke.

Dean shot her a returning smile. "And I know you feel guilty for your part in all of this."

Olivia grimaced because she did.

"But I think those things are making it hard for you to see this for what it could be. A lesson in sacrifice for your girls. I know you don't want them to learn these lessons this way, and I get that. You want these hard lessons to come from a place that has nothing to do with you."

Olivia nodded in amazement. How could he articulate what she had a hard time understanding about herself, much less saying? Maybe it was all those years of being so eloquent in the courtroom.

"But the opportunity has arisen, and you might as well grab the proverbial bull by the horns, don't you think?" Dean asked.

"So I should involve the girls in this? Aren't they too young?" Olivia asked.

Dean shrugged. "Maybe. But is any age too young to learn to put others before yourself?"

Olivia leaned her head on her arms which she'd propped on her knees that were pulled up to her chest as she pondered Dean's words. She'd been trying to teach her girls compassion and service since day one.

"So if you look at it like that?" Dean asked, now looking hopeful instead of helpless. "This can be an opportunity instead of a challenge," Dean added. "Bart is a good dad when he actually spends time with the girls, right?"

Olivia nodded. He really was. At times. One of the great contradictions that made up her ex. He wasn't a good man most of the time. He was manipulative, a liar, and a cheat, and even spent the majority of his time ignoring that he had daughters. But during those rare moments when Bart actually felt like being a father, he became this fun dad that every child dreamed of. And since he was saying he was okay to spend time with the girls, Olivia hoped for Pearl's sake that meant fun dad would appear. Although Olivia couldn't trust Bart to make any long term parental decisions because the girls were lower than they should be on his priority list, in those moments when he did seem to care, when she could see his love for his girls—however twisted it was—Olivia knew they were physically safe with Bart. Emotionally was a different story, and that was why she'd fought so hard to get full custody. But she believed that while Bart was in the mood to act like a father, things could be great for a few hours. Now that Rachel wasn't interested in time with her dad, Olivia was sure her oldest was remembering more of the times Bart had ignored them. Getting her girls there was going to be the big issue.

"You're right," Olivia said. "I was trying to shelter my girls from this situation that I felt was created by my actions, but there is no way to do that at this point. I was an idiot and married Bart, and that decision will continue to reap consequences forever. But I can keep beating myself up or look for ways to make the situation the best it can be."

Dean nodded slowly. "I think it's the only thing you can do now. And you weren't an idiot. You were in love," Dean said.

"Isn't that the same thing?" Olivia responded as she leaned her head back so that she looked up at the roof of her porch instead of at Dean.

"Not when it's the right person," Dean said.

"Yeah, I guess that's the catch no one talks about," Olivia responded.

Dean chuckled. "Yeah, I guess it is."

CHAPTER FOUR

"ORDER UP," Bess called out to Cassie, the sweet girl she'd hired to man the front of her food truck, Scratch Made by Bess.

Cassie leaned over where Bess was tossing spaghetti in Bolognese on their truck's stovetop to grab the containers of shrimp scamp—one of the truck's best sellers—that sat on the metal ledge at Bess's eye line, then walked them to the big window where the customers were waiting.

"Dina and Ellen, two shrimp scampi," Cassie called out, and Bess smiled that Cassie had gotten the names of both of the women who'd ordered instead of one. The girl had the gift of gab in the best way possible, and people left Bess's truck feeling like they'd not only gotten some incredible food—if Bess did say so herself—but like they'd met a new friend. It was exactly what Bess had hoped for her truck, and Cassie had made it a reality.

Bess moved from the Bolognese to the paper take-out containers she had lined up on the stainless steel countertop next to the stove. Her entire truck gleamed of stainless steel, and she absolutely loved it.

Bess placed some of her house salad in the containers and

then checked on the garlic bread warming in the oven behind her to see that they were on their way to being toasty and would be done just as the Bolognese would be ready to dish up.

"Hi, Olivia." Bess's attention turned to the front of the truck as Cassie happily greeted Bess's friend, the next customer in line.

"Hey, Cassie," Olivia responded. "Can we get one lasagna and one scampi?"

The lasagna was a typical Olivia order, but the scampi wasn't. Olivia and her girls all adored red sauce, and they usually avoided seafood. Who was Olivia ordering for?

"I've heard great things about this scampi," a deep voice responded, and Bess fought her curiosity to leave her station and take a peek at the man with Olivia. Olivia had been seen with her friend and landlord, Dean, around town a couple times, but Bess knew Dean's voice. And the rich baritone that slid into her truck wasn't his.

"Coming right up," Cassie said, and Bess could only imagine the wink Cassie bestowed on them before running the slip of paper with the order over to Bess so that she could put it in line with her other orders.

Cassie stayed by Bess, clearing old pieces of paper out and making sure the order sheets she'd given to Bess were in the right sequence. Bess assumed the line that usually accompanied their truck when it was open must've died down since Cassie wasn't manning the register. Bess was also down to just a couple of order forms that she had left to fill. That meant they must be coming to the small lull that existed between lunch and dinner, when her counterpart, Chef Alexis, would come in.

"Is it two o'clock already?" Bess asked, and Cassie nodded as Bess handed her the four orders of Bolognese for the family who'd ordered before Olivia and the mystery man.

"Go ahead and take a lunch break. I can cover the counter and the back," Bess offered Cassie.

Bess and Alexis split the time in the small kitchen of the food truck. Bess had to be there at eight to prep all of the ingredients for their day and stayed until about two on most days. That's when Alexis came in to take over the evening shift that often went until nine or ten, depending on how much clean-up had to be done. But Cassie's shift didn't need to start so early or go so late since she didn't have to help with the prep or the clean-up, so she just worked during the hours the truck was open, from eleven to eight. It worked out well for all of them.

"Thanks," Cassie said as she washed her hands and then cut herself a portion of lasagna from under the warmer before leaning against the back door of the truck to eat her meal. The lasagna was the one thing Bess didn't make to order because of its long cook time. She hated that it sat under a warmer, but honestly it didn't sit for too long. The lasagna was almost as popular as the scampi, and Bess could go through an entire tray in less than an hour's time. She usually prepped about eight for the day, and they almost always sold out of lasagna by five pm. So the dish was always fresh and delicious, but Bess still hated that she had to use warming lamps for any of her creations.

"Have you given any more thought to hiring another chef?" Cassie asked as she took a bite and then moaned. "How does this still taste so good? I've had lasagna every day for the past two weeks, and I could honestly eat it forever."

Bess chuckled.

"This job definitely isn't helping my waistline," Cassie added.

"We serve salads," Bess offered.

Cassie scoffed. "Why would I choose a salad when I can have this?" she said as she stuffed her mouth once again, and Bess had to laugh. Cassie was a hoot.

But Bess suddenly remembered Cassie's question and knew she had to address it. "Are you feeling overworked?" Bess asked.

Cassie immediately shook her head. "But it seems like you might be. And the line got to be a little long again today," Cassie said. She knew she'd been hired because of those lines and how long they'd been before she'd joined the team. Cassie had been a frequent customer in those lines, so she could attest to how crazy they got.

"When we make things to order, we can only go so fast," Cassie added.

"But with additional hands, the work could go faster," Bess agreed, and Cassie nodded.

"I'll talk to Olivia and see where the budget is. I would like to keep things streamlined and as quick as possible for the customers, so if we have the income, I don't see why not. Do you know of anyone we could hire?" Bess asked.

"On island? No," Cassie said. She had lived on the island her whole life, and because she was a good thirty years younger than Bess, she knew a whole different generation of people than Bess did. It was nice to have her knowledge as well as her work ethic on their team.

"That's too bad. I would love to hire local."

Cassie nodded. "I'll keep my ears open."

"Thank you, Cassie," Bess said as there was a knock at the back door.

Cassie stepped forward so that she wasn't leaning on the door and then Bess called out, "Come in!"

Bright light streamed in as the door opened and Olivia stepped onto the truck.

"I figured Cassie was taking a break since I didn't see her at the front, and I'm guessing we're the only order left to serve?" Olivia said with a smile that reached all the way to her bright blue eyes. Bess loved that Olivia was smiling as much as she had back when Bess had been her English teacher during her senior year of high school. It was an accessory Olivia had been missing for too long.

"You are," Bess said as Cassie sidestepped Olivia, making her way out of the truck. Probably so that she could eat the rest of her lunch sitting at one of the tables outside instead of hunched over her plate in the small quarters of the food truck.

But since Bess had Olivia alone, it was now a good time to talk to her about what Cassie had just brought up.

"Cassie was wondering if we should hire another chef?" Bess said as she tossed some shrimp in a bunch of butter and garlic.

"Do you need the help?" Olivia asked. "I'm happy to pitch in whenever I'm needed."

"Oh no. We've gone through this Olivia. I know I used your help early on, but your job is outside of the truck," Bess said. She had realized quickly that she was overworking her first employee and friend when the woman took shifts on the truck as well as taking care of all their marketing and financial matters.

"She was just saying the line was getting long again. It's not the end of the world, but we've been working on trying to get orders out to people as fast as we can."

Olivia nodded. She knew that was one of Bess's goals.

"Let me look over the numbers and I'll get back to you," Olivia said. Her grin came back in full force, reminding Bess that Olivia was here with someone.

"Was that Dean I heard with you?" Bess asked as she served up the scampi and lasagna before adding salad and garlic bread to both plates. Bess knew the man with Olivia was not the man she'd asked about, but she also wasn't sure how to broach the conversation any other way. Bess, Olivia, and Deb had endured divorces at about the same time. They'd been with one another through the bad, the ugly, and thankfully some good, so it was natural that Bess was curious about Olivia having a new man in her life.

"No," Olivia said, her grin somehow growing larger, and Bess was now even more curious.

"Dax is home," Olivia added, and Bess suddenly understood the smile. Olivia adored her brother, and Bess knew the two of them didn't get to spend as much time together as Olivia would've liked. Of no fault of Dax's. Bess knew Dax had a demanding job that had kept him in Nashville for the past twenty or more years since graduating from high school. And the job meant he'd hardly had time to take trips home. Bess knew that Olivia and Dax were close, despite the distance between them, and that Dax was quite a few years older than Olivia's thirty-eight but still quite a bit younger than Bess.

"Oh that's wonderful," Bess said as she handed Olivia the two plates and then moved to her dessert refrigerator. This called for a celebration.

Bess dug out Olivia's favorite tiramisu and then a chocolate cake that was too rich and decadent for everyday consumption.

"Share these with your brother," Bess offered, realizing that Olivia's hands were full.

"I'll take them out for you," Bess said, realizing it would be nice to say hi to Dax. She hadn't seen him since his last trip home a couple of years before. Bess had never really known Dax from his time living on the island because she and Jon had moved into their home a couple years after Dax had graduated from high school. But every time Dax had come home, he'd stayed with his family who lived next door to Bess, so they'd become acquainted with one another over the years.

"It will be nice to say hi to Dax."

Olivia opened the backdoor, going slowly down the steps

before Bess followed her, doing the same. The metal steps were tricky on the best of days, but with the slight misting of rain they'd had about an hour earlier, the slower the steps were taken the better.

"I can head back into the truck," Cassie called out when she saw Bess come down the steps, but Bess shook her head.

"I'll just watch for new customers from here," Bess offered, and Cassie nodded. She sat at a table by herself with her phone out and headphones in, probably watching the vampire show she'd been working on getting Bess to watch. Bess didn't want to break it to the cute girl that there was no way on this green earth that Bess would watch a vampire show.

A car pulled up on to the side of the road, and Bess worried she'd have to drop the desserts and run back to the truck. But as soon as she looked at the driver of the car, she realized it was Alexis coming in to work and not a customer.

Bess turned back to the tables after a quick wave at Alexis to see that Olivia had left Bess behind and was already seated with her brother. So Bess made her way toward them, Dax standing when he saw where Bess was headed.

"Bess," Dax said, and Bess wasn't sure why she hadn't recognized his voice when he'd been at the truck with Olivia. Maybe because his was the last voice she'd been expecting to hear.

The man outstretched his arms and pulled Bess into a warm hug, enveloping Bess in the smells of salt air and spicy sandalwood.

Bess stepped away, feeling a blush on her cheeks that she hoped she could blame on the heat of the food truck. That was quite the exuberant welcome—she and Dax were usually hand-shaking acquaintances—but Bess had to admit she didn't mind the hug in the least.

However, although Dax smelled and looked incredible—his

wavy, dark auburn hair was swept back off his face but blew in the wind just enough to make it seem relaxed, and his bright blue eyes were nearly mesmerizing, not to mention from her position in his hug, it was easy to feel the hardness of his chest and arms that told Bess the guy worked out—he was at least five, if not ten, years younger than Bess. Was she actually feeling attraction to such a man? She needed to put a stop to it immediately.

"I brought out a few desserts," Bess said as she worked to hide her blush and shifted her attention away from Dax's hug to the white picnic table where the Penn siblings sat.

"I can't wait to try them. I still dream about those cookies you brought over the last time I was home," Dax said, and Bess's blush was instantly back. What was wrong with her?

"I'll have to bring over a batch soon then. Can't leave those dreams unfulfilled," Bess said, her mind mostly focused on trying to control her blushing. Then she replayed what she'd said. Had she said she wanted to fulfill Dax's dreams? The blush was back in full force, and Bess decided she'd lost that battle. Maybe she could salvage the conversation.

"I just meant the cookies.... You need those cookies," Bess fumbled over her words and then shut her mouth. This was only getting worse.

She chanced a glance at Olivia who looked at her with a puzzled expression, and then she had to turn back to Dax. Dax's face was filled with a smile that told Bess he was working to bite back his laughter. So she had sounded as idiotic as she'd felt. Great.

"Well, enjoy the food," Bess said as she turned around to head back to the truck.

What was going on with her? She was a grown woman who had been married for thirty years, not some schoolgirl with a crush. Sure, Dax was attractive. But then again, so were many of the men who Bess came in contact with at her truck.

Bess had no idea the why of it; she just knew she had to deal with it.

———

BESS WALKED with a determination toward the Penn's home. Since she'd told Dax she was going to make him cookies, she now had to fulfill her word, even though all she really wanted to do was hide from Dax for the remainder of his trip home. Thankfully the man was typically only back on the island for a few days at a time, so hopefully by his next trip home, all thoughts of Bess's ridiculous blunder about his dreams would be forgotten.

Bess had only had her bumbling experience with Dax the day before and would've liked to have more time to lick her wounds and get ready to face the man again. But today was Monday, her only day off from the truck, and she figured it would be the easiest day to whip up a few batches of her chocolate chip cookies and take them over to the Penns. Hopefully they'd be out for the day and Bess could drop her cookies on one of the chairs on their front porch and be done with the whole thing.

When she got to their driveway and saw a car she didn't recognize sitting parked in it, she guessed she was out of luck. Dang it.

Maybe Dax would be too busy to come to the door?

Bess walked up the driveway and along a cement walkway that led to the white and green beach home's front door when she heard, "Hey, Bess."

Bess nearly dropped the plate of cookies she held and stopped to make sure she had a good grip on them, then calmed her pounding heart before looking up at the front porch to see that Dax was sitting in one of the seats she'd been hoping to use as part of her escape plan. The one with the back to her home, so it wasn't a wonder why she hadn't seen him.

"Dax. I brought your cookies." Bess held up the plate and then pulled it back in front of her. Again, what was she doing? Why had she held up the plate of cookies like it was a lion cub being announced to the world?

"Awesome," Dax said in his laidback drawl that had only become more significant with the years he'd spent in Nashville. "After that scampi and cake, I was thinking of heading over to your house today to tell you that now I will be dreaming of more than just your cookies."

Bess's cheeks flamed before she realized he wasn't talking about dreaming of her like she'd thought for just a moment but about her food. Duh.

Bess hurried the rest of the way up the yellow flower-lined pathway and up the steps of the porch. New plan. Give Dax the cookies and run home immediately. She didn't understand what was going on with her, and she needed to get control of herself now.

She walked right up to where Dax was still sitting on one of the porch chairs and held the plate in front of him. He'd take it, and then she'd be off. Easy peasy.

But Dax didn't take the plate. Instead he unwrapped a corner of the foil-covered plate and took a cookie, not the plate. He bit into the cookie as his eyes closed, and Bess couldn't help but watch him savor the bite. This was why she did what she did. She loved watching a person enjoy her food. The fact that that person was as gorgeous as Dax didn't hurt the situation.

"It's even better than my dreams," Dax said, startling Bess and reminding her of her plan. If only Dax would take the dang plate.

"That's what I'm here for," Bess said as she offered the plate to Dax once again. Why wasn't he catching her hints?

"To make my dreams come true?" Dax asked, and Bess shook her head so fast and hard, she felt herself go dizzy.

"I was just joking, Bess," Dax said as he laid a strong, warm hand on Bess's forearm, and she about dropped the cookies again. She needed to get a grip.

"Right, yeah. Of course."

Take the stinking cookies!

"Are you okay?" Dax asked. Then, before Bess could answer, he stood and took a step behind Bess, putting his hand at the small of her back to lead her to the chair next to the one he'd been sitting in. "Why don't you take a seat?"

Bess could only blame her next action on her addled mind, probably due to Dax's touch, but she sat. With the plate of cookies still on her lap.

"So a food truck, huh?" Dax asked the same question dozens of others had since Bess started her new business after her separation from her husband, but somehow all of the previous words she'd used to delight people with her new plan for life fled completely, leaving Bess with the perfectly appalling word choice of, "Yup."

Since when did Bess say *yup? Yes*, sure, but *yup?*

"Well, I can see why. You could cook your way right into Heaven," Dax said as he took the last bite of the cookie he held and then leaned over the arm of his chair as well as Bess's so that now he was definitely in her personal space. And although Bess's heart beat at nearly a hundred times its normal rate due to Dax's proximity, she was beginning to realize she wasn't having this reaction because she was hating this experience. Nope. She was reacting like a high school girl with a crush.... And she was loving it.

Well, maybe not the high school part. Couldn't she be acting like a grown woman with a crush? Granted, the last time she'd had a crush had been in high school. She'd started dating Jon early in college, and she and Jon had been friends before that. A beautiful way to start a relationship, but because of that, she'd missed this heart pounding stage of things. And she was very much enjoying herself. Even if she was making a fool of herself.

Bess took as deep of a breath as she could without alerting Dax to her current state, which wasn't much of a breath because of how close he was. Man, did he smell good. Woodsy with a hint of citrus. Bess had always been a fan of citrus scents. Dax's blue eyes were captivating from a distance, but this close? They literally sparkled.

It was then that Bess realized they were probably sparkling with humor since Bess had been staring at the man, wordless, for nearly thirty seconds. Heaven help her, where was her brain today?

"How long are you home?" Bess finally asked a normal, friendly question, and Dax smiled.

If she thought his eyes sparkled before, now they just lit up. Between his broad shoulders and his chiseled jaw, Dax was the kind of man to make the young women of Nashville do a double take. It wasn't a wonder that Bess, a more mature woman who hadn't had the consideration of a man in much too long, was falling apart at his attentiveness.

"A bit," Dax said as he finally leaned back.

Bess wished she could say she was relieved to have her space back again, but not all of her was. Most of her yearned to have Dax close again, maybe even closer than he'd been. Foolish.

"My biggest client is leaving Nashville and wants me to go with him to LA," Dax said suddenly, leaning forward toward Bess again.

Bess's poor heart did a tumble right down to her feet.

Dax grew closer as he watched Bess's face with a grin, only to pull up the tinfoil she'd replaced on the cookie plate, grab two cookies, and then sit back. All with that silly grin on his face.

Oh, he knew what he was doing, and Bess felt a bit of the fighter in her appear. Dax might be handsome and all the words appealing about a man, but she would not be putty in any man's hands, even if he was sweet and made her heart tumble.

Bess closed the covering on the plate and then stood to put it on the table at the other end of the porch, his eyes going wide in alarm. He thought she was leaving ... and he didn't want her to go. Good.

She set the cookies down and then turned to return to her seat. After Dax's little stunt, she wanted to pull one of her own. She made quick work of the rest of the porch to her seat and returned Dax's smug smile as she sat back down.

He chuckled before taking another huge bite of cookie and then leaned back, his arm covering both his own and Bess's arm rests so that his hand every so often grazed Bess's arm. Oh, he was better than good.

"This move is good for my client, but it's going to be rough on me. It would mean a whole lot more travel because I'd still have clients back in Nashville. I wanted to take a break from it all for a few days before I commit to my new lifestyle," Dax said.

Bess heard his message loud and clear. She wasn't sure it was the message he meant for her, but it was one she got all the same. This was clearly a fun flirtation because he wasn't looking for anything permanent. His career was going to take him away soon. Her crush would go nowhere. And after the past many months of her life, Bess had to admit a harmless, exciting crush where no one would get hurt sounded kind of appealing.

Besides, Dax was much too young and good looking for her. She was sure he had women lining up in both Nashville and LA, ready to date him. Women half her age and without all her baggage. Jon was older than her, her father older than her mom, and Levi older than Gen. It was the way things worked in her family. Dax, eight years her junior, was practically a baby. But the determined way he held her gaze told Bess he was going to be a fun crush, nonetheless.

CHAPTER FIVE

GEN HAD a smile from ear to ear as she searched the internet for the best ways to surprise a soon-to-be father. She'd already cried through numerous YouTube videos. Fortunately, she was in her office at her salon or Levi would've known something was up.

She looked at the clock on the top right-hand side of her computer screen to see that she still had about another half an hour before her next appointment. She'd been working on cutting back her hours at the salon ever since she and Levi had realized they'd be taking in Maddie full-time. Gen's eventual goal was to only have to come in two to three days a week, but it was going to be difficult. Gen had been cutting hair on the island for so long that there were many, many people who would only entrust their hair to her. She had standing appointments with regulars every day of the week, so which days did she cut? Which clients should she offend? *None* seemed like the right solution, but Gen also longed to stay home with Maddie ... and one day her new bundle—who was now the size of a peach, according to her pregnancy app. Gen rubbed her stomach and realized she needed to tell Levi about their baby today. She'd held off for a week in order to give Levi and Maddie some time to adjust to one transition before springing another one on them. But now was the time.

Especially since Maddie's babysitter and Gen and Levi's lifesaver, Lily, had already sniffed out the truth. Between Gen's nearly constant nausea, that according to the pregnancy app should be ending any day now, and the deep tired lines around her eyes, Lily guessed on day two after Gen had taken the test that she was in the family way. It made sense, considering Lily had recently given birth to her own bundle of joy, and the signs and symptoms were parts of her recent past. But since Lily knew the truth, Gen had to tell Levi ... now.

But how? They'd waited for this moment for so long. So long. And Gen wanted to get it right.

Gen leaned back, watching as her yellow curtains fluttered around the window in her office that overlooked the street. Many of her stylists had balked at her choice of yellow curtains —it seemed old-fashioned to them—but Gen loved things that felt like they had a bit of history to them. Maybe it did make her old-fashioned, but she liked to think of it as admiring the past. She chuckled to herself as she realized that was probably the same thing.

A car pulled into the only open spot in front of the salon, and Gen immediately recognized the brown Chrysler. She grinned as Lily opened the door of the front seat while strapping on a baby carrier.

Gen thought about going to help the new mother out— having her own infant while babysitting Maddie the toddler couldn't be easy—but she also knew Lily was intent on proving herself. She'd called the babysitting job Gen and Levi had provided a Godsend.

Lily and her husband, Allen, were new to the island. Or Gen should say *new once again*, at least in Lily's case. Lily's sister, Kate, was Gen's receptionist at the salon, and they'd grown up on the island. But after high school, Lily had moved to a small town in Alabama for a nannying job where she'd met, fell in love with and then married the handsome and charming Allen. However, once Lily became pregnant, both husband and wife realized that they wanted to be near more family now that they were growing their own. Allen's newly divorced parents still lived in Alabama, but they were too busy warring with one another to care too much about becoming grandparents. However, Lily's very supportive parents and Kate lived here on Whisling. The draw of grandparents plus an aunt who couldn't wait to love on Lily's new baby was too much to withstand. So they picked up their fledgling roots, Allen could do his job as a kindergarten teacher nearly anywhere, and came to the Pacific Northwest.

They loved it. But they still had some financial issues. Being the sole bread winner for an entire family on an island was a stretch for Allen's modest teacher's salary. So Lily had decided to go back to nannying and was grateful to be able to babysit Maddie in order to earn some much needed income for their family.

And the situation worked just as well for Levi and Gen. While it would have been nice to have Maddie watched by a family member, Bess and all of Gen's family on the island had their own jobs and Levi's family lived away from Whisling. Even Maddie's beloved grandparents, Mal's parents, lived a ferry ride away. So it worked out perfectly for all because although Lily wasn't family, she loved Maddie like family and that was all that mattered.

"Mama Gen!" Maddie called out as she threw open the door of Gen's office.

Gen stood and moved around her desk before dropping to

her knees and holding out her arms to take in her beautiful little girl.

Maddie's adorable blonde curls bounced around her perfectly cherubic face as she raced toward Gen's open arms.

"Maddie Mae." Gen used the nickname she'd penned almost moments after Maddie had moved into their home. Gen didn't know why she'd made up the middle name, but it had rolled off her tongue and just felt right. Maddie had informed Gen her name was Maddie Elisabeth, but when Gen had told her Maddie Mae was a special name just for Maddie from Gen, the toddler had grinned and nodded like she was in on a secret that she really liked. So Maddie Mae stuck.

"I hope you don't mind us barging in like this," Lily said. "We were on our way home from the park and Maddie asked to visit Mama Gen. How do you say no to this face?" Lily somehow also knelt down, even with her baby carrier strapped to the front of her, and held Maddie's cheeks as the latter giggled in delight.

"I know those aren't words you want to hear from your babysitter, but this little girl has me wrapped around her finger," Lily added as she moved to stand, needing to use her arm as leverage against Gen's desk to get all the way up.

"As she has us all," Gen said as she pulled Maddie back into her arms. Then she added, "I'm always up for an interruption from some of my favorite girls." Gen first dropped her gaze to Maddie in her arms and then looked up at Lily and her sweet baby, Amelia, wanting Lily to know she'd included them in the comment as well.

Gen couldn't believe how quickly the woman had wormed her way into her heart. Sure, they'd been acquaintances pretty much since Lily was born, and they'd both lived on the island all of their lives. But they'd really bonded this last week over Maddie and the secret they held together. Gen knew it meant a lot to Lily that Gen had revealed her pregnancy to her first. Lily had felt horribly that she'd asked about it—she had no idea Levi didn't know—but she'd only asked because she wanted to give some pregnancy pointers.

"And since you all are here, I could use a little advice," Gen said as she lifted Maddie into her arms as she stood, then went to the door of her office to close it for some privacy. "How do I tell Levi? We've both waited for this moment for years, and I want it to be perfect."

Lily nodded as she took a seat, but she kept on rocking her body, probably trying to soothe Amelia to sleep. "Have you checked the internet?" she asked.

Gen nodded. "Pinterest, YouTube, the usual suspects," she said.

"And?" Lily asked as she flipped all of her long, black hair behind her shoulders. Gen was surrounded by pretty women at her salon all day, but Lily was in a league by herself with her dark hair, pale skin, and stunning violet eyes. However, she seemed oblivious to her own beauty, making her not just gorgeous but very likeable. It was quite the intimidating combination, but Gen was beginning to grow used to it.

"Nothing great," Gen said as she pushed her own auburn hair behind her ear. Working at a salon, Gen had had a number of hair looks over the years. But she always seemed to come back to a variation of her natural red shade in the end. "Not that I don't love what I've seen, just none of it seems like Levi."

Lily nodded. "You've been trying for a while, right?" Lily asked.

Gen nodded dramatically. A long, long while. Too long. But she couldn't complain now that she finally had a babe within her belly.

"And how have you always imagined telling him?" Lily asked.

That caused Gen to pause. Gen hadn't even thought about

that. It had been so long since she'd even dared to hope that she could one day tell her husband they were going to be parents ... again. My how her world had changed, seemingly overnight.

"I guess with a pair of baby shoes?" Gen said as she thought about her much younger self scouring the online sites of a number of shoe stores any time she was even a day late for her period. "Levi has a thing for shoes."

Lily smiled. "I've seen the symptoms. A new pair of shoes on all of the days he hasn't been at a worksite before he comes to pick up Maddie. None of them scuffed in the least."

"You've diagnosed him correctly." Gen returned Lily's smile, and the second woman stood to join Gen where she still stood close to the door, holding Maddie.

"So do the baby shoes," Lily said.

Gen's smile widened. Lily was right. But the big problem Gen had been trying to avoid came rearing its head once again.

"But the island. It's too late to try to order anything online for today, and I can't go out and buy a pair of baby shoes without getting the rumor mill going. I haven't even called or gone to the doctor yet because I wanted to tell Levi about the baby before Mrs. Mallory could."

Lily laughed at the mention of the older woman who was a well-known busybody—yet somehow still adorable—who drove the whole island crazy. But they had to love her.

"I'll get the shoes. They'll have to be a bit girly for people to believe they're for Amelia, but maybe a pair of high top sneakers?" Lily asked.

Gen's eyes went wide.

"That would be perfect. Thank you," Gen gushed.

Lily waved a hand, acting as if it was no big deal.

"It's the least I can do for weaseling your secret out of you before you were ready to tell anyone," Lily said.

Gen shook her head. "There was no weaseling," she said.

"I'm so glad that you know. I don't know that I would have gotten through today if it weren't for you."

Lily placed a hand on Gen's arm that held Maddie. "You are giving me much too much credit. But I'll take it," she added with a grin. Then she moved her hand to Maddie's arm. "Do you want to go shopping, Maddie?" Lily asked, and Maddie nodded enthusiastically. How could a person not immediately fall in love with this girl?

"We getting shoes for Amelia?" Maddie asked, and Gen's eyes went wide as she tried to remember exactly what she'd said in front of Maddie's cute little ears. It was obvious that Maddie had understood quite a bit of what she and Lily had spoken about.

"For Amelia's new friend," Lily said so that they didn't have to lie.

Maddie seemed happy with that response while Gen was glad her secret was safe for at least a few more hours until she had the time to talk to Levi.

Gen gave Maddie another squeeze, but after looking at the clock, she knew she'd better give her daughter up, at least for the time being. Gen's four o'clock appointment would be there soon.

"Is it bad that I haven't gone to the doctor yet?" Gen asked as she set Maddie on the ground.

Lily opened her hand so that Maddie could place her little one within hers. "I think you're fine. Many women don't go in for months. I had a friend who didn't know she was pregnant until she was twenty weeks," Lily said.

Gen nodded. She'd heard stories like that and had wondered how in the world it could happen. But now that she was probably around fourteen weeks and had had absolutely no idea until a few days before, she could see exactly how in the world it happened.

"But I'm older ..." Gen began, and Lily put her free hand on Gen's shoulder.

"Gen, you just found out. You have a lot going on. Most of the time these babies bake just fine on their own. Take things one step at a time. Tell Levi, call the doctor. You'll be fine," Lily said in her matter-of-fact voice that Gen was sure worked on every one of the children she'd nannied.

Gen nodded and then smiled. She was going to tell Levi he was going to be a father tonight. Gen had always wondered what it would be like to watch Levi rock their baby to sleep, what he would be like in a birth room. But after years of trying for a baby, Gen figured she'd never know. Then when Maddie had come along in her unusual circumstances, Gen had held on to that. At least Levi got to be a biological father and Gen had the opportunity to be a mother. She'd miss the infant stages, and boy would she miss carrying a child in her belly. But she'd come to count her blessings.

Now they would get all of it. What an incredible miracle.

Lily and Maddie walked across the salon floor as they, especially Maddie, received greetings from Gen's stylists. Gen knew Maddie also had a number of them wrapped around her finger if the dolls and clothing she'd received in the past week were any indication. They paused at the receptionist desk where Lily talked to Kate, and then Gen had to stop watching them. Ellie Baker, Gen's four o'clock, came walking into the lobby of the salon, so Gen began her way to her station to ready it for the color Ellie was sure to ask for. Ellie had been coming in for the exact same cut and color every two months for three years.

Gen stopped for just a moment at her station to see that things were in place before walking to the color room to begin Ellie's color preference. Gen smiled to herself as she contemplated her bustling salon, her sweet little girl who had just left, her hot husband who was out on a worksite on the other side of the island, and now this new addition in her belly. Life was good.

GEN HAD TEXTED Levi to tell him she'd grab Maddie on her way home from the salon. Fortunately, Ellie had been her last appointment of the day, and because she'd been asking for the same thing for so long, it hadn't taken as long as most cut and colors. Gen was out of work by six, about the same time Levi would be done for the day, and she wanted to get Maddie so that she could also stop by for the pair of shoes. Lily had sent her a picture of the shoes, and Gen was already in love. The white and red sneakers were perfect. This was going to be perfect.

She and Maddie would walk in from work, Maddie holding the shoes, and they'd tell Levi he was going to be a daddy again.

Gen's heart flipped. This was real.

Thirty minutes later, with her daughter and the pair of shoes stowed safely in her car, Gen felt her hands shake as she unbuckled Maddie from her car seat. Levi's truck was already parked on their blue-iris-lined driveway, so this was it. Gen knew the changes coming in the next few moments were all good, all things she'd been praying to receive for years. Nonetheless, they were huge changes, life-altering changes, and Gen's heart raced at the thought.

Levi would be pleased, right? Gen had just assumed because this was what they'd both wanted for so long that of course he would be thrilled. But the timing of it was weird. They'd only had Maddie for a week. Their world had already just been knocked off kilter. Granted, Gen couldn't have been more overjoyed to raise Maddie with Levi, but it had already been one huge change. And now this? Was it too much?

Gen lifted Maddie into her arms before slinging her purse over her shoulder and then giving Maddie the box of shoes. Well, it was too late to worry about any of that now. She had a treasured life in her womb, and Levi had to know.

"Do you want to give this to Daddy?" Gen whispered into Maddie's ear as she put her down just inside their garage door. Gen would venture to guess that Levi was in the kitchen, getting started on something delicious for dinner. When Gen had started her salon, much of the cooking had fallen to Levi since he was usually the first home from work. They'd endured quite a few terrible dinners before Levi had decided to learn to cook, but many hours of cooking shows later, Levi was now practically a pro. Everything that he prepared was wonderful, and Gen now even preferred his cooking to her own.

Maddie seemed to know exactly where her dad would be as well because she raced down the hall toward the kitchen, leaving Gen with barely enough time to kick off her shoes and follow the blur of blonde curls.

When Gen entered their gray and white kitchen, Levi was holding the box of shoes as he stood next to a simmering pot on the stainless-steel, gas stove. He looked from Maddie to Gen with a perplexed look on his face.

"Did Maddie steal Amelia's shoes?" Levi asked.

Gen let out a giggle. She wasn't often a giggler, but her pent up anxiety allowed for little else. She needed Levi to know the truth and for them to move on from this moment. The thinking and rethinking of everything was killing her. She needed to share this beautiful new burden with her husband.

"These are too small for Maddie, right?" Levi asked, staring at the shoes in his hands. Maddie had been in shoes with soles ever since Gen and Levi first met her. The infant shoes Levi held were obviously for a much smaller child.

"So why does Maddie have these?" Levi had asked three

questions in a row without receiving a single answer. Gen realized it was time to speak up.

"They're for someone else in this home," Gen said before placing a hand over her belly.

Levi looked up at Gen, freezing, shoes in one hand and spatula in the other. His gaze seared into Gen, and she knew he was taking a moment to process things.

"Gen," Levi finally whispered as he dropped both hands, placing the spatula on the stovetop and giving the shoes back to Maddie.

Gen nodded, knowing the unspoken question her husband was asking. His eyes said it all.

"Seriously?" he asked, tears filling his eyes, and Gen felt her own well up with tears. How could Gen have been nervous? This baby was a blessing, an actual miracle. The timing of it didn't matter.

"Seriously?" Levi asked again, and Gen realized he needed an answer.

"Seriously," she replied quietly.

Levi bounded across the few white tiles between them and lifted Gen into his arms. "A baby?" he asked as tears spilled down his cheeks and mixed with Gen's as they held one another.

"A baby," Gen said. Her voice broke over the word and the emotions she felt rushing through her.

"We're having a baby?" he asked again, and Gen nodded her head against his.

Levi pulled back just enough that he could press his forehead to Gen's. It was one of Gen's favorite spots; she was able to look into Levi's eyes and was close enough that whenever she felt like it, she could kiss him.

"I love you," Levi said with such a surety that it made Gen quiver.

"I love you," Gen returned before Levi claimed her lips and showed Gen just how much he loved her.

"I love you," Maddie said from her spot on the kitchen floor, and Gen pulled away from Levi to gather Maddie into her arms. This baby was as much Maddie's as it was the rest of theirs. They'd come about their hodge-podge family in an unusual way, but in that moment, Gen knew things were just the way they were supposed to be.

CHAPTER SIX

"I DON'T WANT TO," Rachel said, louder than she had the time before.

Olivia knew her oldest was seconds away from blowing up.

"So we can't go?" Pearl asked, the child near tears.

Olivia was at a loss as to what to do.

She'd tried to present the outing to Bart's in a way that neither daughter could refuse. It would be time together with their dad at the beach. Lots of treats and playing in the sand. But Rachel had outright refused from the get-go. Olivia had been clear that the girls needed to be there together—she'd presented it to appear that it was for their sake, she didn't want Rachel to dislike her father any more than she did—so Pearl knew Rachel's refusal meant she couldn't go either.

Rachel looked from Pearl to her mother before crossing her arms across her chest and then scowling at her sister. "You can go by yourself," Rachel said before turning and stomping her way to the opposite side of the porch to sit on the swing.

"No, I can't. Mom said we have to go together. It will be good for us, right, Mom?" Pearl asked.

Olivia grappled for the right words to say. She'd begun this conversation outside in hopes that the fresh air and sunshine would make her girls more agreeable. Olivia had tried to point out to Rachel that Pearl would act as an excellent buffer for her. With Pearl trying to claim all of Bart's attention, Rachel could just get the treats and beach time and practically ignore their father, while Pearl got the time she craved.

Olivia had also hoped since they were outside that if things got tough—like in that moment—Buster could ease the tension. Too bad Buster seemed to be out on a run with Dean. But that was Olivia's fault. She hadn't checked to make sure Buster was there before talking to her girls.

"I do think it would be good for you girls to go to the beach with your dad. It's been a long time since you've seen him," Olivia said to Rachel who sat on the swing with her arms around her curled up legs, her burnt copper hair flowing over her shoulders. When had her little girl become such a beautiful preteen?

But the determination in Rachel's eyes was clear. She wasn't budging on the subject.

Olivia turned to Pearl whose wide brown eyes were full of too much hope. How was Olivia supposed to choose? Crush Pearl or further hurt Rachel? It was an impossible task. One of many she'd faced as a single mother, but it didn't get any easier.

"But if Rachel doesn't want to go," Olivia said to Pearl as she stroked Pearl's dark brown hair that was the exact shade of her father's.

"I can go by myself," Pearl said with a smile that didn't quite look real. She knew it was a stretch to ask, but that was how badly Pearl wanted to go.

"Pearly ..." Olivia began, but thankfully she was interrupted by Buster's barking. Finally.

The dog came bursting into the backyard, and both girls hurried forward to see their friend. Olivia noticed that Rachel held back, allowing her sister to go in for a hug before taking her own. Rachel knew not going was hurting her sister, and it was easy to see she didn't want Pearl to hurt. But she also, for whatever reason, could not go. And there was no way Olivia would make her. But what about Pearl?

"Dean!" Pearl called out, and Rachel echoed. Both girls looked nearly as excited to see Buster's owner as they were to see Buster.

A shirtless Dean walked through the yard, bestowing a fist bump to both of Olivia's girls since he was too sweaty to give hugs. Then he joined Olivia on the porch. Olivia worked hard not to notice the contours and ridges of Dean's arms, chest, and abs. But it was like staring into the sun during an eclipse. Olivia knew she shouldn't do it, but the sight was too marvelous not to tempt her beyond measure. She knew she wouldn't mind a hug, sweat and all.

Buster's bark pulled Olivia out of her Dean trance, and she was reminded that she was in the middle of a very serious conversation and a precarious situation. When the girls were done with Buster, they would expect for Olivia to somehow set things right. And she had no idea what to do.

"How's it going?" Dean whispered. As always, he'd picked up on the currents of the situation without Olivia having to say a word. She marveled at Dean's sensitivity to her predicaments.

"Not well. Neither will budge," Olivia whispered back.

Dean frowned, his face looking the way Olivia felt.

"Can we take him on a walk, Dean?" Rachel asked, stepping away from Buster just long enough to see the leash Dean still held in his hand. Pearl was still squatting beside Buster, hugging him with all she had.

"I'm guessing Buster is tired after his run with Dean," Olivia said, and Rachel nodded reluctantly as if she knew that answer was coming but still had to try.

"Maybe we can take Buster to the beach with us when we go see Dad," Pearl offered as a way of winning her sister over to her side. But judging by the scowl that returned to Rachel's face, that wasn't an option.

It did give Olivia an idea, though. One that might work.

Olivia glanced at Dean before looking back at her daughters. He gave Olivia a quick nod, and Olivia had to move past her awe of the man in front of her to present the new plan to her girls. Dean knew what she was asking of him and was willing. Judging by his smile, he was even happy to do what Olivia had had to beg the girls' father to do.

What a difference.

"I don't know that Buster can go to the beach that dad wants to go to," Olivia began, and Dean chimed in, "Buster has special beaches."

"Why does Buster have to go to a special beach?" Pearl asked, her head tilted in confusion.

"There are beaches just for dogs," Olivia said, and Pearl's mouth dropped open. Even Rachel seemed intrigued.

"So Buster goes to beaches with lots of other dogs?" Pearl asked.

Olivia nodded and decided to let Pearl take the lead for a minute while she was so excited by the prospect.

"But Dad can't go to that beach?" Pearl asked, and Olivia didn't want to lie. Bart could go to the beach, she just doubted he would want to considering his dislike of all things four-legged.

"Dad wouldn't want to. He hates dogs," Rachel said.

Olivia thought about trying to dull the words, but they were already out there, and they were the truth. Besides, Olivia needed Pearl to set her sights on a different plan than the one that involved Bart. Bart's declaration that he see both girls or neither was the reason behind all of this. So if Bart came out looking a little less than rosey but both of her girls were content, Olivia would be okay with that.

Pearl pursed her lips in consternation, and Olivia knew her youngest was deep in thought.

"But Dean could take us to the beach with Buster, right?" Rachel asked hopefully, looking first to her mother, then to Dean, and then to her sister.

"The beach with lots of dogs?" Pearl asked, and Dean nodded.

"But Dad can't," Pearl said softly, and Olivia hated that Pearl had to give up her afternoon with her dad. She was asking for so little, but Olivia knew this was the way it had to be for now. Hopefully one day Rachel would want to see her dad or Bart would stop acting like an idiot. But for now, Olivia hoped Pearl could be so excited about this new plan that the old one wouldn't feel so important.

"What about we go to the beach with Dad one day and Dean another day?" Pearl asked with a smile.

Olivia thought that was a perfectly valid request but one she couldn't give to her sweet girl.

"I don't want to go with Dad, Pearl. But we could go with Dean and Buster," Rachel said.

Pearl's smile fell. "Do you hate Daddy?" Pearl asked Rachel, and Olivia wondered if she should step in. But this wasn't her place. Her girls needed to work through this in their own ways sometimes. And she'd be right here if things got too hard for them.

Rachel nodded.

"But I love him," Pearl said, and Olivia felt her eyes begin to burn. How could one situation cause so many tears? How many times had Olivia cried for the girls' and her loss? Would the tears ever stop?

"But we're sisters," Rachel said. "We have to stick together, like Mom said. And I can't see Dad yet."

Pearl looked to their mother and then back to Rachel.

"Okay," Pearl said as she nuzzled Buster for another hug. "But I get to walk Buster on the special beach."

Rachel opened her mouth to argue, but then she must've thought better of it because she closed it and smiled at Pearl.

Olivia knew this conversation was one much too mature for a seven and ten-year-old. But Olivia had put them in this situation, and they had somehow made it through ... together. Her girls were incredible.

And once again, Buster and Dean had saved the day.

"Alright girls, two more minutes and then it's bath time," Olivia said.

The girls groaned for a second before deciding to put their last minutes outside to better use. Rachel ran for the tennis ball in the middle of the yard and threw it. Buster chased it and then brought it back to Pearl. Buster understood the turns of this game even better than her girls did.

"I'm sorry to have sprung this on you," Olivia said quietly as she turned her attention to Dean. "Are you really okay with it?"

Dean smiled as he watched the girls with his dog. "Having two sets of extra hands to entertain Buster? Of course."

Olivia knew Dean was trying to flip things so it wouldn't seem that Olivia owed him, but she did. She was always indebted to him these days. And if it were anyone else, that kind of obligation would be overwhelming. But with Dean, Olivia didn't mind. It was kind of nice to have someone to share her worries with.

But the situation had brought to light that there were some deep-seated issues, especially what Rachel felt for her father. Although Olivia had been seeing a therapist on her own, she was beginning to think they could all use it. Olivia knew she wouldn't be where she was without her own therapy sessions ... and Dean.

"I don't think I can thank you enough, Dean," Olivia began.

"Then don't try," Dean said with a grin as he nudged Olivia's shoulder playfully. "It's what friends do."

Right, friends. It was a good reminder to Olivia that that was all she was to Dean, and it was all she could handle in her life anyway. Olivia wanted to fix and love herself before she entered into a new relationship.

"I had thought the situation was impossible. And it would've been without you. Well, I guess mostly Buster." Olivia had to bring in some teasing or she was sure to show just how much Dean meant to her.

And she wasn't really falling for him. Probably. Maybe. It was just that he kept on saving her. She was the damsel in distress falling for the hero. It was bound to happen, and now that she knew what was happening, she could just get over it.

"Buster tends to save the day," Dean returned lightly before taking a step away.

And now it was time for good night.

"Time's up girls," Olivia called out, and although they both complained the whole way, her girls were in the door and heading toward the bathroom a few seconds later.

"Thanks again, Dean," Olivia said as the beautiful specimen of a man walked down her porch and toward his back door. If he would just wear a shirt, Olivia was pretty sure she could keep her rogue thoughts under control. Who was she kidding? Dean was so much more than his impressive chest.

"I'm here for you, Olivia. Always," Dean said, and Olivia had to shut her front door to gain some space. As her heart flipped, Olivia knew she could say or think anything she wanted, but her heart knew the truth. She had fallen in love with Dean.

CHAPTER SEVEN

DEB WIPED her hand across the thigh of her white bandage dress that she'd bought just for this occasion. Deb didn't do nervous often. She was usually too in control of every situation to let nerves get in the way. So when nervous did happen, like this evening, Deb didn't handle it well.

She had agreed to meet Luke, date number one from her new dating experiment, in the lobby of the Washington Grand, the home of her favorite restaurant in Seattle. Deb still wasn't sure this date was a good idea though.

She'd been messaging and talking to Luke for almost two months. He had been one of the first men she'd met on her dating site, but was this the way it was done? Come to a mutual location and meet all of a sudden? She guessed she couldn't ease her way into it any more than she had. What steps were there beyond emailing, texting, and then phone calls? They now had to meet or stop their interaction. And it was the second prospect that had pushed Deb to do the first. Deb felt a connection with Luke. She might even like him. And that scared her. Especially after Rich.

She should've tried this whole meet-in-person step with another guy first. One that she liked less. Maybe Peter, who worked for and lived with his parents.

"Deb?" the deep voice Deb had heard over the phone questioned, and Deb looked up to see the exact man she'd been waiting for. A part of her had worried that the deep chestnut hair from Luke's profile picture would now be receding and mostly gray. Or that his piercing gray eyes would've dulled. Or that his sexy broad shoulders would have dwindled away. But they were all still there. And by the way his blue button up shirt hung, Deb would even wager to guess that the abs shown in the one shirtless picture Luke had posted were very much still there as well.

Deb's stomach flipped as Luke took her hand and helped her to stand.

"You look stunning," Luke said, and the honesty in his voice shook Deb.

She felt immediate tears well up in her eyes. When was the last time she'd received a genuine compliment from a man? One that was sincere without asking for anything in return?

She turned away from Luke to let her eyes go wide and her pesky tears dry before turning back to him and saying, "I could say the same about you. Although, is stunning a compliment for a man?"

"Coming from a woman like you? Absolutely," Luke said with a smile and a pump of his eyebrows before he tucked Deb's hand into the crook of his arm.

"Do you mind?" he asked, and she shook her head.

Mind holding onto the muscled arm of maybe the most handsome man she'd ever seen with her own two eyes? Nope.

Luke led them to the escalator that took them up to the second-floor lobby and then into Luciano's, the best pasta outside of Italy and Bess's food truck.

"I'm guessing you painted today?" Luke asked after the maître d' had sat Deb and Luke at their table right next to the window. It was still twilight, and it was like the entire Seattle skyline was on display just for them. Deb knew as darkness fell, the view of the twinkling lights of the city would be nearly as beautiful.

"How did you know?" Deb asked. As an artist, she worked with all different mediums, although her favorite was oil painting on canvas. But Luke didn't know that, did he? She tried to recall their conversations and couldn't remember revealing that about herself. Of course he knew she was an artist, but she couldn't remember the details she'd given him about her career.

Luke gently touched the skin between her thumb and pointer finger where some blue paint had somehow survived her vigorous washings.

"You left me a few clues," Luke said, and Deb wasn't sure what she enjoyed more. Luke's touch or the fact that he was seeing her. Really seeing her. This man was incredible. And she was going to ruin this date. She could feel it. She should've practiced with Peter.

"Paint can be a bit pesky," Deb said after she'd swallowed, but her throat still felt dry. She moved the hand that was still right next to Luke's to commandeer her glass of water. She was going to need it.

After draining half of her glass and trying to avoid Luke's smile that said he knew just what he was doing to her, the waiter finally came to take their order. Fortunately, Deb had been to Luciano's a number of times or she would've been lost since she had yet to crack open the menu. Luke ordered a shared appetizer of fried calamari, but even with the heaviness of the coming dish, Deb still went for the classic fettuccini alfredo. It was a classic for a reason.

"Did Bailee pass her test?" Luke asked. Although Deb and

Luke hadn't gotten into too much detail about her career, Deb hadn't been able to hold back when it came to bragging about her children. Luke had seemed all too happy to ask questions and at least appear interested in Deb's responses, so Deb had kept on talking.

"Oh dear. Did I really tell you about that?" Deb asked, and Luke laughed.

"I asked how she was taking to college life. It was really my fault," Luke said, and Deb appreciated the laugh lines that crinkled around Luke's eyes. Deb wanted a man who laughed. Rich had been that man for a long time, but Deb realized it was long before he'd gone to London that his laughter had come far less frequently, especially when he was alone with Deb.

Deb chuckled. "Well, she passed it with flying colors. Although now she's convinced she studied too hard and thinks she should take it easy."

Luke barked out a laugh that had people turning in their direction, but Deb couldn't care less. A man who could enjoy himself was high on her list of what she'd hoped for her future. But what exactly did Deb hope would come from dating Luke or any of these other men? She had thought far enough into her future to know she wanted to date again, but was she dating because she wanted to have fun or did she want to find a specific man. And maybe ... did Deb want to give marriage another shot? She needed to make that decision soon because she had a feeling more time with Luke would push her in that direction.

"Did you get that file worked out for your client?" Deb asked because she knew it was now her turn to remember things about Luke's life. And she did. Every text conversation between the two of them had been saved in her phone, and the spoken conversations on the phone had been seared into her heart.

"I did. I'm so sorry that I lead such a boring life. You have news about your daughter, and I get to guess about your gorgeous paintings. But you ask me about files," he said, and Deb laughed.

"When you put it like that. Why am I out on a date with you again?" she joked. Before dating and marrying Rich, Deb wouldn't have been caught dead dating a CPA. They seemed boring, and boring had been a cardinal sin in young Deb's book. Now she wanted that. Not boring, but everything else a CPA represented. A solid job that kept Luke in one place, stability, no flights of fancy.

And Luke was all that Deb had hoped a secure CPA would be. But she also knew that he loved to play and watch sports, and he even enjoyed whitewater rafting and rock climbing. Plus, he was incredibly good looking to boot and not boring at all. Deb wondered if she'd found the Salvator Mundi, arguably the most sought-after and definitely the most expensive painting in the world, of dating. Luke seemed practically perfect.

"Because I'm charming.... And I may have guilted you into it," Luke said, causing Deb to laugh again. She missed laughing like this. Enjoying time with a partner and just ... laughing.

Deb stopped in her laughter when she realized Luke was watching her. His smile was sly but somehow also sweet, and she wondered what he was thinking.

"Do I have something on my face?" Deb asked as she put a hand up beside her mouth. She had been a little overzealous with the bread and calamari, but the food at this place was meant to be eaten with gusto, or at least that was Deb's method of thinking.

Luke shook his head once, his smile never wavering. "I'm just glad you said *yes* and that we're here together," he said, and Deb felt her stomach somersault.

Luke's words were shockingly honest, something she hadn't

been expecting. Even when she and Rich were at their best—and Rich could charm the socks off of Deb—he never said anything like this. Telling Deb she was the most beautiful woman in the room was more Rich's style. Then when he was angry, he'd tell Deb how gorgeous he found other women, pricking Deb's jealousy. It was almost as if he were taking back his compliment from before. Rich's compliments usually came with a price. Somehow she knew what Luke had said didn't.

"Me too," Deb finally said after sifting through her thoughts. She found herself falling for Luke, which should scare her. And although some parts of her were screaming to be wary—she'd fallen too fast and hard for Rich— other parts, surprisingly, some very reasonable parts of her brain, were telling her Luke wasn't anything like her ex.

Their waiter came back with their meals, and they began to eat in comfortable silence. The flutters of excitement that came with a really good first date were still there for Deb, but the uncomfortable nerves were all gone. Was this a first date miracle? Deb figured after what Rich had put her through, maybe she deserved this.

"I was thinking we should do a day date for our next date," Luke said, and Deb couldn't hide her wide smile that immediately spilt over her face. Luke wanted a second date, and he wasn't going to play games by making her guess until the end if he liked her or not, make her wait for a call, or any of the other things men had done to her in the past to make sure she knew her place. Luke was telling Deb she had a place in his life.... And it was a spectacular place to be.

"That sounds nice," Deb said, and Luke grinned at the casualness of Deb's words because it was easy to see from her smile that she thought another date would be more than nice.

"There's this—" Luke began, but Deb felt her purse vibrate, causing her to look away from Luke and down at her purse. Deb

NEW BEGINNINGS ON WHISLING ISLAND   87

would've liked to ignore any and all calls on a date, but since she had kids, she didn't have that luxury. Sure, they weren't little and in need of her constant care. But with Bailee still a just a freshman in college, Deb knew her daughter might need her to be on call at any moment. Besides, Deb's children had been the opposite of needy so far, and their calls hadn't come as frequently as Deb would've liked. If either was calling now, something could be up, and Deb wasn't about to ignore that possibility.

So Deb pulled her phone out of her purse and, sure enough, Bailee's name lit up the screen.

"I should take this." Deb looked regretfully at Luke, but he just smiled.

"Of course. I would never expect you to not take a call from your kids." And the man was a Saint on earth. He not only supported her relationship with her children, he also seemed to read her mind.

As Deb stood, Luke did the same, and Deb wasn't sure why that action made her want to cry. She knew it wasn't necessary. She was a modern, independent woman who didn't need a man to stand when she left the room. But there was something so sweet and quaint about the action, it hit Deb in her heart. It was just one of the many ways during the evening that Luke had shown he respected her. And that, Deb could get on board with.

Deb answered the call when she was about halfway across the restaurant. She didn't want to speak until she was out in the second-floor lobby of the hotel where she'd seen clusters of gray couches, but she knew if she waited that long to answer, she would miss the call.

"Hey, Bailee," Deb said, feeling the smile that Luke had put on her face still there. If this was what dating was like these days, Deb was so grateful she'd signed up for it.

"Hi, Mom," Bailee said cautiously, and Deb knew the news coming next wasn't going to be good.

What had Bailee done? Deb thought about the car her daughter was sharing with her brother since they were now both attending a small private college just outside of Seattle together. She worried that Bailee might've crashed it. Deb then realized that more than the car could be hurt. Was Bailee okay?

"What's going on, baby girl?" Deb resorted to the nickname she knew Bailee didn't appreciate, but Deb was now worked up and worried. Those two emotions brought out sentiments, whether Bailee liked it or not.

"So I just got off the phone with Dad," Bailee began, and somehow Deb's body became even more tense as she sat on that plush, gray couch.

It wasn't an accident, so at least Bailee wasn't hurt, but if she was bringing news from her dad to Deb, Deb knew whatever was coming had to be bad news. Maybe even terrible news.

"You know how we have a week off next month?" Bailee asked.

Yes, Deb knew. She had been looking forward to this school break for months, long before she'd sent both of her kiddos—Wes had decided to transfer from UDub—off to their new college, Perry University, this past August. This fall break was the first time that both of her children would be back with her for more than a dinner since they'd left for school in late summer. Sure, her offspring were only a ferry ride away, but between homework, school activities, and friends, it was hard for them to get away from it all. The upcoming break was already a treasure to Deb.

"Dad just called Wes and told him he wants both of us to come spend our fall break with him and Halley." Bailee said the name that made Deb's skin crawl. It was one thing for the man to have an affair with some young flight attendant, but he'd been an idiot who'd gone and married her. And now he was trying to make that woman a fixture in her children's lives? Not if Deb had any say.

Deb swallowed and tried to calm herself, even as she felt rage within her boil.

"What do you think about this?" Deb asked Bailee.

"I guess it's understandable. Dad told Wes that you get to see us all the time since we're at school here and he's all the way in London," Bailee said, her voice going high, the way it did when she was nervous about the words she was saying. Her poor children did not deserve to be in the middle of this mess, and it was up to Deb to ease Bailee's worries.

"Sweetheart, I am behind any decision you make. One hundred percent. This is up to you and your brother. I don't want you to feel that you have to stay here for me," Deb said, even though what she really wanted to do was jump on the first plane to London and strangle her ex. The man had left them. No one had forced him to go to London, and he could always move back home if he wanted to see his kids more frequently. But now he was using the consequences of his own choices to strong-arm his children into choosing him over Deb.

Deb pulled the phone away from her mouth as she cleared her throat, a common sign that she was working hard to bite back her frustration.

"Then maybe we should go?" Bailee asked, her voice so full of concern that Deb forgot about her own emotions.

"Bailee. Sweet girl ..." Deb began, but she heard a shuffling on the other end of the line and then the deep voice of her son saying something to Bailee. Deb was still having a hard time reconciling this strong, masculine voice with her baby boy.

"Hi, Mom," Wes said, causing Deb to grin. She didn't often get to talk to her Wes on the phone. She swore he didn't quite understand the concept that you could speak into the device instead of just tapping out a text message, so when she did hear his voice, it was always a delight. Even if she was seconds away from hurting Wes's father.

"Hey, Wes. How are you doing?" Deb asked, even though she knew he wasn't on the phone to exchange pleasantries. But she really wanted to know how he was doing.

"Okay. Fine. Classes are good," Wes said, giving the answer he always gave when it came to Deb asking about his well-being. She always wanted to pry deeper—she knew there was much more to his life than school—but her relationship with Wes was an interesting one for her to traverse, and Deb couldn't just go after what she wanted when it came to him. She needed to tread lightly in some moments, while in others, he was more than happy to share. She had a feeling this was one of the former moments.

"Are you really going to be okay with us going to London? We don't want to leave you, but what Dad said is pretty true. He hasn't gotten to see us since summer the way that you have," Wes said. Deb worked on being rational when all she wanted to do was scream out that she had only seen them for a few Sunday dinners. The way Rich was wording things made it seem like the kids had never left her home and Deb was being the selfish one here. After she'd given up the very last week of her very last summer with her daughter so that her kids could go to London for his stupid wedding.

"And I guess Halley has been on him about getting more time with us. But they've been flying like crazy and haven't been able to make it out to Seattle yet," Wes said.

Deb bit her lip to keep from shouting all of the indelicate things she was thinking. Yes, both Rich and ...—Deb found herself having a hard time thinking the name of her replacement—Halley worked for the airlines and could've come to visit her kids for free. However, now they were playing the *we haven't seen you in longer* card to commandeer Wes and Bailee's first college break and force them to London. It wasn't fair. None of this was fair. The fact that Deb had to make this transition from everyday mother to empty nester all on her own, the fact that Rich had married a new woman, the fact that they were trying to steal her children away. It was so unfair. And it was all Rich's fault.

Deb felt her stomach thick with anger, but she had to hide it from her kids. She had to. For their sake.

"But they'll have time off during your break?" Deb asked in what she hoped was a civil tone. If Rich and Halley thought they could take her children across a continent and an ocean only to work most of the time the kids were in London, they had another thing coming to them.

"They will," Bailee said excitedly, and Deb realized she was on speakerphone.

Bailee was excited. And Deb wasn't about to crush that spirit, even if she did want to crush Rich.

"Fantastic," Deb said, even though she thought it was anything but. If Rich and Halley were not going to be around, Deb still had a reason to fight this proposed arrangement.

Now that the kids were both in college, the custody arrangement of the divorce didn't cover things anymore. She and Rich were supposed to act like grownups and arrange big moments like their kids' breaks together. Too bad Rich was a lily-livered coward and worked through their children instead.

"So you'll really be okay?" Wes asked.

Deb knew there was only one answer to that question, even though she wasn't going to be. If this were about her, she would fight, kick and scream until she got her way in this. But it wasn't about her. This was about her kids. And they were happy to be going to London and visiting their father for their break. The first time in months that she was going to be able to have both kids under her roof for more than an evening was being stolen from Deb. And her throat went dry at the thought. But she still had to be okay. At least until she got off the phone.

"I'm fine. I'm happy for you. Both of you. Have fun in London. Do all of the touristy stuff you missed last time," Deb offered, trying to sound cheerful.

The wedding week had apparently not offered her kids any time to explore, and they'd missed their chance to ride the London Eye, the one thing they'd both hoped to do.

"Take lots of pictures for me," Deb said as she felt her eyes go glassy. She had to get off the phone now.

"We will," Bailee promised, her voice sounding nearer than before. Now that they had finished the important parts of the talk, it seemed as if Bailee had been given control of the phone again.

"Well, I'm on a date, so I'd better get back," Deb said, and Bailee gasped.

"Right now?" Bailee asked.

Deb chuckled, but she worried it sounded more like a bark. She was still so angry.

"Why did you answer your phone? Get back there, and I need pictures too," Bailee said before Wes groaned. "No pictures, please. But have fun, Mom."

It had taken Deb a few days to muster up the courage to tell her kids that she wanted to get back out there again. But she shouldn't have worried about it. Both teased her that she was on a dating site, but other than that, it had gone smoothly. Maybe Rich getting married so soon after their divorce had driven the point home to her kids that Mom and Dad were over for good, or maybe they just saw that both parents were much more content apart. Either way, neither child had taken issue with Deb dating again. In fact, Bailee had been thrilled.

"Bye, Mom," her children said in unison, and then they were gone.

Deb allowed her phone to drop from her ear, and she stared at it in her lap. She may have been in a hurry to get off the phone, but now that she was, she was in no hurry to get back in to Luke. She knew anger and tension had to be radiating off of her with the way she felt at the moment, and she knew Luke would surely notice her change in demeanor immediately.

Deb drew in a long, calming breath, but it wasn't helping. She still wanted to get on the first plane to London and tear Rich a new one. How dare he! He knew he was playing on her kids' emotions by talking to them directly instead of going to Deb, the way they'd agreed to. And he knew Deb would have no recourse with the courts, or at all, after he'd riled up the kids so much that they were thrilled about this trip.

She and Rich had been married for over twenty years, so Rich knew exactly what this first break meant to Deb. Yet he'd still stolen it.

Ugh!

Deb felt her hands begin to shake, and instead of gaining any control over her emotions, the opposite was happening. She was moments away from losing it.

"Deb?" Luke's voice, which was typically like a balm, raised Deb's hackles even more. What was he doing out here? Couldn't he have given her more time?

"I was worried when you didn't come back in. Is everything okay?" Luke asked.

Deb closed her eyes before looking behind her to where Luke stood close to the entrance of the restaurant.

To lie or not to lie? That was the question. But Deb quickly realized she didn't have enough energy to do anything but spill the truth.

"My ex is taking my kids for their first break from college

since the divorce, Bailee's first college break ever," Deb deadpanned. "And he didn't talk to me. He worked it out with the kids and, like a coward, sent them to tell me."

Deb clenched her teeth as she felt her blood boil. Hearing the situation in her own words was only like adding gas to an already flaming fire within her.

"I'm sorry," Luke said. "That's got to be tough."

Deb didn't know what she expected Luke to say. The words were fine enough. But they felt placating in a situation where Deb did not want to be placated. It almost seemed as if he expected her to be okay now that this was all over. But of course she wasn't. Rich had stolen what was most precious to her, and here Luke was saying *that's got to be tough.* Duh!

"It's beyond tough," Deb said. Then she faced forward again so that she was facing away from the restaurant and Luke, toward the clear glass half walls that divided the second-floor lobby from the vaulted ceilings of the first-floor lobby.

"I'm sorry if I said the wrong thing. This is new for me," Luke said honestly as he drew closer. But that was the last thing Deb wanted. She wanted time, and she needed space.

"I've got to go," Deb said. Even as she stood, she knew she was making a mistake. Luke was the best guy she'd met ... well, maybe ever. She was an idiot to walk away after she'd treated him so badly. But she had no choice. Her anger had taken over.

"Are you sure?" Luke asked as he stepped around the sofa so that he was now only a step away from Deb.

Deb nodded and then walked away as briskly as her heels would allow before she could change her mind and fall into Luke's arms, the way a big part of her wanted to. She was sure those arms could help to heal some of the terrible fire inside of her. How she knew that after less than a date, she didn't know, but she was sure of it.

As Deb walked, she could feel Luke's gaze on her back,

willing her to give them a second chance. Because walking away now would surely be the end of them, right? Their beautiful second date would never happen. But Deb's anger made her choice, and she was down the escalator and racing for her car before she knew it. In the end this would be better, her anger promised. But the rest of Deb wasn't so sure.

———

DEB LOGGED into her internet dating app and knew it was a mistake. Although thousands of guys waited for her to press on their faces and make a match, she knew the only person she wanted to match with had already seen her at her worse. Then to top things off, she'd walked away from him.

Luke hadn't called, messaged, or texted since that dinner almost a week before, and Deb didn't blame him. She had barely noticed his lack of communication for the first two days because her rage at Rich had taken over everything else. But after the anger had dissipated, Deb realized her mistake and logged into her dating app, hoping Luke had left a message there. But nada.

And now, five days later, still nada. Deb really missed Luke. For the week and a half leading up to their date, every morning she'd awakened to a stupid dad joke that was so silly, it actually made her laugh. They'd texted back and forth throughout the day, letting the other know about crazy, funny, or happy things that had happened to them. It was the closest Deb had felt to someone in a long time. And now he was gone.

So she'd done the only thing she could think to do: gone on too many first dates with other men in an attempt to forget all about Luke. A plan that had failed miserably.

There was Darryl at the coffee shop who was dull. The guy had been cheated on by his wife, so Deb was sure the common ground would help them in their dating quest. But by the time

Deb left the coffee house, she was the one who felt cheated ... of a good time. What kind of guy was able to make a cheating tale dull? Cheating was many, many terrible things, but dull wasn't one of them.

Lunch at the sandwich shop with Todd had been just as terrible. He'd been his high school quarterback, and if Deb had to hear one more story about his glory days, she was sure she'd upchuck the turkey on rye she'd used to keep herself busy while Todd had gone on and on. It hadn't helped that Todd's wide receiver from high school had shown up in the same sandwich shop, and Deb had gotten double teamed by the stories. She had a feeling the wide receiver showing up wasn't a coincidence and thought about giving Todd a head's up that his friend showing up wouldn't help him on the dating front. But Deb refrained when she realized this act *was* Todd. If a woman didn't like it, she wouldn't like Todd. Which Deb didn't.

And then there was drinks with Maxwell. Deb still wasn't drinking alcohol since the incident she'd had during her divorce when she'd lost it with Bailee. Deb knew she was still too angry, if the ending of her date with Luke had told her anything, to consume anything that would make her lose control. Her anger was volatile enough. But Maxwell was hot and much younger than Deb, so she figured she could make a few sacrifices to go on a date with him, even if it meant going to a nightclub and watching him drink while she ordered diet cokes. After Darryl and Todd, Deb needed to mix it up a bit anyway. And hopefully prove to herself that Luke was not the only worthwhile guy on the entire site.

So she went to have drinks with Maxwell. In a dry-clean-only black dress that made her look ten years younger, if Bess could be believed. She showed up at the dark nightclub in Seattle in four inch heels, somehow made it to Maxwell's table without breaking her neck, and after all of that ... Maxwell was just as unappealing to Deb as the other two men. And to top off the night, in his sloppy, drunken state, he dropped a drink all over Deb's dress.

Deb looked at the app, knowing she could have another three, four or even five dates in the next week—the men were never-ending—but also knowing the connection she'd found with Luke wasn't something she'd find again. The moment she'd seen his picture, Deb had known. Call it a gut feeling or women's intuition, she'd just known Luke was going to be different. And he was. But Deb had blown it.

Deb sat up from where she'd been lying on her couch. She'd begun in a seated position, but after all of the discouraging thoughts, she'd somehow ended up lying on the arm of her black couch. And although the sectional was comfy, Deb's neck wasn't as limber as it once had been, and she found herself sitting back up as she turned her neck this way and that in order to get the cricks out. When had she come to an age when things could start to hurt within moments of abusing them? It seemed all too recently that Deb could've fallen asleep on that armrest and woken up feeling refreshed. Man, getting older really stunk on some days.

A knock sounded on her front door, and Deb looked at the clock because she wasn't expecting anyone until noon when Olivia was going to come by to drop off some papers that Bess needed to get to her accountant. Since Deb was going into Seattle every other day for her all-too-frequent dates, Bess realized she could capitalize on that and use Deb as a free courier. She was surprised to see that it was already almost noon.

Deb rounded the black ottoman that doubled as a coffee table for her living room and walked past the dark wood bookcases and credenzas that were now filled with knickknacks and tons of clutter. Rich would've hated both, and Deb smiled a little at that thought. It had taken some months, but the place no longer felt like it belonged to Rich. Even in the time Rich had lived in London, Deb had tried to keep their home a place where Rich would feel not only welcome but at ease. As soon as Deb realized Rich was never coming back, she immediately started to let the clutter build up—her first move at redecoration—and added her own paintings to every available wall. She knew it was a bit much, Rich had felt it was boasting for her to show off her talent in their home, but Deb deserved to boast. She worked hard at what she did. Sure, she had some God-given talent, but the paintings didn't just create themselves. Deb's sweat and sometimes tears were involved in each and every art piece, and she deserved to revel in her talent instead of making sure it stayed hidden away in her studio.

The last painting she came to before opening the front door was one of her favorites. She'd painted it from a memory she'd had many years before. She'd taken Wes and Bailee to a nearby park when they couldn't have been more than five and two. Bailee had toddled around in the grass while Wes had tried to climb anything and everything available to him. Deb had captured a moment in her mind when Wes had climbed to the tip tops of one of the large oak trees in the park as Bailee waited patiently, looking proudly up at her brother. It was sweet and sentimental all at once, some of Deb's favorite emotions to portray on canvas.

"Olivia," Deb said as she opened her door to let the red-headed beauty in. Olivia was the kind of woman every other woman envied. She had the svelte figure of a ballerina as well as the grace. She walked gently, but the piercing look in her blue eyes told Deb she was a lot more cunning than her beauty and grace let on.

"'Thanks for taking these to Seattle, Deb," Olivia said as she stepped into Deb's front entryway, then followed Deb into the living room.

"Not a problem. I was glad I could save you the trip," Deb said as she sat. Then she realized she should probably offer Olivia some kind of refreshment. It had been a while since Deb had had anyone over who wasn't so comfortable in her home that they would just go into her kitchen and get whatever they wanted.

"Do you want coffee or something?" Deb offered.

Olivia shook her head. "I came here straight from Bess's," she said by way of explanation, and that was all Deb needed to know. No one came out of her best friend's home unfed or without every refreshment they needed or wanted ... or sometimes didn't need or want. "I told her we could just mail or scan and email most of this paperwork, but I think she feels a lot more comfortable knowing this entire envelope will be handed directly to Danny."

Deb nodded. She wasn't quite as old school as Bess, but she understood Bess's need for person to person contact. So Deb was happy to oblige.

"I don't mind. I can at least make some use out of my frequent trips to Seattle. We both know the dates have been pretty worthless," Deb said before pursing her lips.

"Bess said something about a dating app?" Olivia said, and Deb rolled her eyes.

"The bane of my existence at the moment," Deb said, and Olivia's eyebrows shot up in confusion.

"Are you on one of these?" Deb asked as she held out her phone that was open to the app.

Olivia shook her head, causing her red hair to fly. "I can't even think about dating," the beautiful woman said, and Deb narrowed her eyes in confusion. Olivia had moved out of her husband's home many months before. She should at least be thinking about moving on.

"I know that look," Olivia said. "I've even given it to myself a time or two. But between the girls and the mess that I am ..."

Deb wanted to interject that Olivia wasn't a mess. But Deb knew how much happened behind closed doors and in broken hearts to never say anything like that. She was sure so much was going on with Olivia that she'd never know and maybe wouldn't be able to understand. And by dishing out a blanket statement like the one she'd thought, no matter how well-meaning, she could do more to hurt than serve the recipient. So Deb kept her mouth shut.

Olivia clasped her hands together before laying them in her lap. "I'm just not ready to entangle anyone else up in all that's going on with us."

Olivia dropped her eyes to her lap, and Deb wanted to scoop the woman up in a hug. Sure, she and Olivia had become friends over the past few months, but Olivia was still nearly young enough to be Deb's daughter. And in moments like this, Deb's maternal side had her craving to make everything better for Olivia. But Deb knew that kind of healing wasn't something she could initiate.

Sometimes Deb wondered if her anger had helped her to heal faster than those around her dealing with similar circumstances. Bess still seemed unsure of her divorce, which Deb hated, and was reluctant to cut all ties. Olivia was also not ready to move on completely. Whereas Deb felt as if she couldn't move on fast enough. Her anger was like a fire under her that continually spurred her forward.

Olivia seemed thoughtful after her words, and Deb had heard enough of the rumors to wonder if Olivia's thoughts were on her handsome landlord who seemed to be over at Olivia's home much more than necessary, if the gossip could be believed. Deb usually didn't give much credence to the island gossip, but she kind of hoped this stuff was true. Olivia deserved a good man after Bart. Deb didn't know Bart too well, but most on the island had been charmed by him enough that Deb had wondered if there was something fishy behind his exterior. Someone who worked so hard to charm the world was hiding something. At least in Deb's book.

Deb gave Olivia a few more moments with her thoughts before deciding it was time to bring her out of the doldrums. And what better way to do so than for Deb to tell Olivia all of her own problems. She hoped to at least amuse the younger woman with some of her dating tales.

"Well, I wish I could give online dating a glowing recommendation," Deb said, and Olivia looked up from her lap.

"But most of the time it's just as horrible as everyone says it is," Deb added, and Olivia grinned.

"I didn't really date much," Olivia admitted. "I married my high school boyfriend."

Deb shook her head. "Well, I've dated enough for the both of us, I'm sure," she laughed, and Olivia joined her.

Deb had dated and dated and dated before she'd met Rich. Deb had been pretty sure she was going to be a perpetual dater until Rich took her off the market. Now that she was back on the scene, she'd expected to enjoy at least the freedom of it all. But maybe single men had become a rotten bunch in her twenty-plus years off the market. Or there were only duds, other than Luke, available. Because, unlike pre-Rich Deb, now-Deb felt the urge, maybe even need, to get off the market once again.

"Have you had any good dates?" Olivia asked as she looked over Deb's phone and then pointed at the picture of Luke. "Um, please tell me you're going to go out with this guy."

Deb sighed as she admired the picture of Luke once again. "One good date. With that guy," Deb said.

Olivia beamed. "He's extremely good looking," Olivia said with a cute pump of her eyebrows.

"He is. And the date was going pretty great until I ruined it," Deb said. Then she shook her head at her folly. Why couldn't she have gotten the call about her kids during any of the other dates? Why did it have to be that night?

Olivia opened her mouth and then closed it. Deb was sure she was going to say something along the lines of *whatever you did couldn't have been that bad*, but it looked like Olivia was learning the same lesson Deb had. It was safer to never assume.

"What happened?" Olivia asked, quickly adding, "If you don't mind my asking."

"I don't. Basically the kids called with news that Rich was trying to strong-arm them into going to London for their first break of the year. I flipped my lid and took it out on Luke."

"Oh," Olivia breathed.

Deb nodded. *Oh* was right.

"You like him," Olivia said, and Deb nodded again. She couldn't get the man out of her head, something that should scare her considering what the last man who'd infiltrated all of her thoughts had done. But Luke was nothing like Rich. Deb had seen that even when they were still just texting. Phone calls and their one date had continued to prove that Luke was different from any man Deb had ever known.

"But no use crying over spilt milk, right?" Deb said as she stood and began to gather some of the mess that had accumulated on her couch since she now lived alone and no one really used the couch besides her. Olivia occupied one of the two seats that weren't littered with blankets, books, magazines, and even a couple clean paintbrushes. Deb only cleaned up when she wasn't sure what to think or say. When she had to find a purpose for her hands.

"Can't you clean up the milk?" Olivia asked, and Deb paused with a blanket in one hand and a stack of magazines in the other.

"I've always wondered about that phrase. Of course you don't have to cry. Just clean it up," Olivia added.

Deb set the unfolded blanket back where it had been and allowed the stack of magazines to fall from her hand back onto the couch. "Do you think I should call him?" Deb asked. Sure she'd considered the idea for like a second once before, but it had felt like she'd caused too much damage for Luke to ever forgive her. Why take a second chance on Deb when there were so many more women out there on the app for him to have a better first chance with?

"I do. You like him, and it seems like your other dates haven't gone so well," Olivia said.

They hadn't.

"What do you have to lose?" Olivia asked.

My pride, Deb thought right off the bat. Giving Luke an upper hand, admitting she was wrong.

But the more Deb thought about those things, the more she realized if she was going to really make things work with any guy, she'd have to sacrifice those things at times eventually. Might as well start practicing now? But why would Luke forgive her when there were so many more fish in the sea? Unless maybe he was having as hard of a time finding a connection like theirs once again as well? Deb could only hope. And call him.

"I'd better go," Olivia said as she stood and looked at her watch. "I've got some errands to run before I pick up my girls from school. But good luck, Deb. For what it's worth, I think you deserve another chance."

Deb gave her friend a hug before following her to the front door.

"Thank you, Olivia." Deb meant it. She now had the nerve to call Luke. Who knew when she would've mustered that up if it weren't for Olivia's visit? "Let me know when I can return the favor. I can already imagine your entire profile," Deb said with a smirk.

Olivia chuckled. "Yup. Not happening," she said as she walked onto Deb's porch.

"Never say never," Deb said before closing her front door and leaning against it.

She honed in on her phone, which was resting on the ottoman.

A phone call. It would be easy. Dial Luke's number and talk. She could do this.

Deb stomped over to her phone, somehow feeling a little more powerful with each determined step.

She could do this.

She picked up her phone and sat in her favorite seat on the couch. She then held her phone up, and the staredown began. Deb didn't break eye contact with her phone for a good minute before realizing she was just stalling. Her phone wasn't going to back down ... because it was an inanimate object.

She needed to make this call before she lost her mind.

Deb unlocked her phone and then went into her contacts before she could back out. She clicked on Luke's name and then pressed his number. The call had started. It was too late to back out now.

The phone rang once, twice, three times. Luke had never not answered Deb's call, so she wasn't sure how many rings it would take to send her to voicemail. Was he not going to answer this time? What was Deb going to say to Luke's voicemail?

Deb heard a click, the telltale sign that Luke wasn't going to answer. He'd let her go to voicemail. Did that mean he was ignoring her call? Did Luke not want a second chance? Then Deb heard his voice. "This is Luke. Leave—"

Luke's voice was interrupted by a buzzing, and Deb realized she had another call coming in. Did she dare take this call and not leave a message for Luke? But what was she going to say over message anyway? *Call me back?* Hopefully Luke would see her missed call and call Deb anyway. If he didn't? She'd have to take it from there.

Deb looked at her phone to see who was calling, and her heart flipped. It was Luke.

Deb clicked over to the other call as fast as her fingers would allow. She cleared her throat before saying, "Hello."

"Hey, Deb?" Luke's deep voice filled the airwaves between them. "I was hoping you would call."

He was? Deb's little heart leapt again, and it was only now that she realized how hard she'd fallen in such a short time. She really liked Luke. She wanted to make this work.

"I need to apologize," Deb said. "I shouldn't have left the way I did."

"If you need to apologize, I should do the same. I shouldn't have come out to find you. I've kicked myself for that move for days. I should've given you more space," Luke said, ever the gentleman.

"You couldn't have known," Deb said.

"And yet I should have. I knew as soon as I walked out of the restaurant that you were fine physically. But you needed more time. I've had more than adequate training after living with three women for years. I should've turned right back around and let you come to me when you were ready," Luke said.

Deb couldn't help but smile. "It sounds like you know women well," she said.

"I wouldn't be so sure my two daughters would agree with that statement. But yes, living with them has taught me a thing or two," Luke said.

"Does that mean you'll give me a second chance?" Deb asked, only able to truly hope he might after how wonderfully their conversation had gone.

"That depends," Luke said, and Deb's heart dropped. She had thought it was going so well. "Will you give me a second chance?"

Deb giggled and breathed a sigh of relief. Luke hadn't given up on her.

"Do you have plans tomorrow evening?" Luke asked.

Deb was about to tell him *no* when she realized she did. She was supposed to meet Victor for coffee right after he was done with work. But then again, six was kind of late for coffee. Deb smiled as she realized a way to rearrange her plans. She could go to coffee with Victor at lunch, drop off the papers for Bess, and then take her profile down from the app. Because she was done with trying to juggle all of these dates. The appeal of the app had once upon a time been the fact that Deb could meet so many men at once, but the appeal had faded because Deb found herself wanting a great date with just one man at a time. Preferably Luke. And now she had that chance. She wasn't about to blow it again.

"Tomorrow sounds great," Deb said.

"I get off of work about five thirty. Do you want me to come to the island this time?" Luke asked.

Deb grinned. She'd purposely set every first date in Seattle. Having a man meet her on the island was a bit intimate, and she'd assumed it would take several dates to get to the bring-them-to-Whisling point. But she found herself not wanting to take any more time before letting Luke see her hometown. She not only wanted to show off the island to him, she also hoped to show him off a little. Having Luke come to the island would mean a little rearranging of her plans, but she could get back to Whisling in plenty of time after her coffee date and errand for Bess.

"I'd love that," Deb said. "I can pick you up at the ferry. Just text me when you get on one."

"It's a date," Luke said before ending the call.

Deb's stomach flipped in anticipation. That it was.

DEB SAT across from Luke at Winders, one of the delicious seafood restaurants on the island. There were several on Whisling, and all of them were good. Deb chose this particular one because it was the only place she could get a reservation for a seafront view with so little notice. She was owed favors from several of the owners because she'd outfitted all of the restaurants with a few of her paintings, but when she'd found the already open reservation at Winders, she'd decided to take it instead of calling in one of the favors.

Deb's very favorite restaurant on the island was not a sit down place; it was Bess's food truck. But although she really wanted to take Luke there, she didn't want to eat outside or take Luke back to her place. It was much too soon for that. So for now, Winders would have to do.

"What's good here?" Luke asked as he perused the menu.

"Everything," Deb said honestly. "I guess it depends on what you feel like."

"I'm thinking seafood," Luke said.

Deb laughed. "Good choice."

"Maybe ..." Luke looked over the menu again, and Deb decided to help him out.

"The crab legs are incredible, but I think I'm going to go with salmon tonight," Deb said.

Luke nodded. "Better date food. I like the way you think. I'll do the same," he said with a grin.

Deb loved that Luke wasn't afraid to say things like he saw them. He wasn't into playing games, and after being married to

and bamboozled by such a charmer, Luke was completely
refreshing.

"Deb," Otis, the owner of the Winder, greeted as he came to
their table to give Deb a kiss on either cheek. Otis could often be
found at the Winder during the dinner rush; he loved to mingle
with his patrons.

"Otis. Good to see you," Deb said with a smile before
turning to Luke.

"This is my friend, Luke," Deb added.

"By the way he's looking at you, he's more than a friend,
Deb," Otis warned cheekily, and Deb felt herself blush.

"Has Deb boasted about what a talent she is?" Otis continued, and Deb felt her cheeks go redder. Otis was worse than a
proud papa.

"She hasn't," Luke said, playing right along with Otis and
then looking at Deb with mock outrage. "Deb, you've been a
neglectful date."

Deb shook her head as Otis motioned for Luke to stand. "I
guess I'll have to take him on the tour. We've got some of Deb's
very best pieces here," Otis said before leading Luke toward one
of Deb's paintings that was above the table of another couple.
Obviously Otis had no need for Deb.

Otis spoke to Luke and then to the couple before turning
back to point at Deb. Deb had hoped staying at the table would
keep her out of the limelight, but no such luck. The couple gave
Deb a golf clap of congratulations before Otis moved on
with Luke.

"Did you need a few more minutes before you order?" the
waiter asked as he returned to Deb and Luke's table with their
drinks.

"I think we'll both have the salmon," Deb said, and the
waiter nodded.

"Great choice," he said before leaving to go toward the kitchen.

Luke came back to their table a few minutes later.

"I hope you don't mind, but I ordered for you," Deb said.

Luke grinned. "How could I mind? A masterful talent like you could do very little wrong," he teased.

Deb felt her cheeks flame again. "Otis's words?" she asked.

Luke nodded. "But I have to agree. You are incredible, Deb."

"It's a job," Deb said because she was unsure of what to do with such high praise. Heaven knew Rich hadn't given the same to her.

"It's a calling," Luke said as he sat back down across from her.

Deb met Luke's intense gaze, wondering what all he was trying to tell her with just his eyes. "What do your girls think of you going on another date?" Deb asked as a way of changing the subject. She knew Luke was always up for talking about his girls.

"They're the ones who dressed me," Luke said with a somewhat embarrassed grin. "So I guess you could say they're a little excited."

Deb looked from Luke's gray suit, which fit his fine shoulders, to his yellow tie, which brought out the gold in his eyes.

"Excellent work, girls," Deb commended.

Luke chuckled. "I wasn't looking for a compliment," he said.

Deb grinned. "Well, you got one anyway," she said as their food arrived. The smell of the garlic butter on the salmon made Deb's mouth water immediately, and even though it might not have been the best date etiquette, Deb dug in immediately.

"Both girls consider themselves budding fashionistas, so they took the assignment seriously," Luke said, but only after he, too, got to taste the salmon. "This is incredible, by the way."

"Isn't it? Otis hired a star talent right out of culinary school. He found a gem."

Luke nodded. "I'll have to bring Grace here. She's thinking she might want to skip the college route and go to culinary school."

"How do her parents feel about that?" Deb asked. She was a little nervous about her question because it was the first time she'd brought up Luke's ex. Well, not the very first time. She had tried to subtly inquire about her during one of their first real text conversations—the kind that went on for a hundred texts back and forth—but the question had been promptly ignored. Deb had taken that to mean the exes were having a hard time navigating their relationship the same way she and Rich were because she had also avoided talk of Rich. But now seemed like the right time to bring her back up. If she and Luke were going to go anywhere beyond this date, things were going to get more serious. And that meant knowing a bit more about what she was getting into. She'd have to give Luke the same consideration as well. Even though her kids were out of the house, Deb was still having to deal with Rich as a coparent, ugh. Deb could only imagine how often Luke's ex would be in the picture considering both of his girls were still in high school.

"Her dad is mulling over the idea. But I'm sure her mom would be thrilled. Katya was a veritable home chef and the reason why Grace loves to be in the kitchen so much," Luke said. It was easy to see the wistfulness in his eyes.

Not what Deb had been expecting, and she had to admit the look in Luke's eyes hurt. Deb wasn't sure she should press, but it almost seemed like Luke was still in love with his ex. Was that why he didn't want to talk about her? Deb couldn't handle being the other woman, even if the first woman was out of the picture.

It was only after all those thoughts that Deb caught a minor detail that might mean a lot. Why had Luke said *would be*?

Didn't his ex know about Grace's future plans? Unless she was completely out of the picture. Deb needed more info, asap.

"I take it you don't often talk to the girls' mom?" Deb asked.

Luke shook his head and then paused mid-shake, his eyes filling with pain. "I haven't told you," he said quietly as he set down his fork.

Deb did the same as Luke reached across the table for her hand. What had Luke not told her? Granted, it was only a second date, so she guessed she couldn't be too upset if he'd kept stuff from her. But Deb still didn't like it.

"It's a subject I typically avoid. It feels like everyone in my life already knows about it, and they only want to talk to me to get the gritty details."

Deb understood that. She often felt that way when people asked her how Rich was doing these days. They didn't really care; they just wanted to know if Deb still wanted to kill him.

Deb nodded, hoping she could help Luke to go on. She didn't know where this conversation would take them, and she didn't care for that. Because she really liked Luke. She adored the way his chestnut hair curled just above his left, gray-blue eyes, even when the rest was relatively well tamed. She liked his calming voice and the way he looked at her when he first saw her on each of their dates, like he was the luckiest guy in the world. Even though Deb knew she was the lucky one. But whatever Luke was about to tell her was big. And Deb didn't like it. But she still wanted to know. It was a difficult conflict of feelings.

"Katya," Luke said with an emotion Deb tried to pinpoint. It wasn't adoration, but it wasn't the contempt with which she said Rich's name. What did that mean?

It took Deb a few seconds while Luke mulled over his next words, but she figured it out. It was reverence. Luke said his ex-wife's name with reverence.

"She was diagnosed with ovarian cancer when Ashley was twelve and Grace was eleven," Luke said softly.

Deb fought the urge to gasp. Katya wasn't Luke's ex. He was a widow. Deb hadn't even considered that to be a possibility. She wasn't sure why. Maybe because Luke was such a vibrant and lively man, it seemed almost impossible that he'd been touched so closely by death.

"She fought hard. For so many years beyond what the doctors gave her. She hated that the girls would only have memories of her while she was sick, but at the same time, she wanted them to have as many memories as they could."

Deb felt her eyes fill with tears at the idea of leaving Wes and Bailee. They were her world. To know something was robbing you of a future with them? Deb swallowed back her cry and blinked her tears away. This was about Luke and his family.

"She passed a little over two years ago." Luke scratched his head as if he didn't know what to say beyond that. Deb felt lost as well, but she decided it was up to her to continue their conversation since Luke didn't seem to want to.

"I'm sorry," Deb began when she realized there were no better words to convey what she was feeling.

She squeezed Luke's hand that she still held across the table and then looked into his eyes, hoping to find some clue as to what to say to help him. To help them.

Deb thought about telling Luke she was sure the girls would treasure their memories or she could only imagine how hard it had been for him to lose the woman he loved, but all of it seemed wrong. Deb couldn't understand. She knew nothing when it came to losing a beloved family member to death.

"Happiness is hard to find after tragedy." Deb said the only truth she knew that felt relevant to Luke's situation.

"It is," Luke said. "But that's part of why the girls were so thrilled to dress me for this date. They said today was the most excited I've been to go out with someone since their mom."

Deb didn't bother to hide her grin. She was pretty sure Luke wanted her to be pleased about that statement, and she was. But she was also scared. Coming into a relationship after a divorce was hard, but it was what Deb had expected when it came to dating men her age. This, however, was far different. No one in their family had wanted Katya to leave. If given the choice, all three of them would want her back. Deb felt terrible for their loss. But she was left wondering: where did she fit into the equation?

CHAPTER EIGHT

"STEPHEN," Bess said as she embraced her firstborn on her doorstep. Sunday dinners with all of her children were getting to be fewer and further apart in the past few months. Between Stephen's PHD, Lindsey's new job, and James's social life, Bess found herself with just one out of three on many Sundays. But that wouldn't be the case this Sunday. All three had promised to show up, and Bess had gone all out.

"It smells amazing in here," Stephen said as Bess led him into the kitchen where she had both a red and white sauce simmering on the stove. The red sauce would be a dipping sauce for the homemade breadsticks she had in the oven, and the white sauce would cover the cheesy shells sitting next to the stove. She'd already pan fried half a dozen pieces of chicken for the chicken parmesan that was in the oven, and she had a side of butter and garlic pasta, just the way James liked it.

"Whoa. And it looks different," Stephen said as he looked around the newly painted kitchen.

For the first time in Bess's life, she'd hired help to do the redecorating of her home. She'd been wary of hiring the work out at first because she was quite picky when it came to the look of her home. But between the busyness of the food truck and Bess's need for her home to not only appear but feel different now that it was just her home without Jon, hiring someone to do the work seemed necessary. Deb had tried to convince Bess to hire a decorator, but that wasn't going to happen. Bess had a vision for what she wanted to change; she just needed someone to do the legwork. So she'd had Levi's right-hand man, Greg, pull down the wallpaper and paint the walls and cabinets a bright white—like the farmhouse kitchens she'd been seeing so much of—as well as exchange the hardware on all the cabinets and drawers to a slim, gold handle. She'd kept her large, white sink that she'd always loved for cleaning her big pots and pans, as well as the large picture window that overlooked the aging trees in her front yard. But other than that, everything looked completely different. She'd found a gray marble countertop that went with the rest of the theme and had even had Greg refurbish her beloved table. It was now as white as the rest of the kitchen, and although it had been the hardest change to make, she knew she had to. The memories associated with the table were nearly as strong as any in Bess's mind, and letting go of Jon also meant letting go of that table.

"Do you like it?" Bess asked Stephen, who immediately nodded.

"This is literally Jana's dream kitchen," Stephen said, the hurt on his face easy to see.

"How are things going with Jana?" Bess didn't want to pry, but she knew Stephen would never bring up his ex-fiancé unless Bess did. And she felt partially at fault for the demise of their engagement. If she and Jon hadn't split, maybe Jana and Stephen would still be together as well. But Bess knew her guilt needed to be set aside because it helped no one. Nothing about the past could be changed. Bess had asked Jon to leave, and Jana and Stephen had broken up as a result of the hurt Stephen had felt from his father's betrayal. At least they were broken up temporarily. Bess still had hope for her son and the sweet girl he'd loved for so long.

"She's willing to go to therapy with me," Stephen said slowly as he ran his hand through his rich dark hair. The thickness and texture of Stephen's hair was just like his father's, but the color was all Stephen's own. It wasn't quite brown but it still wasn't black, a beautiful color in between that Bess had always loved.

"That's good. For both of you," Bess said, trying not to smile too big. Stephen had been needing to seek outside help for a while and had been dragging his feet. Thankfully, wanting to be with Jana was enough of a push to get Stephen going in that direction. Even if he and Jana stayed apart, Bess really hoped this therapy would help Stephen move on.

"It is. Jana knows I need it. And if we're going to be together, *we* need it. But I don't think she's sold on the idea of *us* yet," Stephen said honestly as he sat at the new white table, crossing his arms in front of him.

"I wouldn't expect her to be," Bess said softly.

Stephen nodded. "I hurt her. And she says part of her wants to forgive me but part of her is scared. She can't commit to forever with a guy who will run at the first sign of trouble."

Bess wasn't quite sure that was fair to Stephen. What had happened was more than the first sign of trouble. His role model, his father, had fallen from his pedestal, and poor Stephen had had to deal with the repercussions of that fall. Should Stephen have let Jana in? Absolutely. But Stephen's whole world had fallen apart. Bess couldn't help but want to defend him.

"It was a little more than that," Bess said softly, hoping not to offend Stephen or Jana.

"I'm pretty sure she knows that now. Now that I've let her in a little more. She really does feel bad for me. And she wants to be there for me. But because I didn't let her before ... she worries that this change of heart is temporary," Stephen said.

That was a valid concern.

"We have our first therapy appointment this week. We'll hash it out and see where the pieces fall," Stephen said as Bess turned to the stove to make sure nothing was burning. She poured the white sauce over the shells and then put them in the oven. The meal should be ready in ten minutes, and she was pretty sure her other children would be there just in time. Stephen had caught the ferry that came in just before the others since he didn't have his car with him.

"That's a mature outlook," Bess said.

Stephen smiled. "I guess it is. Hopefully Jana will notice," he said. Then he stood. "Do you need help with anything, Mom?"

Bess looked around at her kitchen, knowing she wanted to tidy up a bit before they sat down for dinner.

"Do you want to set the table?" Bess asked.

Stephen grinned. "I'd be happy to."

The two set to work, and soon the front door opened once again, the house filling with immediate noise when Lindsey and James came in arguing about who had won their silly game guessing what time they'd walk through the doors of their child-hood home.

"I said six oh two," Lindsey argued as they both came into the kitchen.

James shook his head in disagreement. "You said six ten. I said six oh two," he said.

Bess chuckled. Children might grow and leave the nest, but that didn't mean they grew beyond their silly disagreements. Bess loved the reminder that her children would always stay her children, no matter how big or old they got. They were her babies.

"You're wrong," Lindsey chided.

Bess felt it was time to intervene. "Agree to disagree?" she asked. It was what she'd often said to the kids to get them to stop arguing when they were little. At least when the issue didn't really matter, like this one.

James and Lindsey looked at one another before turning to their mother.

"Fine," James muttered, and Lindsey nodded her assent as well.

"But only because in my heart, I know I'm right," Lindsey said as she took a few steps away and sat at the table.

James rolled his eyes and looked as if he was going to say more when Bess took her youngest into her arms to give him a bear hug before whispering, "Let it go."

James nodded, and Bess had to look up too far to see that her baby was agreeing with her. She wasn't sure she liked that all three of her children had outgrown her, her youngest by nearly a foot.

"Thank you. I'll give you more of the leftovers," Bess whispered again, and James grinned widely before joining his sister at the table.

The siblings fell into conversation, thankfully not of the arguing variety, as Bess served up plates, and all of her children helped to take them over. She was grateful she'd raised children who didn't expect to be served. They knew they needed to be up and helping if they expected to eat.

Conversation first went in the way of Lindsey's new job and then focused on James and his lack of being able to commit to anything: an apartment, a career, and especially a girl. Bess kept silent for most of that conversation, knowing James was still young. The part about James's reluctance towards finding a job did worry her a bit since he was a senior this year and really should be zeroing in on what he wanted to do after college, but she figured a little bit of a lost moment was okay for now. When it mattered, James usually came alive, and Bess was counting on that happening soon.

Lindsey asked about Jana, and Stephen just told his sister he was working on it. Bess was grateful she'd already talked with her oldest or she would've been completely in the dark. The woman was too good not to go after, at least in Bess's opinion, and she was pretty sure Stephen felt the same way.

"Have you talked to dad lately?" Lindsey asked her brothers, and Bess felt her ears perk up but tried to keep her face from showing any emotion. She'd known Stephen was having a hard time accepting his father back in his life after he'd cheated on Bess. But Stephen had promised he'd try, and she knew Jon was doing everything in his power to keep that relationship from failing. Jon had always been an excellent father. Most of the time he'd been an excellent husband as well. It was just that they'd gotten lazy over the last few years, neither putting their relationship or the other first. But Bess would've never imagined the sweet man who'd carried her over the threshold and stayed up into the night with all three of their babies would be a man who could also betray her. But he had.

James nodded as Stephen muttered, "Yeah," around a mouthful of pasta.

That was amazing news.

Stephen chewed and then swallowed.

"He said he signed the papers and your divorce is final?" Stephen looked to Bess, and Bess nodded.

She'd been surprised by the lack of emotion she'd felt that day when her attorney had told her the entire process was complete, a week after she'd signed the final papers. She was no longer a married woman. She'd expected pain, sorrow, or maybe even rejoicing. What she hadn't expected was to feel calm and peace. She wasn't sure what that meant other than she felt she'd made the right decision. She'd needed to divorce Jon to move on from what he had done. She'd heard dozens of stories—people liked to share all of their life's tales with Bess after hearing what she'd experienced, invited or not—of couples working through infidelity and coming out stronger on the other end. And Bess had entertained that thought. So many nights she'd stayed awake wondering if ending her marriage was the right thing to do. But for her, it had been. Bess and Jon needed to step away from one another for their sake and the sake of their children. There was no easy decision when it came to ending a marriage, but for Bess it had been the right one.

"I'm glad he let you go. It was the least he could do, considering ...," Stephen said.

Bess wasn't sure how to respond to that. She'd had an initial conversation with each of her children about Jon's cheating and then a few more conversations with Stephen because he'd needed it. But Jon's infidelity wasn't something she wanted to talk about every time they spoke about their father. It wasn't fair to Bess and her healing, and it definitely wasn't fair to Jon. He was so much more than that specific incident, especially for his children.

"We came to a mutual understanding that it was best for us," Bess said before turning to each of her children to gauge how they were handling the topic.

James seemed unaffected, just as interested in his chicken as he'd ever been. Lindsey nodded thoughtfully as she met her mother's gaze but didn't seem upset in the least. And even Stephen didn't look hurt when Bess landed her eyes on him. He gave her a soft smile of understanding, and Bess knew she'd done the right thing for herself and her family, even if Jon hadn't been as sure about the divorce. He'd called her that final day as he'd picked up the pen to sign the last of the documents. Bess had let silent tears fall as he'd asked her for one more chance to make things right. She'd insisted this was the way to make things right, and Jon had signed without any further argument. Before he ended the call, he said, "I'll always be here, Bess. And I'll always love you."

It was the last time they'd spoken, and Bess had to admit the peaceful manner in which they'd completed their divorce must have added to her calm. For that, she'd forever be grateful to Jon.

"It's still weird," James said as he looked up from his plate and joined the conversation.

"What's weird?" Lindsey asked.

"To have a single dad. He asked me about Tinder the other day," James said, and Lindsey gagged.

"You told him to stay far, far away from the app, right?" Stephen asked, horror filling his face.

"Can you imagine?" Lindsey said when she finally stopped pretending to lose her dinner. "What if he matched with someone we knew or, oh my gosh, one of my friends?" Lindsey began to gag once again, and Bess wasn't sure she felt all that great either. She'd known Jon would date again, she probably would too, but she wasn't sure why she'd assumed she'd be ready to date first. Maybe because she was the one who'd finally pulled the plug on their marriage? But she guessed she wasn't, if Jon was already joining dating apps.

"I told him Tinder was for hooking up." James said the words too lightly, and Bess felt her stomach flip. She didn't like the idea of her husband of thirty years going onto a dating app to "hook up." But he was his own man now. However, she hoped she knew him well enough to assume he wouldn't be like that.

"I guess he had no idea," James continued. "He thought it was a normal dating site. He'd just heard some of his students talking about it and decided to ask me before he got the app."

James laughed, and Stephen joined him. Lindsey still looked as horrified as Bess felt. Fortunately, she did know Jon well enough, and he wasn't looking for a purely physical relationship. But he was looking for something. Bess swallowed. Did that mean she should be looking for something too?

"So he's dating?" Stephen asked the question Bess would've never dared to.

James shrugged. "I guess. Those sites go pretty fast once you sign up. I have friends who go on two to five dates a week. It's like a buffet of women," James said, and it was now time for Bess to interject.

"James," she reprimanded, and James looked toward her with a guilty expression. He knew what he'd said was crude, but she wasn't sure he knew just how demeaning to women his comment had been.

"Sorry, Mom," James said quickly, but that wasn't quite enough. Bess had to make sure James knew better.

"Buffet of women?" Bess asked, and James hung his head in shame, the same way he had when he'd broken Bess's favorite snow globe when he was ten.

"You do understand how disgusting even the idea is," Lindsey said, and James nodded slowly.

"It's just something the guys say. I shouldn't have said it," James said.

Bess shook her head. "You shouldn't have even thought it, son," Bess said, deciding right then and there she wasn't going to sign up for one of those dating sites. She'd always felt uneasy about them but understood that it was hard to meet people to date these days. But James had been a little right in his assessment. Not the words, but the idea. There were so many women, and men, on the site, why would you settle for just one when you could just keep on scrolling and find a dozen more. Bess knew the sites worked for some, like Deb and maybe Jon, but they weren't for her.

"I know, Mom. I really am sorry. The words just fell out, but

I promise I don't think of women in that way. I'm not even signed up for any of them," James promised.

Bess smiled. She knew her son hadn't meant any real harm by his words, but just because we don't mean harm with our words doesn't mean they don't cause harm.

"I know, James. I just want to be sure you are showing how much you respect women with every word you say and each deed you do," Bess said to James, who nodded in agreement. Then she turned to Stephen.

"I'm trying," Stephen said, and Bess could see the guilt on his face at the way he'd treated Jana.

Bess nodded and then looked at Lindsey.

"Me?" Lindsey asked.

"Yes, you. You're the most important. Because if we as women can't respect ourselves and our peers, how can we expect anyone else to do it?" Bess said, and Lindsey nodded slowly, a few of her brown curls falling out of her ponytail to frame her heart shaped face.

"Yeah, I guess that makes sense. I think I do?" Lindsey said. Then she tilted her head as she pondered. "No, I do," she finished after a moment of thought.

"Good," Bess said, allowing James to take over the conversation. Evidently it was football season, and all three of her kids were diehard Seahawks fans.

Bess's thoughts went back to Jon and the fact that he was dating. Hadn't he just told her he'd always be there for her? But had she really thought that had meant he'd never love another woman again? That he'd wait on the tiny possibility that Bess would one day return to him? No. That was silly for her to think and would've been foolish for him to follow through with. Of course Jon had to date. He couldn't be alone forever. But it all just felt so fast.

"They need a better kicker," Stephen said, and Bess

pretended like she cared by nodding along with Lindsey. But James came to the kicker's defense as Bess's thoughts wandered once again.

Jon was divorced. He had to be thinking about moving on. The same way Bess should be thinking about moving on. She just hadn't yet.

She remembered the way she'd felt with Dax on his porch. Well, maybe she'd thought about moving on a little. But she wasn't ready to act on those feelings, was she?

Definitely not with Dax. As if the gorgeous man who had women falling all over him was interested in a frumpy woman who wore an apron half the day and leggings the other half. Besides, the guy didn't even live on the island. Talk about unavailable. Olivia had told Bess that because Dax was going to be doing a lot of traveling back and forth between Nashville and Los Angeles, he hoped to be able to stop for a few days on Whisling in between some of those trips, especially after all of the time he'd spent away for so many years. Bess had hoped for a millisecond that she could be a small reason why Dax would want to come home more often than he had before, but she soon realized how silly those thoughts were. The few interactions she'd had with the man since her divorce had left her flustered and feeling foolish. There was no way he could be interested in Bess. But she did have to admit she was highly attracted to the man. Maybe that meant she was ready to move on? To date? Someone other than Dax though. The attraction there was definitely one-sided.

"Are you going to get that?" Lindsey asked, and Bess looked at her daughter with a raised eyebrow.

Get what?

A knock sounded on the door, and Bess realized it must've happened once before as well, but Bess had been too far gone in her thoughts to even notice.

"Oh, yes," Bess said as she stood and walked to the foyer to see who had been knocking.

The way that Bess's front door opened blocked the sightline from her kids to outside, and Bess was eternally grateful for that when she saw who was standing on her doorstep.

"Dax. You're back," Bess said, not liking the breathless quality her voice took on any time she talked to the man. But could he be a little less attractive? His auburn hair had gotten a recent cut—it was short on the sides but still long on the top— and Bess liked the look ... a lot. Dax had styled his hair up and away from his face, giving Bess a great view of his blue eyes and strong jaw. What was it about a chiseled jawline that was so attractive? But it was.

"Hey, Bess. I couldn't stay away for long. Now that I'm trav- eling so much anyway, might as well make a pit stop on my favorite island. Besides, I needed to bring this back." Dax held out the disposable tray that had held the cookies she'd given to him over a month before.

"It's meant to be thrown away," Bess said, and Dax looked down at the hard paper platter that Bess was pretty sure wasn't even the same one she'd given to Dax.

"Really?" he said, even though it was quite obvious.

"Really," Bess said, not able to help the way her cheeks brightened or her mouth lifted into a smile.

"Hm, well maybe this was all just an excuse to come over to see you again," Dax said, and Bess felt her mouth go dry. She inhaled deeply through her nose, the smells of her delicious dinner hitting her hard, and then realized why Dax was there. The man wasn't there for her; he was there for her food. He must've smelled their dinner cooking from next door—she knew smells wafted around the neighborhood with ease—and his stomach, not his heart, had led him to her doorstep.

Oh man, her foolishness took no time to make another

appearance. All it took was the presence of Dax. But she was a grown woman who had power over her attractions, so Bess smiled and opened the door wider.

"Why don't you come in? I can serve you up a plate," Bess said as she stepped back from the door so that Dax could get in.

Bess needed to get it through her thick skull once and for all that a man like Dax could never actually be interested in Bess as a woman. Her food, on the other hand? She was sure every man wanted that.

With a grin, Dax stepped into Bess's home, but his eyes went wide with surprise when he saw Bess's full dinner table.

"Hey," Lindsey said with a smirk as she looked Dax up and down.

"Hi," Dax said as he smiled at each of Bess's children.

"Dax, this is Lindsey, Stephen, and James," Bess introduced as she pointed to each of her children. "This is Dax Penn, from next door."

"Hi, Dax Penn, from next door," Lindsey said sassily. Bess shot a look of warning at her daughter from behind Dax's back before stepping in front of him and waving toward the table.

"Have a seat, Dax," Bess instructed before she went to load up a plate with probably too much food for any one man to eat.

"So, Dax, from next door," Lindsey said, obviously not heeding Bess's warning. "What brings you to Whisling?"

Stephen sat back and then crossed his arms across his chest as James leaned forward to lean on his elbows. Evidently everyone was waiting for Dax's response.

"I grew up here. I came back to visit last month while I was in the middle of moving and enjoyed my stay so much that I decided I needed to make the visit much more often," Dax said, giving Bess a pointed look as she set his full plate of food in front of him.

Bess felt her stomach flip at that look. But she wasn't the

reason he wanted to come back so much. She couldn't be. During his last trip, he'd been home a few more days after the cookie incident—he'd had ample opportunity to seek Bess out—but Bess had only seen him at her food truck. And even when he'd come to her truck, they hadn't done more than exchange pleasantries. Then he'd left for over a month with absolutely no communication. Not exactly the actions of a man interested in her. Bess shook her mind free of her fanciful thoughts and reminded herself she needed to focus on the little group around the table.

"This looks delicious, Bess," Dax added, fixing Bess with his warm gaze. Dax needed to stop doing that if all he wanted from Bess was food.

"Thank you," Bess said, but she was stopped from saying more when Lindsey stood from her seat beside Dax.

"You should sit here, Mom. Next to your *friend*," Lindsey said, emphasizing the word all too much and making Bess's face flame once again. This was why people shouldn't date with children. Not that she and Dax were dating, but from the stance of her boys and the cheekiness of her girl, one would guess they were. Her kids needed to stop.

Bess thought about telling Lindsey her move wasn't necessary, but that would only draw more attention to Lindsey's unwarranted action. So Bess just sat.

"Moving at this point in your career? Does that mean you're between jobs?" Stephen asked, his eyes boring into Dax.

Fortunately, Dax was focused on his food, so he didn't notice Stephen's glare or the way Bess shot one back at her son. She hoped her wordless warning told him to chill out.

"No," Dax said, looking up. "Same job. Two locations now."

"What do you do?" James asked, leaning forward as he joined in on the interrogation.

What had gotten into her kids, and how could Bess get rid of it?

"I'm a talent agent," Dax said before scooping a bite of shells into his mouth.

"Do you serve these on the truck?" Dax asked, his eyes full of appreciation, and Bess shook her head.

"You should," Dax said, and Bess grinned.

"Mom's full of all kinds of talents," Lindsey interjected from left field, and Bess's eyes went wide.

Lindsey just smiled back at her mom before mouthing, "He's hot!"

Bess felt her face flame as she checked from the side of her gaze to see that, thankfully, Dax's head was down and focused on his food once again.

"Have you been to the truck?" Stephen asked another question, his tone low and full of condescension.

"Almost every day I'm on the island," Dax said matter-of-factly.

"What?" Bess asked. This was news to her. She'd seen Dax at her truck a couple of times, but she didn't know he'd gone every day. Granted, she didn't work on the truck every day.

"Alexis is great and all, but I was always a little disappointed when you weren't the one preparing my food," Dax said. "You're just a cut above the rest, and I missed seeing your beautiful face."

Out of the corner of her eye, Bess could see Lindsey mouth *beautiful face* as her boys' stances went rigid.

"So a talent agent. Do you represent anyone we've heard of?" Stephen asked all too haughtily.

"Stephen," Bess reprimanded out loud for the first time because his comment was that rude.

"It's a good question, Mom," James added, and Bess wished she could stare daggers at her sons without Dax seeing her do it.

But Dax's attention was now completely on those who sat around the table. He had stopped eating and had actually put his fork down to answer Stephen's question.

"Probably a few," Dax said, and Stephen scoffed.

"Like who?" James pressed as he leaned even further into his elbows, his chest dipping so low it almost hit his plate.

Bess ached to throw two breadsticks right at each of her knuckleheaded sons' heads.

"Shelby Yates, Blake Young, Ellis Rider are a few," Dax said, and Lindsey laughed in the faces of both her brothers.

"Big enough names for you?" Lindsey asked James mockingly, since all three of the names Dax mentioned were some of the biggest in country music.

"Oh, and I just signed Julia Price." Dax added the name of arguably the most sought after actress in Hollywood. "I guess she heard I'd just relocated to LA, and she wasn't happy with her current representation."

Lindsey's mouth dropped open, and James leaned back in his seat. Even Stephen seemed a bit in awe.

"I didn't know that," Bess said as she gifted Dax a warm smile.

"No one does yet. Julia's publicist will be announcing it tomorrow," Dax said, returning Bess's smile with one just as warm. Maybe a little too warm, if you asked Bess. She thought about fanning herself, but it would be highly inappropriate in front of Dax ... or her children.

"So you're highly successful," Lindsey said with a smirk directed at both of her brothers.

"I guess," Dax said with a shrug of one shoulder, an act full of humility. "But my professional feats could never be compared to your mother's. I mean, this is what she does on her off-time?" Dax held out his hands to display his mostly empty plate.

"Right? Mom's a winner," Lindsey said with a wink at Bess,

making Bess feel a little like she was being sold to the highest bidder. Which, if Dax was the highest bidder, Bess would have to say she didn't mind. But Bess highly doubted Dax was even in the running for showing her any kind of attention, other than the kind that admired her food.

And Bess didn't mind. She loved that he loved what she created. Well, she mostly didn't mind. She had to admit, she was quite attracted to the man next door. Even if he was too young, too handsome, and too ready to head back to LA for Bess's good.

"And with that sentiment, we'd better be heading back to the ferry," James said as he rolled his eyes toward his sister. Even the baby of the family had caught on that Lindsey was trying to set their mom up with their fine-looking dinner guest. "We brought Lindsey's car, so we'll have to catch the eight-thirty back."

At James's announcement, all embarrassment and annoyance at her children fled. Her kids might be frustrating at times, but Bess didn't want them to be anywhere but with her.

Bess nodded in response to James as her kids began to shuffle and Lindsey grabbed her purse from one of the kitchen stools. Living on the island was full of so many wonderful features, but having to take a ferry to and from the mainland sometimes wore on Bess. Especially when it meant her kids had to head out before she was ready to see them go. But living by the ferry schedule was a fact of life for every resident of Whisling Island, and Bess was no exception. Since the ferry only took cars over on a few of its daily trips, if her kids wanted to drive to the ferry station in Seattle and then from the dock on Whisling up to her home, they had to make sure to catch the rounds that allowed for cars. Thus, they had to leave at eight-thirty instead of on the latest ferry that headed back to Seattle at eleven.

"I guess I'll go back with them," Stephen said, even as he continued to eye Dax suspiciously. "Do you mind dropping me off at my place so I don't have to catch the bus home from the docks in Seattle, Lindz?"

Lindsey tapped her lips thoughtfully as Stephen rolled his eyes. It was the same thing Lindsey had done to her brothers for years whenever she had the upper hand. Lindsey lived for these moments.

"I guess. But you'll owe me," she said with a wide smirk. "Maybe to the tune of asking Alex if you can give me his number."

Stephen groaned. "Lindsey, you know how I feel about you dating my friends." Stephen shook his head, but Lindsey just smiled.

"I also know how you feel about taking the bus," Lindsey said sassily.

Bess fought the urge to chuckle. Laughing right now would only exacerbate Stephen's annoyance.

"Why didn't you bring your car?" James asked as the rest of them got up from the table and started heading toward the front door.

"I was hanging out with Jana, and I had her drop me off at the dock. I assumed my dear sister would be happy to take me home." Stephen narrowed his eyes at the sister in question who continued to smirk back.

"I would love to take you home, Stephen. All I'm asking is a tiny favor in return," Lindsey said in a sing-song voice that Bess knew would annoy Stephen more. How was it that siblings always knew exactly which buttons to push?

Lindsey opened the door as Stephen groaned again.

"Fine. But if he doesn't call you, not my problem," Stephen said as he and James followed Lindsey out the door.

"Why wouldn't he call me? Do you know something I don't?" Lindsey asked as she stopped walking and turned to question her brother. Now it was Stephen who was smirking.

He also knew just how to get under Lindsey's skin and maybe get his way after all.

Bess followed her kids onto the front porch where she received hugs from all three.

"Listen to your brother's advice on guys," she whispered in Lindsey's ear as she hugged her.

Lindsey grudgingly nodded because she knew, in the end, her brothers were usually just looking out for her. Although Stephen could be a bit overprotective at times.

"Be nice to your sister," Bess whispered as she hugged Stephen, and Stephen pulled back, giving her his *innocent look* that he'd perfected over the years.

Bess shook her head and smacked his shoulder before turning to James.

"Oh, the leftovers," Bess exclaimed, about to go back and pack them up when Lindsey looked at her watch.

"Sorry, James. No time," Lindsey said, and James's face fell. Bess knew he counted on at least an extra meal or two from the food she gave him when he left on Sunday evenings.

James pulled his mom into his arms and said, "I guess that means I'll have to be back next week." Bess couldn't help the huge grin that came over her face.

"Me too," Stephen said as Lindsey nodded, filling Bess's heart with a peace that only came from knowing she would get to see her children again soon.

"And make sure you're ready to spill the update on Mr. McHottie in there," Lindsey said all too loudly as she pointed toward the kitchen that was just a few steps away.

Bess's face flamed red as she realized she'd all but forgotten that Dax was still in her kitchen amidst the chaos of sending her kids home.

"Good night, Lindsey," Bess said as she ushered her daughter toward her car.

"Night, Mom," she called back as her brothers followed down the driveway.

Bess paused a moment before shutting the door behind her children. She willed her face to cool before she went back into her home to see Dax. It was impossible for him to not have heard Lindsey's last declaration. What would Dax think? He had to know Bess knew better than to hope for any romantic attachment with him, right?

Well, there was only one way to find out. Bess stood up straight and marched herself right back into her kitchen. Maybe if she held her head high enough, Dax would never know the embarrassment she was feeling?

As Bess walked into the next room, she found a clear and clean table and Dax standing in front of her sink, slipping on the gloves Bess wore to do her dishes. Was this man about to clean up after dinner? Bess hadn't had a man wash the dishes ... ever. The kitchen had always been her domain. And although she loved to cook, she disliked cleaning up all of the mess as much as the next woman. But Jon had never even thought to volunteer to do the dishes. He worked while Bess took care of the home.

So a man washing Bess's dishes? This was a foreign concept Bess was still working on wrapping her mind around.

"What are you doing?" Bess asked Dax, in case she might've somehow mistaken him putting on dish gloves and now turning on her sink.

"I thought I'd clean up," Dax said before turning back to look at Bess. "As long as you don't mind?"

Bess shook her head slowly. "No, not at all. Thank you," she said as she began to gather up the dishes around the kitchen, putting the empty ones in the sink and then placing the left-overs all in one tray that she planned on sending home with Dax. It was the least she could do.

"You know your way around a sink," Bess said as she stood

back to watch Dax wash and rinse the same dishes she would've chosen to hand wash. He then proceeded to load the rest into her dishwasher.

She was pretty sure Jon would've messed up every portion of this task. She realized her thoughts had strayed back to her ex, her now-dating ex. She needed to stop comparing every man to him, whether good or bad. Pushing thoughts of Jon from her mind, Bess focused on Dax. Well, not like that. She was still sure Dax was nowhere near interested in her; she was just focusing on her present versus her past.

"My dad washes the dishes every night. He passed down the torch when I was a teen," Dax said, smiling at Bess with a look that should've graced the covers of the magazines his clients often showed up in.

Bess realized that she'd somehow moved closer to Dax in the past few minutes as she'd checked on him to make sure he didn't need any help or instruction on how to do things in her home. She was a bit of a stickler when it came to cleaning, but Dax's standards were proving to maybe even be higher than her own.

And holy heck was that attractive. As if the man didn't have enough going for him.

Bess wasn't sure whether she should offer to help or continue enjoying the view, but she decided on the former since it wasn't Dax's responsibility to wash every dish in her house.

"I can take over now. You've done more than your fair share," Bess said as she moved even closer to Dax, ready to take over the gloves.

Dax shook his head. "There's no point in starting a job unless you're going to finish it well."

Bess dropped her hands, which had been ready to take the gloves. She was surprised by Dax's determination to finish the dishes as well as by his words. She found herself really liking both. Which was ridiculous. Dax was just being a good neighbor.

"Words to live by," Bess said, and Dax nodded.

"I like to." He scrubbed at a particularly cheesy dish, his attention on that instead of on Bess. Which Bess didn't mind at all. It gave her all the more time to admire his profile, from his strong jaw already sporting a five o'clock shadow to his wavy hair.

Dax suddenly looked her way and caught Bess staring. He gave her a knowing smile, making Bess realize that he'd known exactly what she was doing the whole time. Bess felt heat rising up her neck once again and wondered if she'd ever blushed so much in her entire life. She honestly hadn't even known herself to still be capable of blushing at her age. But apparently all she'd needed to bring it out was a Dax.

"Um," Bess stammered, feeling the need to say something now that she'd been caught. "The leftovers," she said oh so eloquently before drawing in a deep breath. She could do this. "James was supposed to take them, but we forgot about them until it was too late. Would you like them?"

Bess moved back toward the island where the tray of left-over food sat, using that as her excuse to back away from Dax.

"Of course. We all know how I feel about your food, Bess," Dax said, his voice low and rumbly, causing Bess to feel things she really shouldn't. He was just talking about her cooking. That was it. But then why did it feel like so much more?

Wishful thinking. That had to be it.

Dax began to pull off the gloves, and Bess realized her entire kitchen was spotless without her having hardly lifted a finger.

"Thank you again," Bess said as she took in the clean room around her. Evenings like this, where she'd cooked half the day and then cleaned for another hour after everyone had left, usually left her with an aching back. But she felt none of that ache as Dax moved toward her.

"When you cook for me, I'll always clean," Dax said, his voice still doing the rumbling thing that wasn't good for Bess's sanity.

"Uh huh, sounds great," Bess said as she turned to grab the tray of food and shoved it toward Dax. She needed to get the man out of her kitchen before she did something silly. Like grab him and kiss him.

Had Bess just thought that? There would be no action more unlike Bess than kissing her neighbor without any inclination of him wanting said kiss. This was why Dax needed to get out of there. A gorgeous man who complimented Bess *and* cleaned her kitchen? That was dangerous.

"Bess," Dax said softly, and Bess looked down to see the tray of food still in her hands. Dax had sidestepped her offering and was now right beside her, causing Bess's poor stomach to attempt some acrobatics it hadn't in years.

"Do you have any plans tomorrow?" Dax asked.

Bess felt her eyes go wide before schooling them. Dax could be asking for anything. Help with cleaning his kitchen since he'd just cleaned hers, a cooking lesson, anything other than the thing an irrational part of Bess was hoping for.

Relax and think about your plans for tomorrow, Bess commanded her racing brain and heart.

"I'm working the lunch shift at the truck tomorrow, so I should be done by two or three, depending on how busy we are. But I'm pretty free after that. Did you need help with something?" Bess asked, trying to sound as neighborly as she possibly could.

"Yes, I do. I'd love for you to join me for dinner. I can't promise the fare will be anything as delicious as what we had tonight, but I want to take you out, Bess," Dax said, and it took everything in Bess not to give Dax the incredulous look she was feeling.

Dax had just asked her out. This made no sense. And Bess should know because she'd been telling herself all the many reasons why Dax could never be interested in her for the past couple of hours.

Wait, did Dax feel the need to feed Bess because she'd fed him? Was this some kind of neighborly reciprocation? Had Bess been married for so long, she could no longer distinguish a friendly gesture from a date? Oh man. She was going to blame this one on Lindsey. Her daughter had been the one to fill Bess's head with thoughts of her hot neighbor. No, she couldn't blame this wholly on Lindsey. Bess had been attracted to Dax the moment he'd shown up outside of her food truck with Olivia. But she needed to make this right.

"You don't have to do that, Dax. I'm happy to feed you without you feeling the need to feed me. Cooking is what I love to do," Bess said, trying to make eye contact with the gorgeous light blue eyes that gazed back at her but finding herself looking all around her kitchen instead.

Bess felt the tray of food being lifted out of her hands, and she looked down to see that Dax had taken it and set it back on the island behind her.

"And what I'd love to do is take a gorgeous woman out to dinner, Bess. This has nothing to do with you cooking for me and everything to do with me wanting to take you on a date," Dax said as he took a step closer so that Bess's hand, which was still up in the same position as when she'd been holding the tray, brushed against his waist.

She dropped her hands quickly as her mind worked on replaying what Dax had said. This gorgeous, successful, kind man wanted to go on a date? With her?

"What do you say?" Dax asked when Bess realized she'd been quiet for a long time. Probably too long.

What did Bess say? Was going out with a man who was far better looking than she was a mistake? A man who didn't live here and who would probably be leaving the island once again in mere days? Yes. So really there was only one answer Bess could give.

"I'd love to."

CHAPTER NINE

"GOOD MORNING, BABY GIRL," Gen said as she awoke her beautiful daughter. Gen lifted Maddie into her arms and nuzzled against her sweet-smelling hair, allowing the loveable girl to wake up little by little. This was one of Gen's favorite times of the day, when she got Maddie all to herself. Because Levi had to be at work before Gen did, he was usually rushing in the mornings. Whereas Gen had all the time in the world to get Maddie ready for the day.

"Morning, Mama," Maddie said, and the word filled Gen with so much warmth and pleasure, she worried she just might burst. Nothing could've prepared Gen for how fully and utterly she'd fallen in love with Maddie. But she had. A part of her even wondered if she could ever love the growing babe in her belly as much as she loved this little girl in her arms.

But by all accounts, especially the ones Bess and her aunt had told her, Gen didn't need to worry. Her heart and ability to love would grow with each child. Gen's love for Maddie would stay unlike any she'd ever known, and Maddie would forever be the child who'd made Gen a mother, but she would feel love for her next child in a new and just as beautiful way.

As Gen held Maddie in one arm and cradled her growing belly with her other hand, she felt an immense ache in her chest that reminded her of the two people she truly wanted to turn to with all of her questions but who were no longer here. Bess had been incredible in every way, but sometimes Gen wondered what life would've been like if she had her parents back, even just for one more day. Man, she missed them. But if there was one thing the last fifteen years had taught her, this was the way life was now, and dwelling on what could've been only served to hurt Gen's heart. She would always hold the memories of her parents in her heart, but wishing that she'd had more time or focusing on what she'd been robbed of helped no one. Especially Gen.

But she loved moments like this one, where she could remember both of her parents with a smile. Becoming a mom herself reminded Gen that she'd had the very best examples of parenthood. And she hoped she could make them proud. One thing she was sure of was that her mom and dad would've adored Maddie.

Gen let Maddie out of her arms and onto the ground as Maddie toddled sleepily to the photo of Mal that Gen and Levi had framed and set up on Maddie's bookshelf. Maddie took the photo into her arms and then gave her mom a kiss. Gen had only had to initiate the tradition once and Maddie had kept it going every morning. Gen liked to imagine Mal got to be with them for that moment each day.

"What do you want to wear?" Gen asked after Maddie set down the frame and then walked to her closet.

"Um," Maddie said as she thoughtfully tapped her cheek, causing Gen to stifle a giggle. This little girl was everything good.

But she was also as stubborn as a mule and had decided a week before that she was ready to dress herself. Now it took

Gen and Maddie at least ten minutes a day to figure out what Maddie was going to wear every morning. And honestly, Maddie usually looked like ... well, like a two-year-old had chosen her outfits. But the little girl couldn't have been prouder.

Maddie dug through her closet and presented Gen with a flowered pink and yellow leotard that should really only be worn to ballet class, a red and green striped tutu, as well as one of Levi's old, purple berets that Maddie had officially become obsessed with. Gen swallowed as she eyed the prospective outfit. Gen really didn't want to be the kind of mother who wouldn't let her daughter express herself, but did that mean she had to be the kind of mother who let her daughter go out of the house in this?

"I love it," Maddie declared, and Gen realized she didn't have a choice. She helped Maddie get dressed, brush her teeth, and tame her hair into two small buns on either side of her head. Even in the horrendous outfit, Maddie looked adorable.

"Are you ready for breakfast?" Levi called out from the master bathroom, letting Gen know her shift with Maddie was done and it was now her turn to get ready.

"Yes!" Maddie shouted. "I want toast and cereal and eggs and strawberries and pancakes and oh, oh waffles!"

Gen giggled as she left Maddie in the hall between their bedrooms and the kitchen and walked back to her bathroom. She paused when she met Levi, who was just leaving their bedroom.

Levi shook his head as his eyes roved over his wife appreciatively.

"Have I told you how incredibly sexy you look today?" Levi asked as he took a few steps toward Gen and wrapped his arms around her before pressing a kiss to her neck.

"Have I told you I find that hard to believe considering my hair looks like a bird just flew out of it, my pajamas are in fact one of your old t-shirts, and I have officially reached the stage of pregnancy where I'm showing," Gen said, even as she returned her husband's embrace.

"Mmm hmm," Levi murmured as he tightened his grip on Gen. "Just the way I like you."

Gen laughed as she tried to step out of Levi's arms, but he held her just where she was as he passionately looked down at her lips.

"And it looks like I need to remind you that we have a very hungry two-year-old waiting for you," Gen said as she tried to pull away again. This time Levi let go, but not without voicing his displeasure with a groan.

"I love you, Gen Redding," Levi said as he took a step back.

"I love you, Gen Redding," Maddie mimicked, and Gen looked around Levi to see that Maddie was waiting patiently in the hall behind her father.

Gen grinned as she responded, "I love you, Maddie Mae. And your daddy too."

Maddie's smile shone as she scurried down the hall toward the kitchen.

"We need to watch what we say in front of that one," Gen said as she grimaced, wondering just what else Maddie had overheard in her days of living with Gen and Levi. Not that they'd said anything terrible, but they could've said things that shouldn't be repeated by a toddler.

"Yeah," Levi said with a nod. "But it is kind of cute, right?"

"Absolutely adorable," Gen said as she headed toward their bathroom. She wanted to look a little more presentable for work than she did at the moment, but her stomach really was beginning to pop and most of her pants were feeling quite snug. She would usually opt for a dress, but she had a doctor's appointment later that day, complete with an ultrasound where they would hopefully be finding out the gender of their little bundle.

And she'd rather not have to pull up her entire dress for the ultrasound tech to get to her belly.

Gen picked out her baggiest pair of pants that wasn't sweats, what Gen really wanted to wear, and tried them on. They slid on easily, but the button at the top was another story. Gen tugged, but the centimeter that separated the button from the button hole would not disappear.

It was officially time for the trick.

Gen was grateful to have many friends and family who'd gone through pregnancy over the past several years, and most were very free with their advice. Some of the stuff wasn't great, but when Olivia gave Gen a tip about fastening her pants with a rubber band, Gen knew it was a tidbit to file away for later.

Gen looked through her bathroom drawers and came up victorious with a rubber band that she proceeded to wrap around the button of her pants then through the button hole and then back around the button. And they were finally fastened ... kind of.

She hurried through the rest of her getting ready process since getting dressed had taken up a big chunk of her time, and she joined Levi and Maddie in the kitchen just as Levi was cleaning up the cute, little girl. From the red streaks beside her mouth, Gen was going to guess Levi had given Maddie at least one of the breakfast foods she'd requested. The girl did love her strawberries.

Levi dropped a kiss on the top of Maddie's head as he let her down from her booster chair and then turned toward Gen, dropping a kiss to her lips.

"Remember we have the ultrasound today," Gen said as Levi headed toward the garage door that was just off the kitchen.

"I could never forget," Levi said with a happy grin. "I can't wait to meet our little boy."

"Or girl," Gen said, and Levi laughed. She knew he wanted

a boy because it seemed perfect after Maddie, and Levi had always dreamed of teaching his son everything he knew. But she also hoped he'd be excited to have a girl. She was pretty sure he would be, but it gnawed at her a bit that he seemed to always have to joke that this baby in her belly was a boy. What if it wasn't?

"Or girl," Levi said as he opened the door to the garage.

"Have a good day, Maddie Mae," Levi called out. "And I'll see you soon, Gen." He winked, and then he was gone.

"Have a good day," Maddie mimicked, and Gen swept the little girl into her arms as she looked around her all-white kitchen that used to be her pride and joy. Gen had taken great pleasure in choosing the white countertops that were marbled with just the tiniest bit of gray and the pure white marble tiles that cost more than Gen was willing to admit. She'd taken nearly a month to decide on just the right white color for her cabinets. She knew she'd driven Levi crazy when they'd remodeled the room a couple of years before, but the kitchen was all Gen had to focus on after her long days at the salon. Well, and Levi, of course. Working on the kitchen had felt like the outlet she'd needed as she came to terms with the idea that maybe she needed to pour the energy she'd invested into starting a family into another venture.

But now that pristine kitchen had a green booster chair strapped to one of the pretty, white fabric-covered, barstool-height chairs that sat next to her kitchen island. There was now a dishrack that old Gen would have called an eyesore next to their kitchen sink, but it was the easiest way to dry Maddie's many sippie cups and would soon be holding the baby's bottles. Color dotted every corner of the kitchen Gen had worked to keep all white. And Gen wouldn't have it any other way.

"Are you ready to go to Lily's?" Gen asked Maddie, who cheered in response. Gen was so grateful to be able to send

Maddie to a place she loved so much. It made leaving her each morning a little less terrible. Because ever since Maddie had joined their family, and Gen had found out she was pregnant, Gen had wanted to be that mom who stayed at home. Maybe not every day—Gen did love her job—but at least a few days a week she wanted to be home with her babies. So far that had been impossible, but Gen really hoped in the next few months she could arrange her schedule so that she could do so. She was ready for that next step.

Gen piled Maddie and their three bags—Gen's purse, Maddie's diaper bag, and Gen's work bag—all into the car. She securely fastened Maddie in her car seat, and they were off.

Once Gen dropped Maddie off at Lily's, the day flew by, and Gen found herself opening the door to her OBGYN's office a few hours later.

Whisling Island was relatively small but large enough that there were a few of each kind of doctor. Gen had chosen to go with the same woman who'd delivered all of Bess's children, even though she was getting up there in years. Dr. Fern's bedside manner left nothing to be desired, and even though she'd probably be retiring soon after Gen gave birth, she was still sharp as a tack.

Gen checked in with the receptionist and found a seat in the small but cozy waiting room. The doctor had converted a turn-of-the-century home into her office space, and the old living area served as the waiting room. The receptionists' area was the old kitchen, or so Gen had been told, and the exam rooms had been bedrooms. The doctor had kept the beautifully ornate fireplace, which sat to Gen's right, even though Gen had never seen a fire lit in the space. Gen was guessing it was too risky considering all of the children who accompanied their moms to appointments.

A large portrait of the home from a hundred years before

hung above the fireplace, along with other old pictures and paintings of the way Whisling used to be. Gen loved the way she felt like she was taking a history tour every time she came to the doctor's.

Gen glanced down at her watch just as the door to the office opened and Levi came walking in.

"Just in time," she said as Levi sat, putting an arm around the back of her chair and squeezing her far shoulder affectionately.

"I try to be," Levi said, right as the nurse called them back.

The swinging door Gen and Levi passed through to go back to the exam rooms hadn't been changed since the creation of the home and had once been used between the living area and kitchen of the home. The old brown door was solid, with etchings of vines and flowers that Gen itched to stop and admire. But knew she needed to move along.

Barbara, Dr. Fern's longtime nurse, took Gen's vitals before taking her into one of the exam rooms.

"The doctor should be in soon," Barbara promised and then closed the door behind her.

Unlike the waiting area, this room was full of pictures of babies. Gen smiled as she took in the chubby cuties of all colors that hung on the yellow walls. The exam room looked quite sterile compared to the rest of the office, but Gen figured it was probably for the best. It was a doctor's exam room, after all.

She remembered having to wait in this room for her regular gynecological visits for years, hating every moment those babies stared down at her, almost as if mocking her inability to bear a child. But now it was different. She was different. And she knew her miracle was nothing to take lightly. Getting to carry a child to twenty weeks that they'd naturally conceived was a downright dream.

Gen looked over to where Levi sat in an extra chair beside

the exam table and noticed that his leg was bouncing at a pretty rapid rate.

"Nervous?" she asked.

Levi shook his head. "Why would I be?" he asked with a curious cock of his head, but his leg continued to bounce.

Gen pointed at his leg, and Levi stilled it.

"I didn't even realize I was doing that. But no. I'm not nervous. I'm excited, thrilled, ready to meet my baby boy," Levi teased again.

Gen rolled her eyes. She probably should've addressed the whole boy situation before getting to where they were, seated in the doctor's office ready to find out the gender of their baby. But she'd assumed all of this boy stuff was a joke. And it probably was. But the tiniest worry threaded through Gen that maybe, just maybe, it wasn't. That was what she should've addressed before, but it was too late now since Dr. Fern had just knocked on the door.

"Gen, Levi," Dr. Fern greeted as she came into the exam room.

"Hi, Dr. Fern," Gen greeted as Levi smiled.

"You don't know how glad I am that you two are here today. I've been rooting for you both. Don't tell my other patients, but you guys are my favorites," Dr. Fern said with a wink. Then she moved her attention to Gen's chart on the computer.

Gen was pretty sure Dr. Fern said that to every patient, but it felt good anyway. She grinned as Dr. Fern looked back at Gen from her computer.

"Everything looks great. We will be monitoring you a little more closely since this pregnancy is happening a bit later in life," Dr. Fern said, causing Gen to remember the first time she'd been told she was having a geriatric pregnancy. She'd just about blown a gasket. Sure, Gen knew she was no spring chicken, but thirty-eight wasn't geriatric. Except in the world of pregnancy it was.

Gen nodded in response to Dr. Fern and then looked over at Levi who was suppressing a chuckle. She knew that he loved that Gen was being called geriatric and thought it was hilarious. Well, Levi could laugh it up considering he was nearly a year older than she was.

Dr. Fern went through a few more things before motioning to the ultrasound machine that sat in the corner of her office. "And now for the big event," Dr. Fern said as she wheeled the machine toward Gen.

"Do you want to find out the sex of the baby?" Dr. Fern asked as she situated herself on her stool next to the exam table.

"Yes," Gen and Levi said in unison.

Dr. Fern chuckled as she showed Gen how she wanted her to position herself. "Good," Dr. Fern said as she squirted a cold goop onto Gen's stomach and placed the wand against her abdomen.

"Boy, boy, boy," Levi chanted quietly, but both Gen and Dr. Fern ignored him as the picture of Gen and Levi's baby lit up the monitor.

"Oh my gosh. There's his head," Gen uttered, and Dr. Fern nodded.

"I always thought these pictures looked like alien sightings, but I can see our baby," Gen said as tears filled her eyes.

Dr. Fern chuckled. "Here are the legs," she said as she pressed the wand into Gen's stomach, and the baby moved.

Dr. Fern took measurements of the baby's every part, and Gen looked over at Levi who had his eyes glued to the screen.

"Is the baby healthy?" Gen asked. She knew this appointment was exciting because of the gender reveal, but she also knew it was important because of the baby statistics the doctor could only get with an ultrasound.

"Baby looks incredible," Dr. Fern said with a smile. Then she turned to Levi. "And I think you're wrong," she said before turning her attention to Gen. "You are going to have a girl," Dr. Fern added.

With those simple words, Gen swore her heart burst right on that exam table. She was already so full of love for this little baby. A girl. She didn't know she'd cared, and honestly, she hadn't. But now hearing she was having a girl, it all felt so right. Maddie would have a sister, and Levi already made such a good girl dad. Gen would get two little girls who'd she'd love and adore forever. A girl. Visions of more pink and rainbow tutus swirled through Gen's mind. It was going to be so fun.

Dr. Fern handed Gen a paper towel to clean some of the goop and then stood, pushing the ultrasound machine away.

"Congratulations," Dr. Fern said before exiting the room and leaving Gen alone with Levi.

Gen wasn't sure why she was so nervous to look over at her husband. He had to be happy; this was a blessed occasion. But a small part of her wondered why he hadn't made a sound, why he hadn't come over to hug her immediately after getting the news. Being so quiet wasn't like the man she loved.

But Gen knew she was only delaying the inevitable, so she chanced a glance at her husband.

Levi sat with his elbows on his knees, his hands propping up his chin with a small smile on his face. Gen was glad to see the smile, but why was it so small? What was going on in Levi's mind?

She watched as his Adam's apple bobbed.

"A girl," Levi said, his smile getting tighter, and Gen knew she wasn't wrong. She had every right to worry.

Levi was upset that they were having a girl.

CHAPTER TEN

"WHY IS HER NAME *DOCTOR BELLA*?" Pearl asked as they pulled into the parking lot behind the plaza of offices that housed the office of their therapist.

Olivia had been coming to see Doctor Bella ever since she'd realized how broken she was while living in her parents' home. But she hadn't thought it was the right time to bring the girls. She knew Rachel and Pearl were processing in their own ways, and she felt it would be a disservice to them to push them along if they weren't ready for it. She knew therapy would be beneficial for them ... someday.

But after the debacle with Pearl and Rachel and stupid Bart, Olivia felt it was time for her girls to dig a little deeper into their emotions. Maybe heal in a way they hadn't been able to on their own. So Olivia had brought up the idea of Doctor Bella and then let them process the change for about a month, giving the girls time to get used to the idea. Rachel still wasn't quite on board, but Olivia felt that was more a preteen rebellion than an indicator that she wasn't ready to talk to a professional. So today was the day for them to finally take that next step.

"Because she's a doctor and her name is Bella," Rachel said in her tone that Olivia hated. Rachel had turned ten over the summer and was now sure everyone in the world was either a tiny bit less smart than she was or a whole lot less smart. And her tone told everyone just where she thought they stood. Pearl, undeservedly, got the brunt of Rachel's attitude.

"It's the name she likes being called," Olivia said, sending a warning glare toward her oldest. "Just like you like being called Pearl."

"Or Pearly Girl," Pearl said with a wide, innocent grin as the three of them exited the car.

Rachel folded her arms over her chest after she slammed the car door shut behind her as they all headed toward the office. Olivia knew Rachel's overabundance of attitude was a defense mechanism to something new. She'd made it clear she was wary about the situation when she'd demanded ice cream after the appointment, as well as a promise that she would get to go with Dean and Buster to the beach once again. But she was there, attitude and all, so Olivia had hope for this session.

The outing to the beach with Dean had become a weekly occasion since Rachel had continued to decline hanging out with Bart, and Dean was all too willing to help. Probably just another reason why Olivia was in love with her friend and neighbor. But she was ignoring that tiny fact because it was a complication Olivia was nowhere near ready to face.

"I can just talk to you, right?" Rachel asked Olivia as they rode the elevator to the third floor where Doctor Bella's office was located.

"You don't have to do anything you don't want to do, Sweets. But I am promising you that Doctor Bella only wants to help you," Olivia said, and Rachel scowled in response.

"Rachel, we need to talk to Doctor Bella," Pearl said as she skipped through the tiny space on the elevator. "She's going to help you want to see Dad again."

"I never want to see Dad," Rachel mumbled. Then she looked up at Olivia with a terrified expression on her face. "I don't have to see Dad, do I?"

Olivia shook her head. "You don't have to do anything you don't want to do," Olivia reiterated. "Doctor Bella's office is a safe place."

Rachel nodded once, and Olivia wanted to cheer that it finally seemed as if her words had gotten through to her oldest. Olivia had said nothing different from the many conversations they'd had over the past weeks while trying to prepare the girls for this visit, but apparently Rachel was only ready to hear what Olivia was saying in her own time.

The elevator doors opened, and Pearl skipped down the hall ahead of Rachel and Olivia, throwing open the door Olivia had indicated they would enter.

Olivia threw an apologetic look at the receptionist, Shannon, who seemed startled by their abrupt entrance. Shannon smiled in response. She rounded the half wall that separated her from the rest of the waiting room to shake Rachel's and then Pearl's hand.

"It's a pleasure to meet you," Shannon said, treating both girls like adults.

Olivia watched as Rachel's entire posture changed from defensive to proud. Her shoulders were no longer rounded as she stood up tall, pushing her auburn hair—almost the same color as Olivia's at her age—behind her ears.

"It's a pleasure to meet you," Pearl mimicked, and Olivia fought the urge to smile at the grown up way her children were acting. It was adorable but also exactly what they needed. Doctor Bella had found a gem in Shannon.

"Would either of you like something to drink?" Shannon

offered. "Water, juice, soda," she whispered the last word conspiratorially to Rachel, and Olivia could've hugged her. Olivia had warned the office that Rachel was a bit guarded when it came to the entire therapy process, and Olivia could see Shannon was quickly winning her over. Not only did Rachel suddenly seem comfortable, she was actually smiling.

"Can I have a lemon lime soda?" Rachel whispered back, and Shannon gave Olivia the briefest glance to see the latter give the slightest nod before telling Rachel, "Of course."

Pearl asked for the same, and the three ladies sat on the comfy couches as they waited for Shannon to return, which she did within less than a minute.

"The doctor will be out shortly," Shannon informed Rachel and Pearl before handing Olivia the water she'd brought for her.

Olivia shot Shannon a smile full of gratitude before Shannon took her place behind the desk once more.

A middle-aged man who Olivia didn't recognize came into the waiting room from Doctor Bella's office, smiling at Olivia and her girls before turning to speak to Shannon in whispered tones.

The man left about a minute later, and it wasn't that long before Doctor Bella emerged from her office. The small blonde woman whom Olivia had grown to respect hadn't been Olivia's first choice in therapists. She'd been nervous about seeing a psychiatrist who she'd gone to high school with—even though Bella had always been kind in high school, known as the girl anyone could go to for help. But Olivia wasn't sure she wanted to reveal all of the pain she held from her marriage to someone who knew almost all of the same people Olivia did.

However, as Olivia had been calling around getting to know the therapists on the island, Bella had told her that she took doctor-patient confidentiality seriously. The words Olivia spoke in Doctor Bella's office would never be uttered anywhere else.

Olivia had assumed as much, but to hear Bella say so out loud had been an immense relief. So because Doctor Bella had been exactly whom Olivia needed in every other way, Olivia had given the doctor a chance.

And in the end, knowing the same people had actually made things even easier. Although Bella was always the consummate professional, she knew about Bart's charm, even when Olivia couldn't quite describe it, and about Dean's calm demeanor when Olivia tried to explain why the man had been so crucial in her healing.

Olivia would guess that Doctor Bella knew exactly what Olivia felt for her attractive landlord, but she'd never said anything about it ... yet. Olivia had an inkling her feelings for Dean would come up in therapy soon. But probably not in front of her girls.

"Olivia, you didn't tell me your girls were so grown up," Doctor Bella said as she approached the family who sat on her couch.

"I'm almost nine," Pearl said as she sat up straight, setting her soda on the coffee table in the waiting room.

"In six months," Rachel said with a roll of her eyes that Doctor Bella caught and noted, by the way she looked at Olivia. "I'm already ten."

"Almost nine is a great age to be," Doctor Bella said as she shook Pearl's hand. "And double digits, huh? That is quite grown up," she said as shook Rachel's.

Both girls grinned; Doctor Bella had somehow been able to please both of them while offending neither, something Olivia had yet to perfect.

"Let me show you into my office," Doctor Bella said as she opened the door for the girls and led them to a blue couch that had matching arm chairs which sat perpendicular to the couch at both ends. A dark wood coffee table that matched the one in the waiting room sat in front of the couch, and across from the couch was a large desk made from the same wood as the coffee table. On top of the desk were a few file folders stacked neatly, along with photos of Doctor Bella's family. Olivia knew that the doctor had two boys just a few years older than Rachel and Pearl, along with a toddler baby girl, all of whom were proudly displayed in photos on the desk and on the built-in bookshelves on the far wall of the room.

Doctor Bella opened a wicker basket near the built-ins and waved for the girls to come join her.

"I sometimes find talking to people easier when I can cuddle with something. Do either of you want a stuffed animal or a blanket?" Doctor Bella asked.

Pearl grinned and grabbed a large white teddy bear with a big red bow around its neck as Rachel eyed the basket warily.

Pearl ran back to join Olivia on the couch as Rachel scrunched her nose.

"Are you a little too old for stuffed animals?" Doctor Bella asked, even though Olivia knew that wasn't the case. Rachel slept with her own stuffed puppy every night, but then again, cuddling that toy at night was far different from asking for one in a doctor's office with sunshine streaming through the windows.

Rachel nodded, and Doctor Bella brought out a plush pink blanket.

"But the room does get kind of cold. A blanket is nothing like a stuffed animal," Doctor Bella said as Rachel pursed her lips and then eyed the blanket.

Rachel quickly sank her hand into the basket and came out with a white blanket that matched the pink one Doctor Bella held, then ran to the arm chair furthest from the basket and closest to the door.

She sat in the chair and tucked the blanket around her, smiling as she rubbed her hand against the soft material.

"So, Olivia, how was your week?" Doctor Bella asked as she sat in the chair opposite from Rachel and placed her pink blanket around herself in the same way Rachel had.

"It was pretty good," Olivia said honestly, but she knew she'd be keeping some things back. This family therapy would be good for all three of them but would mostly be for her girls. Olivia would still be coming in for her solo sessions, so she knew Doctor Bella was beginning with her only to give her daughters a bit more time to get used to the idea of talking to this woman who they hardly knew. Since the doctor's boys went to the same school as Olivia's girls, Olivia was sure they'd seen the doctor around. But she was also pretty sure they would've never had a reason to talk to her before that afternoon.

"Mine was good too," Pearl said as she leaned forward, hugging her teddy bear tightly.

"Was it?" Doctor Bella asked, "What made it good?"

"I won my class science fair," Pearl said with a proud grin. "If I win the one for my school, I'll get to compete against all of the first, second, and third graders on the island."

"With all nine schools?" Doctor Bella asked, her eyes wide with wonder even though Olivia was sure the doctor already knew the answer to her question.

Pearl nodded, her little chin bouncing so hard off of her chest that her head flew back and hit the couch.

Olivia grinned. Pearl should be proud. She'd worked hard on her project, testing the flavors and lasting powers of gum.

"I did that in first grade," Rachel interjected, always needing to one-up her sister.

Olivia closed her eyes, praying for patience, before opening them to meet the gaze of Doctor Bella who continued to smile.

"Did you?" Doctor Bella asked. "My, you guys are a smart

family." She somehow complimented both of the girls without lessening the accomplishment of the other.

"We are." Pearl accepted the compliment in a way only an eight-year-old could as she scooted back in her seat so that she was right up against the back of the couch.

"What else was good about your week?" Doctor Bella asked.

Pearl tilted her head as she pondered the question. "Oh," she said excitedly as she moved back to the front of the couch so that her feet could hit the ground. "We got to go to the beach with Dean and Buster."

Rachel perked up at the mention of their outing and leaned forward in her arm chair.

"Did you know that there are beaches just for dogs?" Pearl asked.

Doctor Bella nodded. "They are some of my favorite beaches," the doctor said.

Pearl grinned. "Me too. Because Buster can't go to regular beaches," she said.

Doctor Bella nodded sagely as if what Pearl was saying was the wisest thing she'd ever heard. "What do you do at the beach with Buster and Dean?" Doctor Bella asked, and it was then that Olivia noticed all the doctor held was the blanket. She typically had a notepad when she spoke with Olivia, but that was absent from their session. Olivia realized the lack of notepad was probably a way to help her girls feel less like they were talking to a doctor and more like they were speaking with a friend. Which was exactly what her girls needed. The woman was good at her job.

"I play fetch with Buster," Pearl said.

"I do too," Rachel interjected. "I'm the one who remembered to bring his tennis ball this week."

Pearl nodded, conceding to her sister. "But I found the stick to throw in the ocean. It's safer to throw a stick because then if we lose it in the waves, it doesn't matter. Buster loves his tennis ball."

"But the tennis ball is more fun to throw on the beach," Rachel added.

"Was playing fetch with Buster your favorite part of the outing?" Doctor Bella asked Pearl who nodded.

"Not mine," Rachel added without being prompted, and Olivia could've cheered. Who would've thought Rachel would be volunteering information already?

"I like playing with Buster, but I like running with Dean on the beach even more," Rachel said.

This was news to Olivia. She knew the girls liked Dean, but she never would've suspected they could possibly enjoy time with him more than time with Buster.

"Running on the beach, huh?" Doctor Bella asked. "That sounds like fun."

"It is," Rachel said. "We race. We make Dean start way behind us because he's faster and has longer legs."

"That makes sense."

"But he doesn't let me win, and I won once," Rachel added with a proud grin.

Why didn't Rachel tell me any of this? Olivia thought, but she wisely kept her mouth shut.

"I didn't win. That's why I like fetch better," Pearl said.

Doctor Bella bit her lip, probably fighting the same urge to smile that Olivia was feeling.

"Playing with Dean at the beach is much better than playing with Dad," Rachel continued to volunteer, and Olivia wasn't sure whether to feel elation that Rachel was beginning to share her feelings or sadness at the truth behind her statement.

"Why do you say that?" Doctor Bella asked.

Rachel shrugged. "Dad gets bored after one race and goes on

his phone. Dean plays with us the whole time and doesn't say mean things about Mom."

Olivia tried to swallow past the lump in her throat. She hadn't realized Bart had disparaged her in front of the girls. It made sense. It was Bart. But she still felt sick at the thought.

"I hate Dad's phone," Rachel said passionately, and even Pearl nodded in agreement.

"But I love Dad," Pearl said.

Rachel shook her head. "I hate Dad," she said as she glared toward Doctor Bella, daring her to defy Rachel.

"Your feelings are your feelings, Rachel. I won't make you change them if you don't want to," Doctor Bella said. "But hate is a terrible burden to carry. Sometimes your hate can hurt you more than the person you hate."

The heat in Rachel's glare left, but she continued to stare at the doctor.

"Dean is funner than Dad at the beach. But dad is our dad. We should go to the beach with him too. Right, Doctor Bella?" Pearl asked.

Olivia did not envy the position the doctor was now in.

"This is our first time all talking together, so we probably won't work it out today. I think that it's brave of both of you to tell me how you feel and what you want," Doctor Bella said.

Olivia felt her jaw drop open. That had been the perfect move. Olivia knew that the doctor had gone to school for a dozen years in order to know just what to do, but Olivia was envious. What she wouldn't give to be able to say the right thing to her girls, even if she only said the right thing sometimes. However, Olivia felt hopeful because Doctor Bella had promised they could start using parts of Olivia's sessions to learn how to do just that.

Olivia closed her mouth as Rachel said, "You won't make me love my dad?"

Doctor Bella shook her head. "I can't make you do anything, Rachel. You are a strong woman, and you will make your own choices. But if you want me to help you feel better, like there isn't so much rumbling inside of you, I can do that."

Rachel's eyes narrowed as she tilted her head and took in the doctor.

"I don't have rumbling, but sometimes it feels like I have twisting, right here." Pearl pointed to her chest, and Olivia wanted to crush her baby in a hug. How could she have done this to her poor girls? They shouldn't be knowing these feelings, feeling these emotions.

"I'm going to try to help you with that, too," Doctor Bella said.

Pearl smiled. "The twisting is gone right now. But sometimes it comes back," she said.

Doctor Bella nodded. "I'll be ready for it," the doctor responded.

Olivia looked at the clock and saw that their session was already up. She stood, and the girls followed her lead, walking toward the door with her.

"I think we'll be talking again next week. Is that alright with you?" Doctor Bella looked from Rachel to Pearl.

"Yup," Pearl said happily as she exited through the door Olivia held open.

Rachel paused and then looked up at the doctor who was a few paces behind them.

"I guess I'll talk to you again," Rachel said with a shrug before following her sister to the reception desk. They'd kept their sodas with Shannon for safe-keeping and were eager to have them back.

Olivia could've hugged the doctor, she was so pleased with what they'd accomplished. The step they'd just taken might've been small, but it was a step in the right direction. And Rachel was ready to take another one. It was more than Olivia could've even hoped for.

That small step gave Olivia hope that she hadn't ruined her sweet girls. Slowly but surely they might be able to piece their family together once again.

CHAPTER ELEVEN

"I THINK I want to introduce him to Bailee and Wes," Deb said as she stood at the counter in Bess's food truck, helping to prep food for the day. Deb was nowhere near as proficient in the kitchen as Bess, but she could cut up tomatoes and onions with the best of them. That was the only job Bess trusted her with, and Deb didn't blame her.

Deb felt tears well up in her eyes now that she was on her second onion, and she knew many more would follow but she was okay with that. If she was going to cry, she wanted food to be the reason, not Rich.

"Luke?" Bess asked as she put a tray of tiramisu in the refrigerator. "Already?"

Deb had told Bess all about her failure of a first date and then the spectacular one that followed. She couldn't believe Luke had given her a second chance. And although she'd been a bit worried about the fact that Luke was a widower, not divorced, Deb realized the way Luke had become single didn't matter. Just that he *was* single and he was ready to move on. Deb knew Luke probably carried baggage from his marriage, but who didn't? Everything else she knew about the man made her want to move forward, have fun, date a guy she really liked and not worry about the consequences.

"I really like him. I see him being in my life for a while," Deb said.

Bess nodded. "I get that. But meeting your kids ... that just feels ..." Bess said.

Deb scoffed. "Talk about the pot calling the kettle black. Didn't Dax just meet your kids?" Deb asked with a grin.

"I should've kept my big mouth shut," Bess said with a shake of her head as she joined Deb at the cutting board. "He came over for dinner when the kids were already there. Not a big deal. Besides, I'm not considering dating Dax. You are dating Luke. Two very different circumstances."

"Aren't you going out with Dax tonight? Pretty sure our circumstances are way more similar than different," Deb said with a grin.

"But things can't go anywhere with Dax. He's leaving again soon," Bess said.

"Doesn't that make things worse?" Deb knew she was pressing Bess in a way she didn't like, but Bess had done the same to Deb.

"My kids met the guy as a next-door neighbor, not as a prospective boyfriend," Bess said. Then she paused in her cutting to turn to Deb. "Wait, is Luke already your boyfriend?"

Deb shrugged. "We haven't put it into words, but maybe? I told him I was going to delete my dating app, and he said he was doing the same."

"I swear this whole new way of dating is way too young for me," Bess said with a shake of her head as she turned back to her tomatoes.

"Says the woman dating a man ten years her junior," Deb said with a pump of her eyebrows as Bess's cheeks turned pink.

"A date. So different from dating," Bess said.

Deb grinned. "You know I'm happy for you, right? And I really wish you'd let me come over to take pictures of you together with Dax and then send them to Jon. He would croak seeing his replacement," Deb chuckled.

"One, I don't want Jon to croak, and two, Dax isn't a replacement. He'll be back in LA within days."

"Is that what he told you?" Deb asked.

Bess shook her head. "But it's only a matter of time. His job is there."

Deb nodded slowly. She had really been rooting for Dax and Bess. Not only was the guy young and hot, he seemed to worship the ground Bess walked on, something Bess more than deserved.

"And for the record, I am happy for you too. I just worry about your impulsive nature at times," Bess said.

"As you should."

Both women laughed.

"But this time, I think I'm doing the right thing. I'm going out with Luke again tonight, and I want him to know how serious I am about him. That I'm not letting my past hold me back," Deb said.

"So this isn't about you showing Rich you've moved on?" Bess asked, the caution in her voice easy to hear. Which she should be, considering she had the nerve to ask a question like that. Of course this wasn't about Rich. It was about Luke.

Deb paused, setting down her knife so that she could wipe the extra tears away with her wrist. She knew she'd have to wash her hands since she'd touched her face, but she could use a break from the onions for a minute.

That pause gave Deb a minute to reflect and let her annoyance at her friend dissipate. This was about Luke, right?

Bess loved Deb more than almost anyone else in the world—Deb was pretty sure Bess's parents and children still beat Deb by a tiny sliver—and Bess would never say anything just to hurt Deb. If she was concerned, Deb realized she should be too. Especially because Deb really liked Luke. She'd already blown it once. She wasn't sure Luke would give her a third chance, and she for sure wouldn't deserve it. She needed to tread carefully. That was all Bess was asking her to do.

"Go out with him tonight. Have a blast. And if you look within yourself and really feel like it's time for the next step, by all means, Deb, introduce those kids. They'll only have Luke falling all the harder for you. But if any part of you isn't ready ..." Bess let her voice trail off.

"You're right. Once again, Bess. Do you ever get sick of it?" Deb asked as she washed her hands at the back of the truck.

Bess pursed her lips as if she were really thinking it through and then grinned. "Nope."

Deb shook her head while drying off her hands and then headed toward the door of the truck. She had been planning to go back to chopping before realizing how late it had gotten. Time always got away from her when she was with Bess.

"I need to get back to my own work, but thanks Bess. You're the best," Deb said as she opened the door of the truck.

"Yup, I know," Bess said with a smirk.

"Save that confidence for tonight. Get a goodnight kiss out of the date since he'll be leaving so soon." Deb shot Bess a smirk of her own.

"Didn't you say you needed to leave?" Bess asked cheekily, and Deb kept right on smirking.

"Have fun tonight, Bess. Do everything I would do," Deb responded as she let the door shut behind her.

As Deb walked to where she had parked her car, she thought back to where she had been even a few months before. Where she and Bess both had been. Who would've thought they would be here now? The thought made Deb smile. They were happy in their lives, and maybe even more importantly, they were moving on.

———————

DEB HAD TOLD Luke she'd meet him in Seattle again this time since he was the one who had to work until six. Deb's hours were more lax, so she could meet him right as he finished work and they could go to an earlier dinner so that Luke could get home to his daughters at a decent hour.

Deb took a final sniff of the fall flower arrangement Luke had sent the day after their most recent date before she went out the door. Even though the flowers were now probably on their last leg, Deb loved the colors: dark greens, yellows, and reds. But most of all she just loved having someone who remembered how much she loved fresh flowers in her home. It had been too long since Deb had enjoyed a fresh bouquet. She told herself once this one died, she would start to buy them for herself. If Luke continued to send them, all the better. Deb could have two. She realized getting her own bouquet was a way of showing love to herself, something Deb had neglected for far too long.

The ferry from Whisling Island to Seattle went by quickly, and Deb soon found herself in front of the skyscraper where Luke spent all of his days. The mirrored exterior reflected the sun, and Deb thought to herself that the building was only so pretty to her because it wasn't a confined space to spend all her time in the way that it was for Luke. She'd worked in a cubicle for six months out of her fifty-plus years on this earth, and that had been more than enough to teach her she needed a job where she wasn't so restricted. She had nothing against those who worked cubicle jobs—she might even be falling in love with a specific someone who worked one—but the thought of those walls being all she saw for eight hours a day would drive Deb crazy.

Although, she was quite sure Luke had graduated from a cubicle and had earned a full-blown office, complete with a view of the Seattle skyline and even the gorgeous Pacific Ocean.

Deb entered the building that looked a lot like many of the others she'd visited over the years. There were a few lounging areas with brown leather couches and a receptionist who sat at a desk near the elevators. The large reception area was at least two stories tall, and because of the glass walls, the place was quite bright and attractive. Even though the cubicles didn't sound too appealing, Deb could actually see herself painting in that reception area, especially on one of Seattle's rare sunny days like the one they were having today.

"Deb," Luke said with his husky voice as he walked toward Deb. Deb wasn't sure how she'd missed Luke coming off the elevator. It must've happened while she was admiring how much light the window walls of his building let in.

"Hi, Luke," Deb said, feeling weirdly shy. This was the way she'd expected to feel on their first date, not their third. She wanted to step in to hug Luke, but she also felt timid about it. Why was she feeling like this? Deb wasn't used to not charging forward into a situation, and she wasn't quite sure what to do.

Luke made the decision for her by wrapping her in his arms, and Deb leaned into his strength. She almost chuckled to herself as she thought about her attractive man—with arm muscles that would make any weightlifter jealous—being an accountant instead of a profession one would expect from a body built so well, like an athlete or even a model. And although Deb knew Luke took his daily bike rides and swims seriously, he wasn't obsessed with his physique the way any other man who looked like him would be. Deb wasn't sure how she'd found Luke, but she wasn't letting go anytime soon.

"So, I'm thinking of going a different route for our date tonight," Luke said as he took in Deb's off-the-shoulder floral dress. "Do you mind if we go a little more casual?"

Deb grinned. She'd been craving some French fries all day. As long as wherever they were going served those, she'd be happy. She told Luke as much.

Luke laughed. "The place I was thinking about has French fries. But also the best burgers in Seattle."

Deb narrowed her eyes as she appraised Luke and his incredible claim. "The best?" Deb asked.

Luke nodded. "I know. It's seems too good to be true, right?" Luke asked.

Deb nodded. Like so much about Luke, this did seem too good to be true. Deb's heart lifted at the idea that if Luke could back the burger claim, maybe the man was really that good too?

"But we'll let you be the judge," Luke said as he twined his fingers through Deb's as they made their way out of the building.

"And bonus? It's just over a block away from my office," Luke said with a grin.

They turned left as soon as they exited the building and began walking on the crowded sidewalk.

Deb reveled in people-watching as they made their way to the restaurant. There wasn't much Deb felt she missed out on by living on Whisling, but during these moments of bustling in the city, she did feel a little bit of a pull to be part of it. Not enough that she would actually move from her beloved island, but the thought sometimes crossed her mind.

"Should we call a car? Are those comfortable to walk in?" Luke asked as he looked down at the wedges Deb wore on her feet.

She wanted to laugh at the idea that her feet couldn't take a few blocks in wedges when, as a flight attendant, she'd stood for hours in heels much thinner. But she was also nearly over-whelmed by Luke's adorable concern. See? Too good.

"I'll be fine. But I love that you care," Deb said, smiling up at Luke.

"This is it," Luke said as they came to a stop in front of a very unassuming restaurant. The entire wall of the burger shop that faced the street was a big, glass window so that Deb could see right into the place. The room was full of round tables surrounded by chairs, along with a few booths positioned along the license plate-covered walls. There was a bar against the back wall and a counter to order burgers to the left side of the bar. It looked like a typical burger place to Deb, and she wondered if she was going to be disappointed.

"Trust me," was all Luke said as they entered the door and went to the counter.

The line was only three people long—that didn't bode well for the food either—and Luke ordered for them both without even looking at the menu.

They took the number the girl at the counter gave them and walked over to one of the many empty booths in the place, putting their number on the table as Deb met Luke's eyes.

Deb realized she did trust Luke. It wasn't a big thing, letting him pick her meal for this one night, but Deb had stopped trusting men after Rich. So feeling this trust was a big deal. Even if it was for something so small.

Her intuition was telling her that meeting Luke was part of her destiny. She felt it at her core. It was why she'd been so ready to introduce him to her kids, until Bess had pulled back on Deb's reins. But so far everything she'd learned about Luke only went along with exactly what she felt. That she had finally chosen the right man. Luke was one of the good ones. So if Luke could be trusted on his bold statement about burgers, Deb would know she was right. It was weird and maybe a little nuts. But it was Deb.

"I didn't say this place had the best ambiance," Luke said when he saw the way Deb was eyeing the license plates on the walls.

Would it really kill them to have a single piece of art?

"But the burgers ..." Luke continued.

"Are the best," Deb finished, and Luke grinned.

"How was work?" Deb asked, feeling it was time to move on in their conversation. At least until the burgers showed up.

"It was a good day. I had to meet with an upset client and was able to smooth things over," Luke said.

Deb cocked her head. "Was this client a female?" she asked with a raised eyebrow.

Luke laughed. "I have more to me than this face," he said as he pointed to his face, circling it with his finger, continuing to chuckle.

"Yeah, you have your incredible body as well," Deb said honestly. Then she laughed so that Luke wouldn't take her too seriously. But how could any female stay mad at Luke after looking at him? Deb knew she couldn't.

Luke laughed harder.

"Oh, and your charm. It's a pretty deadly combo," Deb added.

Luke placed his hand over hers, which was sitting on the table. "You do wonders for my confidence," he said. Deb was about to tell him she was only telling the truth when their burgers showed up.

The waitress placed them on their table as Deb's eyes went wide. The first burger was pretty typical with a single fat patty, some lettuce, tomato, onion, and a slice of cheese. But the second burger was what made Deb shocked. It was at least four times the size of the other burger with two of those fat patties, mushrooms, bacon, and who knew what else. How was one supposed to fit their mouth around that monstrosity? The waitress also brought a basket of fries, onion rings, and fried pickles.

"I can never decide on just one," Luke said when he saw Deb eying the sides. Deb was a sides girl, so she didn't mind. But she was very grateful that she'd added a couple of miles to her run this morning in anticipation of this dinner.

"So, I'm going to warn you. These dipping sauces are good. Really good. But maybe not best-in-the-city status," Luke said as he pointed to the numerous sauces that came with their sides. "The burger, however. I ordered the plain, basic burger because when you load on the toppings like this one," Luke pointed to the monster burger, "the burger itself can get a little lost. I wanted you to know this burger doesn't need all the extras. It's incredible, just like this." Luke pointed to the normal-sized burger that would've seemed huge if it wasn't sitting next to its gargantuan comrade.

Luke pushed the normal burger in front of Deb.

"Try it," he said, watching her with gleeful anticipation that made Deb really, really hope this burger was all Luke claimed it to be. She didn't want to put so much on a burger, but if it was as wonderful as Luke said it was, she could trust him. The thought made her stomach flip, and the idea that she was placing so much of their relationship's future on one silly burger felt a little insane. But it also felt really right. All that was left was for Deb to eat the burger. At least it smelled divine.

Deb took either side of the burger with her hands and began to bring it up to her mouth. The patty looked perfectly cooked, and although Deb wasn't a chef like Bess, she'd had quite a few burgers in her day and would maybe go so far as to call herself a connoisseur.

With her eyes closed, Deb took a bite, and the juices from the burger exploded into her mouth. She tasted char, fat, meat, along with the juices from the tomato, the crispness of the lettuce, and slight spice from the onion. There was a creamy sauce on the burger that had a bit more spice and acidity to break through all of the richness. Oh my gosh. Luke was right. She had placed her trust in the right place. More importantly, with the right person.

Deb grinned wide as she put down the burger.

"It's ..." she began, and then she had to take another bite. It was really *that* good. She chewed a few more times before saying, "the best burger I've ever had."

Luke smirked at Deb, obviously happy about being right. And Deb didn't even care that he was gloating because she still had that burger in her hands and she had every reason to trust the man in front of her.

Deb wondered if Luke would think that she was as nuts as she felt for how much stock she'd put into this one burger experience, but she somehow knew he would understand as well.

She'd have to tell him all about it one day soon, she thought, as a man cheered at the bar for something that had happened on the TV. Maybe in a bit more intimate of a setting.

"Do you want to try that one too?" Luke asked.

Deb would've said no before she tasted the first burger, but now it would be a crime not to try the monster burger. She had to imagine the deliciousness would only be amplified.

Deb nodded, and Luke laughed as he pushed the plate to her.

"How do I ...?" Deb turned the plate as she tilted her head to examine the burger.

"Eat it?" Luke asked.

Deb nodded.

"It gets messy," Luke said.

Deb looked at the burger. She trusted it would be worth it.

She somehow wrestled the monstrosity into submission and

brought it to her mouth. She chomped down and came away with more sauce on her face than in her mouth. But oh my gosh, this was literally burger heaven.

She moaned, and Luke laughed as Deb put down the burger and took the napkin he handed her.

Deb pushed the bigger burger back to Luke—there was no way she could handle more than a bite of that burger—although she'd remember that bite until the next time Luke brought her to this place. Then she set her sights on the sides.

"Why isn't this place packed?" Deb asked.

Luke, who had just taken his first bite and was now as covered with sauce as Deb had been, wiped his mouth with a napkin before answering, "Just wait about half an hour. This place will have a line out the door."

Deb believed it because even the fried pickle she'd just eaten was incredible.

"When did you find this burger?" Deb asked Luke, who had stopped trying to wipe his mouth after every bite and was only getting messier.

Deb felt her heart warm at the sight. There was something comforting about a man who didn't feel he had to be on his best behavior anymore. If Deb got her way, she hoped to continue unmasking more and more of this man who she hoped to spend a long time with.

"About a month after I started at my company twenty-five years ago. One of my coworkers at the time brought me here, and I brought Katya here that same night. It fast became one of our family favorites," Luke said.

Deb smiled at his admission, even as she wasn't quite sure how she felt. She knew she felt an unappreciated stab of jealousy for a few seconds before she realized what Luke bringing her here also meant. Luke was willing to share something with

Deb that had belonged to him and a woman he loved very much. That's what she needed to concentrate on.

After her last date and finding out about Luke's wife, Deb had come to the realization that she couldn't and wouldn't compete with a woman who was no longer here. That wouldn't help anyone. Especially Deb. And no one was making it a competition besides Deb. Why do that to herself and Luke? Katya was a part of Luke and a part of his family. Would Deb really want it any other way? So she chose to embrace Katya, even though Deb was sure she'd have a few bumps along the way. Hopefully that initial spike of jealously would be a lesson learned and would stop happening soon.

"What does Grace typically order?" Deb asked, continuing to talk about Luke's family because she realized that she'd talked a ton about her kids on their last two dates, but she hadn't asked Luke nearly enough about his family.

"The avocado burger. Same as her sister. I swear we personally fund at least one entire avocado farm a year," Luke said.

Deb laughed. "I might fund one as well," she admitted, acknowledging her own love for the green fruit.

Luke shook his head. "I should've known. I can't get away from women who love avocado," Luke said.

Deb smiled. "Did your wife order that burger as well?" she asked cautiously. She wasn't sure how much Luke was willing to share about Katya, but Deb realized she wanted to hear whatever he wanted to tell her. She was falling hard and fast for Luke, and Katya was a part of him. She didn't want to shy away from the subject just because it wasn't easy.

"Katya wasn't big on burgers. She came with us because we all loved it, but she usually ordered a salad, which she said were excellent as well. We all still teased her mercilessly for her choice," Luke said with a wistful smile.

Deb reached out to pat his hand softly. She wanted Luke to

talk to her, and she wanted to comfort him. Anything that would make her more a part of his world.

"She did love the fried pickles though," Luke said as he pointed to the one side that was almost all gone.

"Um, I guess I do too," Deb said as she looked at the nearly empty basket.

Luke chuckled.

"We don't have to talk about Katya if it makes you uncomfortable," Luke said.

Deb shook her head. "It did initially. But I'm dating you, Luke. That means getting to know you. And Katya is a part of you," Deb said, squeezing Luke's hand that he flipped to squeeze Deb's right back.

"No one has said that to me, but it's exactly how I feel. However, it's felt like I've had to hide that part of my life from the women I've dated."

Deb smiled softly. "I've never been very good about letting things stay hidden."

Luke smiled at her in return.

The rest of their evening was filled with stories of their families. Some of Luke's featured Katya, and some of Deb's even included Rich. Realizing Katya was a big part of Luke had helped Deb to realize Rich was a big part of her past, whether she liked it or not. She was still angry as heck at him, but she was beginning to hate him a little less. Which was leaps and bounds beyond what she could've hoped even a week before.

"I really like you, Deb," Luke said as he parked in front of the ferry terminal. He'd wanted to take Deb all the way back to Whisling, but she'd pointed out that that would defeat the purpose of her coming to Seattle so that he could get home to his daughters at an earlier hour. They'd compromised on Luke driving her to the ferry.

Luke took Deb's hand, tugging her a little closer so that their lips met.

Deb sighed in satisfaction as her world collided with Luke's, his hands enveloping her waist. Deb was grateful for and annoyed at the center console of Luke's car which kept them apart. Grateful because this kiss would've gone a whole lot deeper than Deb was ready for if it weren't there, but annoyed because, even if Deb wasn't ready for the kind of kiss that lasted for hours, it didn't mean she didn't want it.

She pulled back when she realized her ferry would probably be leaving at any moment and took in the incredibly good-looking man in front of her.

"I really like you too, Luke," Deb said before getting out of the car with a huge grin on her face.

As she floated toward the boat that would take her home, Deb knew she wasn't just falling for Luke anymore. She had fallen.

CHAPTER TWELVE

BESS HURRIED home from her shift at the truck and jumped into the shower before she contemplated the rest of her schedule for the day. Dax had told her he wanted as much time with her as possible so to let him know as soon as she was ready to go that afternoon.

Bess had had to stay at the truck until a little after two but turned over the reins at that point. She was pretty sure she could do a quick getting ready and be prepared to meet Dax by three. He was keeping the details of their date—*oh my goodness, I'm going on a date*—to himself.

He had warned Bess to wear casual and comfortable clothing that could be worn on a short walk or to a nice restaurant. Bess thought that was asking a whole lot of one outfit, but she was going to try.

She lamented that Deb was also going on a date that evening or else she would've enlisted her friend's help in getting ready. Gen was always busy now that she had Maddie and her growing bump, and Olivia would be picking up her girls from school. Bess figured her best bet in seeking the support she needed to get ready was to FaceTime Lindsey. At the very least, Bess needed help in figuring out an outfit.

"So you need a day-to-night outfit," Lindsey said when Bess described what Dax had told her.

Lindsey seemed so nonchalant about it that Bess wondered if this was a thing. Was Bess that out of the loop? Yes, probably. Oh gosh, and she was going to go out on a date with a man who definitely knew all about these kinds of things. Bess felt her stomach nearly clog her throat.

"Mom, chill out," Lindsey said from the other side of the Facetime call. "It's a first date. With a nice guy. Granted, that guy might be the hottest man I've seen over the age of thirty—"

"Not helping, my dear daughter," Bess said.

Lindsey began to laugh. "He knows you mom. And he asked you out. That means he wants to spend time with you just the way you are. It will be wonderful," Lindsey said.

Bess was glad someone was so sure about that because she definitely wasn't.

Lindsey helped Bess decide on an outfit of jeans and a ruby tunic top that did wonders for her complexion. The problem was finding which jeans would work best, so Lindsey sent Bess deep into her closet. After she'd tried on every pair of pants she owned, Lindsey squealed when Bess put on a pair that she'd bought a few years before but had felt were too tight. For some reason, they'd stayed in her closet instead of being returned. Lindsey loved them and assured her mother that her booty looked *poppin'*. Bess hadn't realized that was her goal, but after the squeal, she figured it was a good thing and decided to go with it.

"Do you remember that leather jacket I got you for Christmas two years ago?" Lindsey asked.

Bess nodded, even though the last thing she wanted to do was pull that jacket out from the back of her closet. First the jeans, and now this? The jacket was gorgeous ... for a woman ten years younger than Bess.

"Bring that with you and put it on when it's time to get gussied up. That's a word you use, right?" Lindsey said, and Bess gave Lindsey a warning glance that just made her daughter laugh again.

"Also, pack that big, chunky, gold and pearl necklace that I convinced you to buy a few months back, and you'll be set," Lindsey said with a grin.

Bess gave a slow spin in front of the large mirror of her master bedroom closet after she'd done everything Lindsey had instructed. She had done her makeup and straightened her shoulder length hair that typically held a bit of a wave. She wore the ruby tunic and *poppin'* jeans.

Lindsey wolf-whistled from her side of the call since she'd instructed her mom to call her back as soon as she was ready to head out the door.

"You look gorgeous, Mom," Lindsey said with a genuineness that Bess didn't often get to hear from her daughter. "Dax won't know what hit him." She paused. "So if you marry him, do I have to call him Dad?"

And there was her jokester daughter.

Bess glared at the screen and walked over to turn the call off.

"Just kidding, just kidding!" Lindsey screeched before calling out final pointers. "Remember the jacket, and wear your heeled black boots."

Bess nodded as she ticked the items in her head. She'd texted Dax a few minutes before, so she was pretty sure he'd be by soon.

"Oh, and Mom, make sure you find out if he's a good kisser," Lindsey said.

This time Bess did turn off the call on her cackling daughter.

The doorbell rang, and Bess felt her heartrate ratchet up to nearly impossible speeds. This was it. She was officially dating. Was she ready for this? Did it matter if she wasn't? Dax was already at the door.

But Bess realized she *was* ready for this. She was ready to have a nice time with a nice guy. She didn't know if she was ready for anything more than that, if Jon had fully let go of the heart he'd held for so long. But Bess could go out and have a good time. She owed that to herself after the year she'd had.

DAX PULLED Bess's chair out for her as they were both seated in the upscale teppanyaki restaurant Dax had chosen for dinner.

He'd really surprised her with his choice of activity and then again with their dinner location, and Bess was loving every minute of their date. They'd had so much fun and such incredible conversations, the kind that could only happen between two people who really cared about one another. Dax had even explained that he had only waited for so long to ask Bess out because he didn't want to move in too quickly after her divorce. He was tempted to ask her out on his front porch that fateful day with the cookies but had decided to wait until Bess seemed really ready for something new. And it was only after this time with Dax that Bess thought maybe she was ready?

"I'm a little bit ashamed to admit I've lived on Whisling my entire life and have never been to the Space Needle until today," Bess said as she remembered the gorgeous city views she'd enjoyed from the top of the building. When Dax had told her that was what they were going to do, she'd been thrilled. It was one of those things she'd always wanted to try, but when tourist attractions were in your own backyard, it was easy to put them off for things more urgent ... or just life. Today Bess had experienced the sights and wonders of Seattle in a way she never had before, and she had Dax to thank for that.

"Did you like it?" Dax asked as he leaned in toward Bess, and Bess felt her stomach flip. The man was absolutely beautiful with his blue eyes that looked a little stormy in the low light of the restaurant.

"I loved it. It was the perfect activity for today. Thank you," Bess said.

Dax smiled. "I aim to please," he said with a confident smile. "And a little birdy may have told me it was something you've always wanted to do."

"Smart little birdy," Bess said, and Dax laughed as the chef came to their grill and began taking orders.

The chef began throwing items on the grill as a waitress brought over soups. Bess grinned after taking her first sip of the rich miso broth.

"Japanese food is one of my favorites," Dax said as the chef twirled his metal spatulas and then flipped them through the air, catching them just before he began flipping vegetables onto the huge, stainless steel griddle.

"Me too," Bess said. "I guess that's one bonus of moving back to the west coast? Lots and lots of Asian cuisine."

Dax nodded. "Nashville had a few hot spots that offered great Japanese fare but nothing like LA."

Bess didn't respond as the chef lit an onion tower on fire, and she leaned back when the heat of the fire hit her.

"How does that trick not get old?" Dax asked.

Bess smiled. It was exactly what she'd been thinking. She'd seen the onion tower at every teppanyaki place she'd ever eaten at, yet it was still a sight to behold every time.

"Speaking of LA, are you going back soon?" Bess asked as the waitress came back with salads and the chef began to dump their veggies onto their plates.

"Probably in the next few days or so. There's only so much I can do remotely, and adding Jen to my client list is only going to make things busier."

"But that's great, right?" Bess asked.

Dax nodded. "It's what I've been working toward my whole life," he said as he stabbed at a piece of zucchini.

"That's incredible, Dax. Not everyone gets to realize their dreams," Bess said as she thought about her own dream of running her food truck. She knew she awoke every morning feeling wonder at the fact that she'd somehow gotten her idea off the ground and was actually beginning to bring in income. There was something powerful about seeing the imaginings inside of your mind come to life, then having that venture make money for you.

"It is. But it also has me thinking about other things. Life passes us so fast, ya know?"

Bess nodded immediately because that was a thought she had nearly every day. How had her life come to this place where her babies were all grown and she had no idea what a *poppin'* booty was? She used to know the right phrases for what you wanted your butt to look like as three adorable kiddos had run around her ankles. Now she was here.

She looked up at Dax. Not that here was a bad place to be.

The chef placed Dax's steak on his plate and Bess's chicken on hers, reminding Bess that she was falling behind in her eating. She still had all of her veggies and half of her salad left in front of her.

Bess filled her mouth with more salad as Dax continued to speak. "I've just been wondering if I've been focusing on the right parts of my life. I think I figured as long as I worked hard, everything else would fall into place. I never figured I'd be north of forty and still single."

That was a wonder to Bess as well. How had a successful, kind, funny and really gorgeous man stayed single for so long?

"I figured the right woman would fall into my lap at the right time. Maybe all I had to do was wait until today," Dax said.

Bess felt goosebumps erupt on her arms. Was he talking about her? Was she the right woman for him?

"I know you're here and I'll be there, but we can figure that out," Dax said. Then he looked at Bess's face. "I'm scaring you off, aren't I?"

Bess shook her head, but she wasn't sure. She wasn't exactly scared; maybe shocked was the appropriate word. She still couldn't understand how she'd even snagged Dax's attention. Now it seemed like he was telling her she was in the running for snagging his heart.

"I promise I don't usually come on so strong, especially on a first date. But I really like you, Bess. You have to know how special you are," Dax said.

Bess's heart flipped. She couldn't remember the last time she'd been told she was special, especially in the genuine way Dax had said the words. With no expectation of anything in return.

"You are a catch, Dax Penn." Bess finally found some words, and they felt right as she heard them spoken.

"That's what I've been told," Dax said with a smirk, and Bess laughed as the chef dished up some fried rice and then shut down his griddle for the time being.

Dax focused on his food, so Bess did the same, but she wasn't sure how much she'd be able to stomach since Dax continued to shoot longing glances in her direction. How could a man like Dax long for a woman like Bess?

Dinner was over way too quickly, and before Bess knew it, they were back on the ferry to Whisling.

"You really planned the perfect outing for me," Bess said as she stood next to Dax on the deck of the ferry.

The days were getting shorter and the nights cooler, so Bess was more than grateful for the leather jacket Lindsey had told her to bring. In fact, she was grateful for all the help she'd received in choosing her outfit considering Dax had called her beautiful two times. And she might've caught him checking out her *poppin'* booty.

"I was hoping that would be the case," Dax said as Bess shivered. Between the chilly evening and the wind coming off the water, even her leather jacket wasn't quite enough.

Bess felt herself encircled by strong arms, and Dax's warmth poured through Bess, heating her up in more ways than one.

Bess had been about to say more regarding the date but found the words weren't coming so easily now that her entire body had relaxed into Dax's arms. How was it possible to feel so comfortable and excited at the same time?

"Am I your first date since Jon?" Dax asked. The man sure didn't beat around the bush. And Bess couldn't be more grateful. After being out of the dating scene for so long, the last thing she needed was a man who played games.

Bess nodded.

"I always thought the guy was a lucky bastard. I can't believe he was stupid enough to let you go," Dax said.

Bess just shrugged from within Dax's embrace.

"You don't know what you've got until you lose it," Dax added, and Bess realized that was the case for her as well. Jon had done a terrible thing to her. One she was just starting to forgive. But the years before had been really good. And Bess had taken the man in her life for granted, imagining he'd always be there.

But she didn't want to be thinking about Jon as she was in the arms of a handsome man who really liked her.

The ferry pulled up to the dock in Whisling as the captain asked over the loudspeaker for everyone to get back into their cars.

Dax let go of Bess to lead her by the small of her back to his car, opening her door for her and then circling the car to get to his own.

"Do you work tomorrow?" Dax asked.

Bess nodded. "The lunch shift again," she said. "But it was really nice to have someone else cook for me tonight."

Dax shot Bess a grin as he started to drive off the ferry.

"I'd like to have someone else cook for you some other night before I go as well," Dax said.

Bess had to admit it was a pretty smooth way to ask for another date. She paused, remembering their most recent conversation. Why did the conversation that lingered in her mind have to be about Jon? They'd talked about all kinds of things in the last seven hours—really amazing conversations that had left Bess feeling alive. But her thoughts wouldn't leave Jon.

"Probably not this week, huh?" Dax asked as he took a left on the main drive on Whisling Island that would take them back to their neighborhood.

"I had a great time," Bess said, and Dax nodded. "I *want* to be ready for another date."

She pursed her lips as she wondered why she wasn't. Dax was incredible. Anything a woman could ever want. He was everything Bess wanted, except for the fact that he lived so far away. But Dax had made it seem as if the distance wasn't a big deal, that they'd be able to figure out how to make it work with ease. So why was it so hard for her to just enjoy this moment and say yes to another date?

"I want you to be ready for another date too," Dax said. "I don't want to take you on another date until you're sure that's what you want. Because you deserve to have exactly what you want, Bess."

Bess felt tears prick her eyes at the kindness of Dax's words. Why couldn't she just fall for him? It would be so easy ... if it weren't so hard.

"Jon is still a lucky bastard," Dax joked as he pulled into Bess's driveway.

"You could've just driven home," Bess said as she pointed to the driveway next to hers.

"Nah," Dax said as he got out of the car and then hurried around to open Bess's door. "You deserve first-class service."

Dax kept his distance as he walked up Bess's driveway with her and then onto the porch.

"I like you, Dax," Bess said, feeling like she needed Dax to know the full truth instead of just what he'd surmised. "But I'm still confused. Jon was a part of my life for most of it. And I'm not sure what life is like without him yet."

Dax nodded.

"I thought that might be the case. I hoped a month was enough, but I should've given you more time. I just really wanted to go on a date with the most beautiful woman I know."

Bess wanted to scoff at that. Dax hob-nobbed with country music stars, movie stars, all kinds of stars, while Bess was a flashlight at best. But she decided to accept the compliment with grace.

"I'm glad you didn't give me more time, Dax. I needed this. I needed you," Bess said, causing Dax to look down at her in a way that made her stomach tumble.

Bess raised herself to her tip toes and placed a careful kiss on Dax's cheek. She wanted to miss her location badly but knew a kiss further south would only serve to confuse the both of them more.

Dax grinned as he backed his way down the porch steps. "Give me the word, Bess. I'll be back."

Man, the guy was dangerously charming.

Dax finally turned around as he reached Bess's driveway and entered his car just to pull it the few feet into his own driveway.

He got out of the car and met Bess's eyes. With just the light of the moon and a few distant street lights, Bess wasn't sure what Dax was trying to tell her with his gaze. But given the context of the evening, Bess was pretty sure it was something good.

"Good night, Bess," Dax called out.

Bess waved and then turned to open her door before she could do something foolish, like run into Dax's arms. Because, heaven help her, she wanted to call him back right now, even if it was premature. She wanted to be ready for a man like Dax. But it just wasn't right yet. However, Bess smiled at the thought. Maybe one day their timing would be right, and Bess could only imagine what a day that would be.

CHAPTER THIRTEEN

IT HAD BEEN a little over a week since the blessed day when Gen and Levi found out they were going to have a baby girl. Each day Gen had awakened with a smile, knowing she was going to have two girls and Maddie was going to have a baby sister. A sister. Gen's life would've been vastly different without her own nearly-perfect sister, Bess. And now her girls would have one another the way Gen had Bess. Gen could think of no greater gift for her daughters.

But Levi. The man had been in a mood, and Gen wasn't sure what to do about it. She was sure his bad attitude couldn't be just about the gender reveal. She figured something must be going on at work, but when she'd asked him about it, he'd responded, distractedly, that everything at work was just great. She then assumed the mood was about something Gen had done because this couldn't be just about having a girl instead of a boy. Her husband couldn't be that shallow. So she tried to go over her past actions but found nothing lacking.

It was only after that final reflection that Gen couldn't deny it. Levi's mood had truly begun the same day of the gender ultrasound. This was all about having a girl. And that got Gen upset.

Was her grown husband really throwing this kind of pity party because he wasn't getting a son?

Gen took a figurative step back and realized her anger would do nothing, so she allowed Levi some time to grieve his lost future. Gen could somewhat understand. The prospect of Gen ever getting pregnant again was pretty much nonexistent. This was their one shot at a baby. And Levi really wanted a son.

So Gen gave him time to grieve. But evidently, ten days was her limit. Because when Levi came through the garage door still sullen that evening, Gen was done.

She waited until Maddie had eaten and was in bed before talking to Levi. He was going to come out of this conversation in a better mood if it killed Gen. She was the pregnant one. Shouldn't she be the one to be this irritable?

Gen cornered Levi as he was washing the dishes.

"Levi," Gen said, and Levi looked up to meet his wife's gaze.

Gen waited for Levi to respond in some way, but he just looked at her.

"Is this about the baby?" Gen asked.

Levi turned his attention back to the pot he was scrubbing.

"Is what about the baby?" he asked.

Gen swore she could see red. He better not be trying to play the denial card.

"This mood. Levi, it has to stop," Gen said, placing a hand on Levi's arm. She hoped it was a gentle touch, but she was a bit too angry to just be gentle.

"Gen, I'm not sure what you're—" Levi began, and Gen squeezed. She was done pretending everything was fine. Levi needed to be done as well.

"Levi. I have not worked my butt off for years to get this family back together only to have you push me away now. I have cried too many tears, stayed up too many nights, had way too many conversations with you and my therapist for us to stop here. So move forward with me, Levi. Now." Gen wasn't going to give Levi the option to quit either. She wasn't sure what was bugging him, but it felt too big to ignore. It would fester. And festering things, when left alone, could often destroy. Gen was not going to allow that.

Levi rinsed his hands, turned off the water, and then turned to face his wife.

"I know you have," Levi said. "I'm trying to work through this. I don't want to burden you."

Gen shook her head as she placed her hands on her hips. "This mood. It's been a burden." Gen wasn't sure if her sassiness was from her frustration or her pregnancy, but judging by Levi's small smile, he was more amused than annoyed at the way Gen was dealing with this.

"Okay. That's fair. I don't know how to say this without sounding like a horrible person, Gen," Levi said.

"Then sound like a horrible person. I've loved you through thick and thin. I'm not going to stop now," Gen said as she crossed her arms under her ever-growing chest.

Levi's eyes met hers, seeking something out. He must've found whatever he was looking for because he began to speak.

"This isn't about not having a boy. It's about having another girl," Levi said, leaving Gen just as confused.

"Do you want to know why I wanted to have a boy so badly?" Levi said.

Gen assumed she knew but let Levi go on.

"We've got a baby girl. A beautiful, perfect baby girl who has stolen my heart," Levi said.

That much Gen knew.

"But Gen. This new baby had to be a boy. Because a boy that came from the two of us, he'd be different. I'd love him so much too. But ..."

What was Levi getting at?

"I'm scared, Gen. I'm scared that this baby in your belly, the combination of me and you, the daughter of the one woman I love more than life itself ... I'm scared she is going to steal every part of me, heart and soul. So then what will be left for Maddie?" Levi asked. "I'm afraid I'll love this baby girl so much, I won't love Maddie anymore."

Tears fell down Levi's cheeks at his admission, and Gen pulled her big lug of a husband into her arms. She got it. She understood what he was saying because she too had worried about having enough love for both of her children. She understood why those thoughts would tear him apart. Maddie not only deserved but needed Levi's love. He was her one surviving birth parent. Gen loved Maddie like her own, but Levi would always be special to Maddie, just the way it should be.

But man was her husband stupid. If he'd only asked Gen, she could've told him that wasn't the way love worked. Why was it that men were so insistent on figuring things out for themselves? He could've saved them all this week and a half of moodiness if he'd just talked to Gen. But they were here now. For that, Gen was grateful.

"What you said would totally make sense," Gen said as Levi pulled out of her hug and leaned back against the sink, "If love were finite. But it's not, you idiot."

Levi began to chuckle.

"What? It's the truth. With this new baby, our love will just grow. When Maddie got here, did you take some of the love you had for me and give it to her?" Gen asked.

"No," Levi said, shaking his head. "But that's different."

"Be that as it may, you don't have to split your daughter love between your two girls. Maddie will always be your first daughter. That doesn't mean you can't love baby number two as much, right?"

Levi shook his head. "Of course not. You're this baby's mom."

"But when you look at your sweet, adorable daughters, their mothers won't matter. Levi, how could you love Maddie any less than you do today? Hasn't your love for her only grown? I know mine has."

Levi nodded slowly.

"That won't change because of this baby. Your love for Maddie can't lessen. It's impossible," Gen said.

Levi seemed to finally understand as a smile lit his face.

"So celebrate this daughter with me and Maddie. We are both thrilled."

"When you say it like that ..." Levi began.

"You sound stupid?" Gen finished.

Levi laughed. "Yeah."

Levi wound his arms around Gen and pulled her in close, just where she loved to be.

"How did I get so lucky to have such a smart and gorgeous wife?" Levi asked.

"I really don't know," Gen said as she shrugged before Levi laughed and then captured her lips with a kiss.

Gen could've stayed there forever, but mother nature's call had become louder and stronger with every passing day of Gen's pregnancy, and she had to go immediately.

She pulled out of Levi's arms and rushed to the bathroom.

Gen would've never believed that Levi's issues stemmed from his worry about not loving enough. Her husband was the most loving man she knew.

As she was about to get off the toilet, Gen glanced down at her pants. That was when she saw it. Bright red spots on her underwear that hadn't been there before.

Her stomach dropped when she realized what it had to be. Blood.

Her eyes began to fill with tears as she willed herself to calm down. It could be anything. It didn't have to be bad.

She hurried out of the bathroom and ran to find her phone.

"Gen," Levi said, rushing to follow his wife into the living room as he noticed the paleness of Gen's face.

Gen dialed the number for the on-call nurse at her OBGYN's and placed the phone against her ear before saying to Levi, "I'm bleeding."

Levi's eyes went wide as he put a gentle hand on his wife's belly.

"She's okay," Levi tried to assure.

Finally someone picked up, and Gen explained what had happened.

"Okay. That doesn't sound great," the on-call nurse said.

Gen's heart dropped. No. No, no, no.

"I think you need to come in, Gen," the nurse said softly. "Gen, I know this baby has been long awaited. Let's hope for the best but prepare for the worst."

Gen replayed those words and then asked, "Do you think I could be losing the baby?"

"Let's hope not."

CHAPTER FOURTEEN

OLIVIA HAD COME AWAY from their first family therapy session with one goal. She'd realized she had been relying on Bart too much. She'd been hoping he'd step up and fill the hole in the girls' lives that he'd created. But Olivia realized she couldn't count on that. Sure, if Bart came around, that would be fantastic. But she knew Bart, and that didn't seem likely.

Besides, she'd done this to her girls. Chosen a charmer with no substance to be their father. So now it was up to her to fix it. She wasn't going to wait for Bart to take them out on fun excursions. She'd do so much fun stuff with the girls, they wouldn't feel the need for their father to do those things for them. Olivia could and would be everything they needed and hopefully all they wanted.

And she was starting with a night out at the movies. The girls were always begging to go to the theater, but Olivia usually had an excuse as to why watching the same movie a few months later at home was much better. Bart had taken them the few times they'd gone to the actual movie theater, and they'd loved every minute of it.

Olivia couldn't wait for Bart this time. She was a single

mom, but she would not allow her kids to suffer because of her and Bart's mistakes. And as wonderful as it had been for Dean to fill Bart's role at the beach, Olivia realized that couldn't be the road she took either. Dean was his own man and would hopefully start a family of his own one day. Even if Olivia held ambitions deep in the recesses of her heart that she could be that woman to start a family with Dean, she knew it wasn't likely. She carried too much baggage, wore too many scars for a sweet man like Dean. So Dean would be a wonderful friend to her and the girls for now, but in the end, Olivia had to be enough.

"Can I get candy?" Pearl asked as they got out of the car and headed toward the theater.

The sun had already set, and Olivia wondered for the third time if going to such a late movie—the movie was starting right about the same time the girls usually went to bed—was a good idea. But there was something magical about the lights of the theater that shone in the night sky. And Olivia needed this night to be magical.

"You can share a box of candy," Olivia said, knowing she couldn't say no to the high sugar treat but also knowing her girls had to go to bed sometime this century. And those movie theater boxes of candy were huge.

"And we can get popcorn?" Rachel asked.

Olivia nodded, causing both of her girls to squeal in delight.

She was doing the right thing.

Olivia held a hand in both of hers as the three of them walked toward the theater, entering the main doors and then going to stand in line for their movie tickets. Olivia had thought about buying their tickets online to save time, but waiting in line was all part of the experience. And that was what they were after tonight.

"I think sour gummies," Rachel said as Olivia realized she'd missed a part of her girls' conversation. It didn't take a genius to figure out they were having a hard time deciding on one candy.

"I want chocolate," Pearl whined, and Olivia shot her a look. She may be trying to spoil her girls a bit that evening, but she would not put up with whining.

Pearl looked properly reprimanded and smiled at her mom, showing that her whining wouldn't continue, as Olivia searched for a quick solution to their problems.

"How about chocolate covered gummy bears?" Olivia offered, and both girls nodded quickly. Thank goodness.

"Hey, that's Dean," Pearl said loudly. Then without warning, she wandered two lines over to where Dean stood with a woman who had her back to Olivia.

Olivia swallowed as she noted the closeness between the couple. The physical distance between them was nearly nonexistent. There was a whole lot spoken with that lack of distance. Dean was on a date.

Olivia's hands went clammy and her throat felt too wide for her neck. It took her a moment to gather herself, swallow, and then realize that Pearl was on the verge of interrupting said date.

"Pearl," Olivia tried to call out, but it was too late.

Pearl had already tugged on Dean's arm and gotten his attention.

Olivia watched as Dean swept Pearl up into a hug and only put her down when there was a wide grin covering the little girl's entire face.

"Can I go say *hi* too?" Olivia could see the way her older daughter longed to join in the moment, and Olivia couldn't deny her.

"Sure. But just say hi and then bring Pearl back," Olivia instructed.

Rachel nodded and then scurried toward Dean, who gave

Rachel a hug of her own and then turned around when Rachel pointed behind Dean to where Olivia stood. Both Dean and the woman with him turned toward Olivia, and she offered them both a wave when she saw that she knew Dean's date.

Charlotte Cummings was a nice woman who lived off of Elliot Drive, the main street that circumnavigated Whisling Island. She had a son who was in Pearl's grade but went to one of the other elementary schools. Olivia and Charlotte weren't friends but were friendly enough that they often waved to one another when they saw each other in public. Pearl and Charlotte's son had been on the same soccer team back when they were both in kindergarten, so Olivia had spoken to Charlotte enough to know that Charlotte had been a single mom for all of her son's life. The father had skipped out days after their baby was born. Charlotte had been young, too young to raise a kid on her own, so she'd moved to the island to be closer to her grandparents who had retired to the island.

Olivia watched as Charlotte interacted with her girls, friendly and sweet as she always was, and then Charlotte looked up at Dean with stars in her eyes. Olivia didn't blame her. Olivia would've looked at Dean the same way if they had a real chance at anything between them. Sure, Dean had crushed on her back in high school and they'd had their moments since, but Dean needed a woman just like Charlotte. The dark-haired, brown-eyed beauty was not only younger than Olivia, she seemingly had less baggage and would probably be ready to have more children immediately. Dean wanted kids, and Charlotte could give them to him.

Olivia, if she was honest with herself, didn't know if she wanted to have any more children. Granted, with the right guy ... but no. She and Dean were a cute fantasy, one that should never be a reality. He was her good friend. The man she'd relied on for everything after Bart. It only made sense that she'd developed a small crush.

Olivia had just gotten to the counter to buy her tickets and waved her daughters back to her. By the time Olivia received her tickets for the kids movie she and the girls were going to, Pearl and Rachel were back, talking a million miles a minute about Dean and his pretty new friend.

"I think she's Freddie's mom," Pearl told Rachel with authority.

"Freddie from your soccer team?" Rachel asked, and Pearl nodded.

"No she's not. Freddie's mom had blonde hair," Rachel said, causing Pearl to look up at Olivia for help.

"She is Freddie's mom. That season was a long time ago. It would be easy to forget the color of Freddie's mom's hair," Olivia said as she got the candy and popcorn for her girls and a large diet soda for herself. She decided she deserved a treat. Olivia was still excited to be doing this for her girls, but it was late— Olivia often went to bed soon after the girls did—and she'd just witnessed her Dean on a date with another woman. *Dean, not my Dean.*

"Told you," Pearl said as Olivia handed off the candy to Pearl and the popcorn to Rachel.

"Be kind," Olivia warned, and Rachel shot her sister a smirk.

These girls would one day be the best of friends. Olivia was sure of it. As long as they survived their childhood.

"She's so pretty," Pearl said as they walked toward their theater, and Olivia did a quick scan of the hall behind them to make sure Dean and Charlotte wouldn't overhear their conversation.

"She's not as pretty as mommy," Rachel said with a frown.

"Rachel, what have I told you about comparing?" Olivia said, even though a small part of her wanted to cheer that her sweet daughter had stuck up for her. But it was more important for Rachel to remember that saying someone was one thing didn't mean another person couldn't be the same thing as well. We didn't have to put another down in order to lift ourselves. It was a good reminder for Rachel's mother as well.

"Not to do it," Rachel muttered as Pearl said, "I don't think she's prettier than mommy."

Olivia sighed. This was a lesson she'd have to work on more. But probably not in a movie theater.

The girls rushed to the seats at the front of the theater as soon as they made their way into the dark space, saving a seat in the middle of them for Olivia. She grinned at the thoughtful gesture. She was going to live these days when her daughters actually still enjoyed her company to the fullest.

As the movie started, Olivia did the very thing she'd warned her daughters not to do. Comparisons were really helpful to no one. But Olivia's brain didn't seem to agree. *Is Charlotte prettier than me?* Because even as she tried to explain away her feelings for Dean, he'd never asked her out. And he had asked Charlotte. Sure, Olivia hadn't been forthcoming with her own attraction to the man. But if Dean really liked her in that way, wouldn't he have risked it and at least tested the waters? But there had been no testing of waters, therefore Dean must not be interested. And the green-eyed monster raging in Olivia's belly told her she very much was.

She leaned her head against the back of her theater seat, trying to focus on the cartoon fairies in front of her instead of the thoughts of her all too appealing landlord.

But what if Dean had asked her out? What would Olivia have said?

She knew what she would've said. No. Because as much as it would've killed her, she wasn't ready for a man like Dean. The kind of man she'd want to give forever to.

So he should go out with Charlotte and enjoy himself because Dean deserved that. And she should be happy with what she had: a great friend who was often a listening ear and an amazing male role model for her girls, who not only made time for them but enjoyed every minute of it. Olivia couldn't and shouldn't want more.

But that didn't keep her from staying up long after the girls were in bed to listen for the moment Dean's car pulled into their shared driveway.

Olivia, like a creeper, snuck over to her window—she'd long since turned out the lights so Dean wouldn't know that she'd waited up for him. She looked at the clock that read ten minutes past midnight.

Did that mean it was a good date? What time did good dates end? What time did bad dates end?

Olivia peered through her blinds as she watched Dean get out of his car. His movement wasn't jaunty. Olivia didn't know why she'd been expecting jaunty, but she had been. At least if it had been a good date.

But his movements weren't tired and slow either. He was moving at a very normal rate. And that told Olivia nothing.

Although what *she* was doing was telling herself everything about what she felt for Dean. But she was going to ignore that for the time being.

Dean walked up his driveway and then paused at the top of it as he faced Olivia's cottage in his backyard. Olivia ducked behind the wall under her window, her heart beating too fast. Had he seen her? Is that why he was looking at her house?

After a minute of letting her heart return to a normal rate, Olivia hazarded another gaze and saw Dean's attention still on her home. But he wasn't looking at the window she was peeking out of. He was staring at her door.

Was he thinking about her? Did he want to come to her door and see if she was up?

Olivia scrambled to her feet, ready to throw open her door, when she reminded herself of all of her earlier thoughts. The thought of losing Dean hurt. But the thought of dating Dean before she was ready or asking him to choose her over Charlotte or any number of the things she'd be hoping when she opened that door couldn't happen. She wasn't ready. She couldn't do that to her girls, to Dean, or to herself.

So instead of going to the door, Olivia walked back to her bedroom and curled up in her warm blankets. Even if Dean wanted to talk to her in that moment, he'd get over it. He'd get over Olivia. And he'd be much better off.

CHAPTER FIFTEEN

"MRS. REDDING, I'm going to need you to change into this gown and the doctor will be in shortly," Melda, the nurse who had taken Gen's vitals, said as she held up a paper thin hospital gown and then motioned toward the bathroom.

The nurse spoke calmly, at complete odds with the way Gen felt. Her insides felt as if they'd been on a wild roller-coaster ride, and she was about two seconds away from crying. Bess had come over as soon as Gen had called and was at her home watching a sleeping Maddie so that Levi could go to the hospital with Gen.

Gen honestly didn't know if she could bear to get the news alone that their baby no longer had a heartbeat. She was pretty sure she wouldn't be able to handle the news at all.

Levi held open the bathroom door, the expression on his face a mixture of incredible pain and a gallant attempt at trying to smile. Gen would've laughed at that face if she wasn't so near devastation. Would they really come this far only to have everything stolen from them?

Gen changed quickly and saw that she had a few more red spots on the maxi pad that she'd put on her underwear before leaving for the hospital. More blood. The thought threatened to ruin her, but she somehow managed another thought. It's not gushing. That had to be a good sign.

With that hope, Gen left the bathroom and crawled into the sheets of the hospital bed. Levi brought a chair to the bedside and held Gen's hand in silence as they waited for the doctor. What news would she bring?

"Hi, Gen," Dr. Worthing, the on-call doctor at the hospital that night, said as she entered the hospital room with a sterile look on her face. Why was the doctor's face so hard to read? Gen wanted to look at Dr. Worthing's face and know if she should be worried or not, but Gen saw nothing. No happiness, no worry, no anger, no contentment ... nothing. Gen wondered fleetingly if that look was something they'd taught in medical school.

Gen didn't respond to Dr. Worthing's greeting since the doctor went straight to work connecting Gen to monitors.

"How long have you been spotting?" Dr. Worthing asked.

"Just for the last couple of hours, I think. I saw it when I went to pee at about seven pm," Gen said.

Dr. Worthing nodded, still showing nothing in her expression or demeanor. But as soon as the doctor connected a large strap around Gen's belly, Gen heard the most blessed sound in the world.

"Is that a heartbeat?" Levi asked, and Dr. Worthing nodded.

Gen let out a breath that helped her entire body to deflate. She had been so anxious, she'd been breathing much to rapidly.

Levi seemed to do the same as he slumped against the chair behind him.

"That's good news, right?" Gen asked.

Dr. Worthing nodded but didn't say more. Could there still be something terribly wrong? The doctor brought the ultrasound wand to Gen's belly and suddenly a picture of Gen and Levi's baby appeared on a monitor next to Gen.

Dr. Worthing studied it as she moved the wand around Gen's belly and then pushed and prodded Gen's baby.

"Bleeding in the second trimester isn't common, but it does happen," Dr. Worthing said as she continued to inspect the monitor for signs of what, Gen wasn't sure.

Why couldn't the nurses or Dr. Worthing have started with this information? Gen had thought all bleeding this late in pregnancy could only mean terrible things. But then Gen reminded herself that for many women, bleeding this late in pregnancy did mean terrible things. And if the nurses had assured her that bleeding was something that sometimes happened only to have come in here and heard no heart beat? Gen felt a tear slip down her cheek just at the thought.

She had been so blessed. What had happened to her was much better than the alternative. They weren't out of the woods, but they had a heartbeat.

"So she's okay?" Levi asked, still gripping Gen's hand.

The doctor nodded. "Everything looks about perfect," she said as she put the wand away.

"Really?" Gen asked, wanting to believe the best but still fearful of the worst.

Dr. Worthing finally smiled. "Really."

Gen nodded, the weight of the evening evaporating away, as Dr. Worthing unstrapped her from the monitors and then gave Gen a paper towel to wipe away the slimy gunk she'd rubbed around for the ultrasound.

"You should get another ultrasound at your next checkup just to be sure. But baby girl looks amazing, Gen," Dr. Worthing assured before she left the room.

"She's okay," Levi breathed as soon as the doctor left.

"She's okay," Gen said as she squeezed Levi's hand.

Gen looked over to see tears spilling down Levi's cheeks as he dropped his face to Gen's belly. "I just couldn't ... if something had happened to her tonight when it seemed like I didn't want her...."

"Whoa, whoa, whoa," Gen said. "I always knew you wanted her, Levi. She always knew that too," Gen added, holding her belly and daughter.

"But what I said tonight ..." Levi said.

"Came from a place of fear."

"I should have been smarter and stronger," Levi said against Gen's belly.

"Luckily you have a wife who's both," Gen teased, and Levi laughed, causing Gen's stomach to shake as well.

"Yeah, luckily I do," Levi said before kissing Gen's belly.

"You know you girls are my whole life," Levi said, and Gen nodded.

"If we lost her ..." Levi's voice broke, and Gen ran a hand through his already tousled hair.

"We didn't. She's here and she's well," Gen said as she lovingly stroked her poor husband's head. They'd been through so much. Gen knew they could've managed this trial too; she was just so grateful they didn't have to.

"I love you, Gen Redding," Levi whispered, his lips fluttering against Gen's belly.

Gen breathed out a deep sigh, feeling weirdly content in that hospital bed. "I love you."

CHAPTER SIXTEEN

"MADDIE!" Allen, Lily's husband, exclaimed excitedly as the toddler ran into the Anderson home without so much as a knock. But since Gen and Maddie came over every morning, Lily and Allen had dispensed with the need to knock on their door. Maddie just pushed her way in, always greeted by Allen first.

Gen had called early that morning to let Lily know what had happened the night before, just in case Maddie was acting weird for any reason. The cute little girl did tend to hear and feel more than most two-year-olds. Lily had just relayed the tale to Allen when Maddie came rushing through their front door.

Allen picked Maddie up from off the ground and twirled her through the air. Maddie giggled uncontrollably, and as soon as Allen set her down, she begged to be picked up again.

Lily giggled along with the little girl—Lily loved when her husband played with children almost as much as the children loved it—but her attention was soon grabbed by the sweet cooing that came from the carrier against her chest where she held her own little girl. Amelia was now six months old, but she still hated being anywhere other than attached to Lily. Her baby was beginning to feel heavy and was doing a number on her back because of the hours she carried Amelia around, but Lily secretly still enjoyed it. Especially because Allen always came through with a massage for Lily every night.

Maddie fell to the ground, her laughter finally overcoming her, and she continued to giggle as she lay on the carpet of Lily's small living room. Allen had a huge grin on his face as he took a step back from Maddie. Lily was sure Allen needed to go finish getting ready for work, but Allen loved kids; it was part of what had drawn Lily to him in the first place. Watching Allen with Maddie told Lily just how marvelous of a dad he was going to be as Amelia got older. Not that Allen wasn't a fantastic dad now. He woke up for every feeding with Amelia, changing her diaper before handing her off to Lily to be fed. But as Amelia grew into enjoying more and more playtime, Lily knew Allen would really come alive in his fatherhood role.

"One more time?" Maddie begged, and Lily could see Allen was about to give in. But he really had to get going. School would be starting in thirty minutes, and no one wanted an unmanned class of kindergarteners on the loose.

"How about we eat some breakfast?" Lily offered to Maddie, nodding for Allen to take the opening and run. Gen had texted Lily that the morning had been a busy one and asked if Lily could feed Maddie breakfast. Of course Lily didn't mind. Maddie, a girl who loved her food, often asked for a second breakfast when she got to Lily's anyway.

Allen grinned at his wife before stepping into their bedroom just off the living room.

The bungalow Allen and Lily rented was tiny, but Lily reminded herself they didn't need much right now. And their home was always so full of love. The front entry of the home went right into the small, outdated kitchen. If there was anything Lily could change about the home, it would be the marigold cabinets and matching countertops. The kitchen was open concept with the living room, a small, bar counter and a difference in flooring the only things that kept the rooms from completely merging into one. The door to the one bedroom (which contained a bathroom) of the home was right off the living room, and that was it. But living on a teacher's salary, especially on an island, was rough. Lily's supplementary income babysitting Maddie served to make things a little less tight, but Lily didn't care about how tight their budget was. Because Allen had brought Lily home to her family. She lived a few streets from her sister and a five-minute drive from her parents. Lily was blessed.

"Can I have ce-ral?" Maddie asked, and Lily nodded with a grin. This was a girl after her own heart. Lily could eat cereal for breakfast, lunch, and dinner.

Maddie ran to the pantry off of the kitchen, opening the door on her own and then pointing up to the purple box of bran and raisins that was her favorite.

Lily got the box and then the milk jug from the fridge, making Maddie her breakfast as the little girl climbed into her own booster seat, which Lily kept on one of the chairs at her table.

Lily sat the bowl of cereal in front of Maddie, and Maddie dug in immediately.

"I was hungry," Maddie informed, causing Lily to laugh. Her soft laughter was joined by deep laughter as Allen joined them in the kitchen.

Allen brought his prepacked lunch out of the fridge before wandering to the pantry to grab a bagel and pop it into the toaster.

"So everything turned out okay, right? With the b-a-b-y?" Allen spelled the last word because they were never safe from the little ears that sat at their table.

Lily nodded, realizing she hadn't quite finished relaying to Allen what Gen had told her. "Thank goodness. Those two have been through enough already."

Allen's bagel jumped out of the toaster, and Allen grabbed the pieces, putting them on a plate before buttering them up.

"They have," Allen agreed as he reached over to kiss his wife on the cheek. And then, as if that wasn't enough, he pulled her into a hug, swaying back and forth with Lily in his arms.

Lily would never tire of how demonstrative Allen was with his love for her, but this wasn't the time for slow dancing in the kitchen.

"You need to hurry or you'll be late," Lily admonished as she looked up at the clock. Allen was always cutting it close on time and drove just a bit too fast for Lily's liking in order to make up for it.

"I'll be fine. But you're right, I need to get going," Allen said as he put his bagel on a paper towel and then bent down to hug Maddie from behind, kissed Amelia's head, and then claimed his wife's lips.

"I love you," Allen said as he pulled away from his wife.

"I love you. Now go." Lily ushered Allen out the door and then listened as he peeled out of the driveway.

Lily shook her head, but she'd known exactly what she was getting when she married Allen. They'd dated for nearly four years and had been with one another for the ups and downs of life. She'd weathered his parents' divorce with him, and he'd weathered a terrible job with her. Allen had been her knight in shining armor when the father of the kids she was nannying tried to make a move on her and Lily had known he was the man for her ever since.

But wasn't that love? Weathering any storm together? And Lily knew she and Allen had that.

CHAPTER SEVENTEEN

DEB RUSHED around her home as she tidied up one final time, her heart racing more from what was to come that evening than the speed with which she was working.

"Mom, calm down," Wes warned as he sat on the couch, careful not to mess up any of the cushions there since Deb had already chewed him out for messing up the couch she'd just carefully placed the pillows on.

Wes and Bailee were home for an evening together. Finally. They'd gone to London for their week with their father and both had had to jump right back into the hustle of school in order to not get behind in their studies. Because of that busyness, Deb had worried that she wouldn't get any time with her children until the holidays. But thankfully, with a little finagling, Deb had been lucky enough to get this one dinner with both of her children three weekends after their break. And she was going to take full advantage of it by introducing them to Luke.

It might've been a blessing in disguise that her children hadn't been available to meet Luke until a month later than Deb had first wanted it to happen. She might've been rushing it then, but she was more than ready for it now. She and Luke were now firmer than ever in their commitment for one another. And Deb was on cloud nine.

So when the evening became available, she and Luke had decided this was it. Carpe diem. Her kids needed to meet him, and she needed to meet his kids. The time was right. They were only growing more serious in their relationship and their feelings for one another.

However, Deb was now second guessing their decision to do everything at once. All of the introductions needed to be done, but maybe not all on one night. Having one of them meet one set of kids would've been hard enough, but bringing them together like this for a family Sunday dinner? That seemed like turning on a ticking time bomb. Were they being idiots?

But it was too late to second guess now. Luke and his girls were minutes away, and Wes and Bailee were right there with her. This was happening. Ready or not.

"If they're going to hate us because of your cushion positioning, I'm sorry to say, Mom, but this is doomed to fail," Bailee teased, and Deb felt a small smile appear on her lips.

"And she's back," Wes said to his mom. "We thought we lost ya to the crazy side for a minute."

Deb took one of her lovely cushions and swatted Wes with it before placing it back just as nicely as she'd had it.

Wes whooped, getting out of Deb's way, and jogged toward the kitchen and the delicious smells coming from there.

Deb wasn't a terrible cook, but she'd decided for this occasion she needed more than her mediocre skills. She'd enlisted the help of Bess, who always cooked a huge Sunday meal for her own family, to make extras of everything for Deb's crew. Her best friend was one of a kind.

"One of the things I miss the most when I'm at school," Wes said as he swiped a brownie from the overflowing plate, Deb too far away to stop him.

"Aren't you supposed to miss your mom's cooking, not her best friend's?" Deb asked.

Wes shrugged. "Whose cooking would you miss?" he asked, and Deb grinned. Her boy was right. Except her boy was no longer a boy, coming in at six-foot-two with broad shoulders and rich auburn hair. If Bailee was to be believed, Wes created quite the stir with the ladies on their campus, much to Bailee's chagrin.

The doorbell rang, and Deb froze. Wes's foolishness had eased her anxiousness for a few minutes, but now they were here. What if her kids hated Luke? What if his kids hated her? They couldn't keep dating. But Deb liked Luke ... a lot.

"Do you want me to get it?" Wes offered, and that got Deb moving. She did not want her son to be on the other side of the door if Luke was feeling the same way she was. Which was a whole lot of nervous. He probably wasn't quite the bundle of nerves Deb was because he was the calm and collected one when it came to the two of them, but he knew how much was riding on this meal as well. And Deb liked to think Luke adored her nearly as much as she adored him.

Deb pushed Wes out of the way as she opened the door with a smile.

"Hello," Deb said a little too cheerily with a smile that was much too wide. She needed to dial it back.

Luke brushed a kiss across Deb's lips in greeting as both of his girls looked away. But Deb did notice small smiles on their faces as they did so. That was a good sign, right?

Luke held a bouquet of roses in one hand and a big tin of popcorn in the other.

"You are a genius," Deb whispered as Luke walked into her home with Bailee's favorite flowers and Wes's favorite snack food. Deb really wished she'd thought to do the same. The best she'd done was find out Luke's daughters' favorite foods and had

Bess prepare them. Thankfully, spaghetti and brownies were right in Bess's wheelhouse.

"Something smells delicious," Luke said as he and his daughters entered the home while Wes and Bailee came into the foyer, causing the entire party to converge in the four-foot-squared space.

"It's Bess," Wes said, already outing Deb before she even had a chance to introduce herself to Luke's girls. Deb nudged Wes in the ribs, and her son had the decency to look like he felt a little remorse.

"I guess introductions are in order?" Deb asked, still sounding too cheery. She needed to cut it out.

"I'm Wes," Deb's son said with a grin, making his way to Luke to receive his tin of popcorn. Okay, Deb now forgave him.

"Luke," Luke said as he shook Wes's hand. Then Wes offered his outstretched hand to Luke's daughters.

"This is Clara," Luke said, pointing his chin to his daughter who was about half an inch taller than the other. Clara had dark hair like Luke's, but her eyes were a bright, sunny blue. Both girls were tall like their father and, as Luke had informed Deb, their mother. Clara had to be a good four inches taller than Deb.

"And this is Grace," Luke said, pointing to his younger daughter who Deb had been told was the spitting image of Katya. Grace exuded the quality she'd been named for as she stepped forward to shake Wes's hand and then turned her attention to Bailee. Grace's once long blonde hair, Deb had seen several pictures of both girls, was now an adorable pixie cut that framed her beautiful heart-shaped face.

"I'm Bailee," Bailee said as she shook Grace's hand, then her sister's, and then Luke's. She received the flowers Luke offered with a huge grin on her face. Bailee really was a sucker for roses.

"And I'm Deb," Deb said, following her daughter's lead to greet their guests.

"Now that that's out of the way, let's eat," Wes said, and Deb smiled. Wes might be a pain in her bottom half the time, but he would also be much-needed comic relief for the evening.

Wes led the group into the kitchen where Bailee had set the table with their best china.

Luke and Grace took their seats, but Clara paused by her seat, taking a look around the kitchen. "I love the combination of blue and white," Clara said as she gazed at the dark blue cabinets and the white marble countertop.

Clara's gaze paused on some of the pieces of art Deb had created just for the kitchen. Although her favorite medium was canvas and paints, Deb had sculpted a couple of white vases and painted patterns on them in the same color as her cabinets. She'd also recently created a huge abstract painting for the wall right next to her table. Bess had asked for something for the same place in her home when she'd decided to take down the wedding photo of herself and Jon that had occupied the space for years, so Deb had made a painting for herself at the same time. Bess's had been white and gray, the tones of her kitchen, while Deb had brought the vibrant blue into her own.

"Thank you," Deb said as she brought over the last of the dishes Bess had prepared and then took her own seat. "Sometimes I wonder if I overdid the blue, but my artist soul longs for color."

Clara sat across from Deb, shaking her head. "I love the blue. And you have just the right amount."

Deb asked Wes to give a blessing on the food before telling everyone to dig in.

"Your dad told me you love interior design. You're thinking about going to school for it next year?" Deb asked, continuing the conversation she'd begun with Clara. She noticed that to her left, Wes and Luke were talking about his recent trip to London to see his dad while on her right, Bailee and Grace were complimenting the others' clothes. Deb had hoped the three girls' love for fashion would help Luke's daughters bond with Bailee.

Clara nodded as she twirled spaghetti around her fork. "I'm really hoping I can get into the Design Institute of San Diego next year," she said.

Deb grinned. "That's quite the aspiration," she said. "I have it on good authority that your dad is quite proud of what you've accomplished and how hard you're working."

"Let's just hope DISD feels the same way," Clara joked, and Deb laughed.

"So is accounting really as boring as it seems?" Bailee asked Luke from the opposite end of the table, causing all other conversations to cease.

"Bailee," Deb reprimanded, but Luke and his daughters both started laughing.

"It is," Clara assured as Grace's giggles only increased.

"It isn't boring," Luke said to Bailee. Then he turned to his girls. "It's an acquired taste."

Clara groaned, telling Deb this was probably an argument Luke often used, and Grace continued to giggle.

"Mom would always tease Dad that when he said 'acquired taste,' what he meant was he was immune to how boring his job is," Grace said. Then she paused, her eyes wide.

Deb realized Grace didn't know if it was okay to bring their mother up in conversation, and Deb knew she had to assure both girls immediately.

"Your dad has told me quite a bit about your mom, but I feel like I'm getting to know her even better just meeting you girls. I'd love for you to share your memories of her with me ... whenever you feel comfortable to do so, of course," Deb said, feeling her voice shake as she spoke. She didn't want to overstep her boundaries, but she also needed the girls to feel she was on their side.

She got a warm smile from Grace, a nod of approval from Clara, and then saw tears glittering in Luke's eyes.

"Do you feel the same way about Dad?" Wes asked, leaning his elbows on the table as he turned to look at Deb.

Deb sat back in her seat, surprised by the question. And yet she should've been expecting it. This was her instigator, Wes, after all. She realized she needed to give her son an answer.

Deb looked for the overwhelming feelings of betrayal and frustration that usually came whenever her children talked about Rich, but they weren't there. Deb searched for a moment longer to find the seething anger, but that too was gone. It was only with that pain and anger no longer blinding her that Deb realized her own children were feeling the acute loss of a parent as much as Luke's daughters were. She'd been so gracious when it came to Luke's daughters' mother, but she hadn't done the same for her own children. She'd only made them feel as if she wished their father had never existed. How was that fair to anyone?

Deb met Wes's eyes, which were full of laughter—he thought he'd made some great joke. But when he looked at his mom, the humor fled.

"I do," Deb said with a nod at Wes, and then she turned to Bailee.

Bailee cocked her head in confusion. "You want us to tell you things we remember about Dad? Things we *like* about him?"

Deb nodded, feeling terrible that she'd let her anger lead her for so long. But somehow, someway, she'd begun to heal and could finally see beyond her own pain.

"I'd like that," Deb said honestly, and Wes narrowed his eyes as he looked at his mom. She could tell he was looking to see if this was all an act that would end as soon as their guests left.

"Really," Deb said.

Wes nodded his approval. "Sounds good to me," he said as he dug back into his food.

Deb smiled as the conversation resumed around the table, all three girls talking about some kind of app that Deb wasn't sure her tech-challenged brain could keep up with and Luke and Wes concentrating on their food.

The meal was going swimmingly. The kids seemed to like one another, she was sure her kids were already half in love with Luke, and Luke's daughters maybe even liked Deb.

She sighed in relief as she pondered another gift this meal had brought. She'd forgiven Rich. Really forgiven him. The anger, the pain, the betrayal. All of it was gone. She wouldn't be attempting to be his best friend anytime soon ... or ever. But she no longer wanted him to implode in a fiery inferno.

Deb didn't think it was just Luke and her relationship with him that had helped her come to this point. Although, Luke had been so patient with her, so she knew Luke had helped. But time had been a big factor, along with Deb pulling herself out of her own bitterness. She had to give herself a little credit, along with Wes and Bailee. Her children had also been a huge push in helping her let go of her pain. Now Deb was free. It was as if heavy chains had been lifted from her heart and soul. Deb hadn't felt lighter in years. She was definitely happier.

Deb met Luke's eyes from across the table, and they exchanged peaceful grins. She could see he was at ease in her home, at her table, and with her children. She felt the same way about him and his children.

As Deb twirled a bite of spaghetti around her fork, she remembered that she had wondered for months after her divorce whether she would ever be the same again. If life would ever be the same. That was all she'd wanted, to get back to who she'd been.

But things weren't the same, and she wasn't the same

woman. Nor did she now want to be. Her pain and trials had made her stronger. She hadn't melted in the furnace of her fears; she'd been fortified. The Deb who sat there at her table that night was a different woman from the one who'd sat there a year before. And that was a very good thing.

CHAPTER EIGHTEEN

BESS SAT in her car after she arrived home from dropping food off at Deb's for dinner that evening. She knew what, or rather who, was sitting in her home, awaiting her arrival. Bess wasn't sure she was ready to face him.

She drew in a deep breath as she looked to her right and gazed at the home Dax would hopefully be coming back to soon. They'd had some flirtatious interactions at the food truck and in their front yards before Dax had headed back to LA, but he hadn't asked her out again. He was giving her the space she needed, proving he was just as much a gentleman as he was charming and handsome. Bess was finding she liked the man more each moment she got to spend with him, but his life was out there and her life was right here.

Sometimes she wondered if she had done the right thing. In fact, she pondered that fact each and every day. A handsome, charming, funny, and intelligent man who was actually interested in Bess had appeared practically on her front door step, and she had turned him away. For all the right reasons—he was leaving and she was staying, she wasn't in the right headspace for a new relationship—but man, did she wish it could just be right. That everything would just work out beautifully.

However, if she was completely honest with herself, she knew the reason she wasn't ready for Dax. Bess wasn't sure she was completely over Jon, even though she knew it was stupid of her to still be hung up on the man. But it wasn't easy for her to walk away from a man whom she'd loved for most of her life, even if he didn't deserve her love. She wished she could just write him out of her life, but he'd forever be connected to her through their children. And that was why she was still sitting in her car instead of hurrying inside to spend time with her children.

Bess turned her attention back to her own home and her immediate future that lurked there. It was Sunday, and that meant Sunday dinner. Stephen, of all her children, had asked if his father could join them for dinner that evening. Even though Bess suspected this act of charity had almost everything to do with keeping Bess from the man next door and not an actual olive branch Stephen was extending to Jon, Bess had to help facilitate it. For Stephen's sake. Any time Stephen spent with his dad was important. Thus Bess was now going to have dinner with her ex. In her home. A Sunday night family dinner.

So here Bess sat, the man she liked in LA and the man who she was trying to move on from in her kitchen. Yes, nothing made sense.

When there were no more excuses left to keep Bess in the car, she got herself out of her seat and walked up her driveway. She looked over to the Penns again, part of her wishing Dax was still around to come out and join them. But that was a fantasy, and Bess guessed it was best left as a fantasy for now anyway. A dinner with Dax and Jon would be uncomfortable, at best. She was just being selfish to want Dax, a person who she knew was fully on her side, at the dinner with her. Her kids, as they should be, were neutral parties, and the man she'd been married to for thirty years kind of felt like the enemy.

Bess got to her front door and opened it, allowing the scents and smells of spaghetti and garlic bread to hit her nose. There was something about the smell of tomatoes and garlic that was just comforting.

"Mom, is that you?" Stephen called out.

He'd been attentive, maybe too attentive, ever since Bess had gone out with Dax over a month before, calling or texting Bess nearly every day, something her oldest had literally never done. Bess tried not to be annoyed that her son only cared to communicate with her now that she was dating. But she reminded herself his concern came from a good place.

"Yes, it is," Bess said as she entered the kitchen, sending a smile to each who sat at her table and then lingering on Jana. She had been the surprise of the evening. Stephen had called Bess about Jon and then had added that he hoped Jana would be coming as well. He'd extended the invitation to her but hadn't been sure whether she would accept it or not. When Bess had opened the door to see Jana with her son, Bess had been thrilled. Stephen deserved this second chance, but Jana was still a saint for giving it to him.

Bess saw that her family had dished dinner up while she'd been away and were now all seated around the table. They were all in the same seats they'd sat in for years with Jon next to Bess's seat. She drew in a deep breath. She could do this. For her children.

She and Jon had exchanged polite greetings when he'd first gotten there, but Bess had had to leave soon afterward to deliver the food to Deb. Now they were here. It was almost like taking a step into their past, except all of the hurt and betrayal was still there. Bess could remember vividly the way she'd felt the day Jon had told her, in this very kitchen, what he'd done.

But she had to push the hurt aside for the time being. She'd worked with her therapist, Dr. Bella, for long enough now that she understood what was healthy and what was not. And Bess truly believed what she was doing was a healthy way of dealing with the situation at hand. She would need to deal with her hurt later—maybe alone, maybe with Jon, but definitely not with her children present.

James offered a blessing on the food and the family dug in, passing plates of pasta, bread, and salad around the table.

Bess served herself a modest portion, her stomach still in a jumble from sitting next to Jon. She doubted she'd be eating much that evening.

"How is your family, Jana?" Bess asked as Jana placed the salad bowl back in the middle of the table.

"They're doing well. My little brother just got an interview with Stanford admissions," Jana said with a proud smile, which Stephen also wore. Stephen and Jana's brother, Tucker, had a special relationship. Bess knew Stephen had worked hard with the boy to get his essays ready to submit, even after he and Jana had parted ways.

"That's incredible," Bess said as she tried not to stare at the noticeable difference on Jana's hand. She no longer wore the ring Stephen had given her. It wasn't a shock, but Bess had been hoping that maybe since Jana was here, things were on their way back to normal for them. Bess still felt she'd had too great of a role in the demise of their relationship since Stephen had only pushed Jana away because Jon had cheated on Bess. If Bess had kept it all to herself then maybe ... but then she remembered that Jon's infidelity had been splashed all over the local news. She realized she couldn't have kept the matter just between her and Jon, even if she'd wanted to. But she still hurt for Jana ... and Stephen.

"My parents are remodeling their kitchen. I need to send

them pictures of what you've done here. I love it, Bess," Jana said.

This time it was Bess's turn to grin. She loved her new kitchen too. She sometimes missed the way it had been, but this change was what she'd needed.

"I would've never thought this table would look good painted white, but I think I like it better now than before. And you know I loved the original look," Jana added, and Bess nodded. Jana had often complimented their table, as had most other guests. The round table that could seat twelve was a show-stopper.

"Did you hear Lizzie had her baby?" Lindsey asked Jana about a mutual acquaintance, and the two fell into conversation about squishable cheeks and baby clothes.

James spoke to Stephen about the Seahawks, leaving Jon and Bess to their own devices. Bess wasn't sure what to say to the man she'd shared her life with who was now a practical stranger, so she focused on her food.

"I've heard wonderful things about your food truck," Jon said as he set his fork down on his plate. "Everyone I see from the island sings your praises. Not that I'm surprised. Your food has always been terrific."

Bess swallowed. That was nice. Jon was being nice. And she could be too. They were past the uncomfortable talks on her porch where she'd told him she needed him to leave because there was nothing left to say. They were beyond worrying about their future together because they knew they had none. She could do cordial, friendly. Just because this was the man she'd wanted forever with and had been robbed of that didn't mean she had to hold it against him eternally. Did it?

She looked around the table to see the pleasant conversations her children were engaged in. Bess couldn't ruin that.

"Thank you, Jon," Bess said as graciously as she could. Then she took a bite of spaghetti because she didn't know what else to say.

"And I like what you've done with the kitchen too," Jon said as his eyes lingered on the painting that now hung next to their table instead of the wedding portrait that had been there for years. Jon gazed at the canvas that was covered with an abstract pattern of grays and whites, something her talented best friend had whipped up in a day, and then looked back at Bess. "I definitely don't miss that wallpaper." Jon smiled, but Bess gasped.

"I thought you loved that wallpaper," she said as she thought about the hours they'd spent putting up the blue, yellow, and white floral pattern that Bess had loved so much.

"I love you, and you loved that wallpaper," Jon said.

Bess didn't miss that he'd used present tense for his first phrase and past tense for the last. That had been intentional.

But did it matter that Jon still loved her? Besides, she already knew that because of his declaration over the phone when he'd signed their divorce papers. So then why did hearing it in person, right at her table, hit her so hard? But Bess couldn't think about that. Not now.

"I did love that wallpaper. But we made the decision together," Bess said. She looked over at Jon, wondering how many times he'd let her have her way even if he hadn't liked it.

"We did. Bess, I would've done anything for you. I still would." Jon shrugged as if his admission didn't matter, but it did. Too much. Bess had known that once upon a time Jon would've done anything for her, but she had thought those days were long gone. There was having love for someone and there was being in love with someone. Bess had assumed Jon only felt the former for her anymore, but now?

"I've even stayed away because you asked me to. Even if I am still completely in love with you," Jon said softly.

Bess felt tears spring to her eyes. This was too much. Especially at a table surrounded by her children.

She got up and made an excuse of going to the sink to wash her hands, but she just needed space to breathe. Space to push Jon's admission out of her mind. If he was still in love with her, why was he dating again? If he was still in love with her, why go through with the divorce? If he was still in love with her ... why had he cheated?

The previous two questions Bess could venture to answer, but it was the last question that got her stuck, each and every time. She couldn't trust Jon nor his love for her until that question had a clear answer. He'd told her it had just happened, he hadn't meant for it to, and other lame and very cliché excuses. But it wasn't enough. Bess had endured hell this last year because of Jon's decision. If she let him back in and he did it again ... she would break. She knew she would. Keeping Jon away was pure survival.

"Mom, do you mind grabbing that second loaf of bread? James already ate the first one," Lindsey called out.

Bess pasted a smiled to her face before walking to the bread, placing it on a plate and walking back to the table.

This was one dinner with Jon. She could get through it and evaluate her feelings later. Her kids had already endured enough of Bess's breakdowns for a lifetime.

"I didn't eat it all on my own," James said, pumping his eyebrows in Lindsey's direction which earned him Lindsey's napkin in his face.

"Lindsey, no throwing at the table," Bess reprimanded, and her smile that she'd pasted on became genuine. She loved having all of her children around her table. Even when they threw napkins.

"Tell James to stop implying that I'm fat," Lindsey said.

James feigned a shocked look on his face. "I would never, Mom," he said.

"You'd better not. Your sister is beautiful," Bess said.

"Yes, she is," James agreed, and Lindsey's scowl lessened.

"Really, Sis. I just meant that you can keep up with me when it comes to bread eating. And we all know I have the kind of figure that makes all women envious," James said, placing his hands on his nearly nonexistent hips and causing his sister and the rest of the table to laugh.

Bess avoided conversation with Jon for the rest of dinner, and all too soon, her kids were leaving. Bess gave all the leftovers to James and then received a hug from each of her offspring and Jana. The crowd moved out the door, but Bess could see that Jon was still lingering.

"I know I blew it, Bess," Jon whispered as he took a hug Bess wasn't sure she was offering. "I know I don't deserve another chance. I know you deserve more than me. But that doesn't keep me from wanting both. I'd love to see a therapist with you. Get help. Because we were dang good together, Bess."

Jon let her go, and Bess felt out of breath. What had just happened?

Bess watched as Jon walked away with her children to his car, and she waved at the group until they drove away.

Jon's words played on repeat in her mind as Bess wondered what she should do. She knew if she was honest with herself, she still loved Jon too. At least a part of her did. But he was right; he didn't deserve a second chance. But did she?

CHAPTER NINETEEN

"MAYBE YOUR MOM wants to come with us this time?" Dean asked as he waited in Olivia's living room for the girls to be ready for their weekly outing to the beach. Even as the days had gotten chillier, the outings hadn't stopped. Although now all of them arrived at the beach much more bundled in clothing.

Olivia sat in her bedroom the same way she always had when Dean had come to pick up her girls for the past month. She'd avoided Dean ever since that movie night when she'd seen that he was out and dating. And he should be out finding someone new, especially if he wanted a family someday. But seeing Dean on a date holding another woman's hand with her own two eyes? Olivia had had to take a step back from their friendship.

But with Dean's invitation, Olivia could see he'd noticed the absence and wasn't going to let her go. Which was so like Dean. The incredible guy that he was still went on the beach outings with her daughters because they didn't deserve punishment— Bart would've discontinued the outings long before—and he also wouldn't let Olivia slink away because their friendship was important to him. He'd given her a few weeks of space, but now he was back, asking her to join them.

Dean was almost too good to be true. And that was why Olivia had to stay away from him. Because she knew what living with what appeared to be *too good to be true* was like. She'd experienced the hell of Bart breaking her heart time and time again.

And although she knew things were different with Dean—she could never see Dean breaking her heart on purpose—that didn't mean he wouldn't ever break her heart.

Because every man could. And the unexpectedness of a broken heart from an amazing man like Dean ... Olivia was too scared to even think about what that would do to her. She had seen heartbreak from Bart coming a mile away, and she'd nearly broken then.

However, this wasn't the moment to be worried about any of this. Dean hadn't asked Olivia out; he was just asking her to come to the beach with her girls. He just wanted to be her friend again. Olivia finally felt at a place where she could accept that olive branch without falling right back in love with the man who needed to be dating anyone other than her.

Olivia realized Dean's question demanded her attendance, so she came out of her bedroom and into the living room to join her girls, who were putting on their jackets, and Dean, who was sitting on her couch.

"Do you want to come, Mom?" Pearl looked up at Olivia with hope in her eyes that Olivia couldn't squelch.

"Sure," Olivia said to Pearl before looking at Dean, the smile on his face a little too self-satisfied. "Let me just grab a jacket."

Fall was nearly over on Whisling, and that meant winter was right around the corner, bringing chilly gusts to the beaches. Olivia adored spring and fall, but both seemed to give way to the next season all too fast.

Olivia slipped on her black windbreaker that had a bit of padding to also help with warmth and joined Rachel, Pearl, Buster, and Dean in the car Dean had waiting for her.

"And then he squished it. It was so gross." Rachel was telling Dean about the boy in her class who'd squished a worm that day, the same story she'd already told Olivia and then Pearl and then Olivia again. To say Rachel was traumatized was an understatement.

"Boys can be foolish," Dean said as he backed out of their driveway and made his way onto the road. "But do you want to know a secret?"

Olivia turned to see Rachel sit up in her seat, straining against her seatbelt to hear Dean's secret.

"Sometimes even big boys like me can be foolish too. That's why we all need a good girl like you to help us make better decisions," Dean said.

Rachel flopped back into her seat. The secret had not lived up to her standards. "I can't make Eli make good decisions. He doesn't listen to anyone. Not even Mrs. Golding," Rachel said as she crossed her arms across her chest.

"You can be foolish?" Pearl asked, her voice full of curiosity.

"I can. And I have been. Almost all men are," Dean said as he took a turn at the bottom of their street onto a road that would lead right to The Drive.

"Daddy was foolish," Pearl said quietly.

Olivia, who had been content just listening to the conversation until that point, now felt like it was time for her to intervene. But Dean beat her to it.

"He was. And I'm not saying you have to forgive him just because all boys are foolish. But maybe you can still love him? Because we all make mistakes. But I'm sure he still loves you."

Dean said exactly what Pearl needed to hear. She needed to believe that her father loved her. And Olivia, bitter as she was against Bart, knew that he did. Just in his own, as Dean would say, foolish way.

"Thank you," Olivia mouthed, and Dean sent her one of his dashing smiles that should really come with a warning. Olivia felt her stomach flip, so she turned her attention away from the attractive man at her side.

Dean soon pulled into a parking space in the lot off The Drive that was used for Ellis Beach, the island's most popular dog beach. Buster jumped out of the car as soon as the door was opened, and Olivia's girls got out nearly as quickly, all three running straight towards the sand.

"I'll find a stick; you can throw the ball first," Rachel instructed Pearl.

Pearl happily tossed the tennis ball down the sand, causing Buster to bound after it.

"Do you three always have such deep conversations on beach days?" Olivia asked, wondering what all she'd missed. She'd assumed it was mostly fun and games.

"No. The girls have never brought Bart up before. I think they felt safe to do so since you were there as well," Dean said as he stuck his hands into the pockets of his jacket.

He and Olivia made their way to the sand, trailing after the faster part of their group.

"I'm glad they did. They both needed to hear what you said. I think they trust what you say about Bart more than what I say. I think they know I will say or do anything to guard them. It makes them a little leery of what I say," Olivia said as she pulled on the gloves she found in her jacket pocket. The beach was even colder than she'd been anticipating.

"But the fact that they know that is priceless. They need to know their mom will do anything for them. That's the protection of childhood every kid deserves," Dean said.

Olivia smiled, even as she thought how lucky some kids would one day be to have Dean as their dad.

"Mom, watch this!" Rachel called as she threw a stick down the beach at the same time Pearl threw the ball. Poor Buster seemed torn but dashed after the ball and then brought it back to Pearl before going after the stick to return it to Rachel.

"So fun!" Olivia called over the wind and waves, and Rachel beamed before both girls threw their items again.

"I haven't seen you around for a couple of weeks," Dean said after the girls got into the groove of their game and no longer required all eyes on them. "Not since I saw you all at the movies."

Olivia felt her cheeks warm at the implication behind Dean's words. He knew exactly why Olivia hadn't been around. She thought about playing dumb—she could always say they saw plenty of one another, which they had in passing—but she knew what he meant. They hadn't had a conversation, just the two of them, since that day. She decided it was time for that conversation.

"Charlotte and I ..." Dean began, but Olivia put up a hand to stop him. She didn't deserve an explanation. And if she needed one, that would imply she cared more about Dean than just as a friend. Although that was the truth, Dean could not know that.

If, and it was a big if, Dean did want to pursue something with Olivia and if he knew she wanted that too, she just wasn't ready. She knew a man like Dean would wait for her, but she wouldn't do that to him. Because who knew when, or even if, Olivia would be in a place to be good enough for Dean? So she had to let him go. Especially if the woman ready for him was a woman as good as Charlotte.

"I really like Charlotte. I was thrilled to see the two of you together," Olivia said exuberantly, trying not to let Dean know the second part of what she'd said was a lie.

"Oh," Dean said as he kicked the toe of his sneaker against the hard sand. "Right. Yeah, she's great."

"Have you guys gone out again?" Olivia asked.

Dean shook his head.

Part of Olivia cheered, even as the smart part told her that wasn't what she wanted at all. She wanted Dean to date Charlotte and find happiness. Heaven knew he deserved it.

"But I'm thinking maybe I should ask her out again. She was nice," Dean said. Even though it wasn't a glowing endorsement, Olivia knew some of the other options Dean had on the island. Charlotte was definitely a better pick than most.

"Maybe you should," Olivia said as Pearl yelled for her attention, and both she and Dean watched the girls giggle as they played with Buster.

Olivia looked at the smiles on her girls' faces and then at the man at her side. He'd done that. And although she couldn't be what he needed—he gave so much more to her than she could ever give to him—she could at least try to express some of the immense gratitude she felt for him.

"Thank you," Olivia said.

Dean looked over at her. "You already said that," he replied with a smile.

"I know, but I need to say it again. I don't know what we would've done without you. These beach days, the cottage, your friendship. You've been our saving grace these past few months," Olivia said.

"You mean Buster has been," Dean joked.

"You and Buster. Really, truly, thank you," Olivia said.

With her last words, Olivia felt as if she were saying goodbye. It was silly because Dean was still her neighbor and landlord, and she knew whatever happened between them, he would always be there for her girls.

But it took a few moments of silence after her last words for

Olivia to realize what she was doing. She was giving Dean permission to move on from their strange arrangement. To completely give himself to the start of whatever he had with Charlotte. And as much as she didn't want to give Dean up—who would?—she had to. For him. *Because* she loved him.

CHAPTER TWENTY

GEN HELD her belly as all of her favorite women in her life greeted her before entering into Bess's living room. It had been months since her hospital scare, and she'd finally made it to this moment: eight months pregnant at her baby shower. She'd been dreaming of this party ever since she and Levi had said *I do*, and it was hard to believe the day was finally here.

The baby—she and Levi were still deciding on a name—kicked hard, letting her mama know what she felt about this party. She seemed to be thrilled too.

"Kate," Gen said as she hugged her receptionist from the salon and then turned to give Lily a hug as well. The sisters must've come together.

"Is Maddie here?" Kate asked, and Gen nodded. Bess had asked if Gen wanted her shower to be a family event instead of something just for Gen, but Levi had vetoed that idea immediately. He had no desire to attend any baby shower, even one for his own daughter. But Gen had brought Maddie along because she knew the toddler would love it. And judging by the giggling Gen was hearing from the next room, she'd been right.

"In the living room. Being spoiled by someone, I'm sure,"

Gen said, and Kate laughed. The girls at the salon all loved
Maddie, along with every other person in Gen's life. Gen appreciated that they'd all welcomed her daughter with open arms,
even though she'd come to them in an unconventional way.
Sure, there was still the odd island gossip who loved the sala-
ciousness of the story, but anyone who really knew and loved
the Reddings were already over how Maddie came to be a part
of their family. They were just grateful that she was.

"I think you should go take your seat of honor," Bess said as
she came into the foyer and ushered Gen into her living room,
which was packed with guests. As Gen passed the kitchen, she
saw Bess's chef, Alexis, hard at work. Deb was also in there,
running this way and that as she tried to keep things tidy.

Gen grinned at Bess's best friend who had lost a little of her
hard edge since becoming exclusive with Luke. The man had
been everything that Deb had needed, and Gen was pretty sure
Deb would be getting a ring on a specific finger someday
very soon.

Bess led Gen to an armchair that had been decorated with
pink streamers and had a banner across the top that read, *Cute
Belly Mama*.

Gen laughed at the description, loving Bess for finding a
phrase to describe Gen besides mom-to-be. Because of their
unique situation, Gen had never had a baby shower before. So
although she was experiencing all of this wonder for the first
time, she was very much already a mom, thanks to Maddie.

Bess often joked that Gen's belly wasn't anywhere near the
size Bess's had been with her three kids. She called herself "big
belly mama" to Gen's "cute belly mama." Thus the inspiration
for the sign.

Gen fell back into the comfy seat—she was past the point in
pregnancy where she could do anything gracefully—and looked
at the women who surrounded her. She met eyes with stylists

who had been with her since the beginning, listening to count-less tales of infertility woe. Then her eyes moved to Kate and Lily who'd been exactly who Gen needed when Maddie came into her life. There were Levi's mom and sister who had flown out just for the occasion, along with Gen's aunt and a few of her cousins who lived on the island. Bess had put up a framed photo of their mom, knowing the woman would not have missed the event for the world. Because even though the walls between Heaven and earth sometimes felt thin, they were still there. The photo was the best way to remind Gen that their mom was there in spirit.

Even though it had been fifteen years since their mom had passed, Gen still missed her every day. And it was moments like today where Gen felt the loss particularly acutely. But thank-fully she'd been left with Bess, the very best sister and some-times pseudo-mom a woman could ask for.

"Let's guess how big this cute belly is," Bess called out as Olivia walked around the room, allowing women to take however many connected squares of toilet paper they felt it would take to be long enough to encircle Gen's belly.

Bess and Deb both seemed to be in really good stages of life, but Olivia was the one who still worried Gen. All four of them had taken their turns wearing pasted-on smiles and stress lines around their eyes for a while after the betrayal of their husbands, but in the past year or so each of their smiles had become more genuine and their worry lines had been joined by laugh lines. However, Olivia's smile was back to looking worn, her eyes a little too sad.

Gen knew Olivia was trying her best to be cheerful, espe-cially on days like today that weren't about her. But Gen had gotten to know the woman well over the last many months, and she could see the strain in her demeanor. Gen wished Olivia could see her own worth.

The group laughed as Maddie took a single sheet of toilet paper as her guess, and Olivia circled back to Gen with her nearly empty roll.

"Do you want to guess?" Olivia asked.

Gen shook her head. "I think it would only depress me," she said.

The group laughed again as Olivia took a seat beside Gen and women came up to measure their paper chain around Gen's belly.

Lily was one of the last to measure her guess and had almost an exact fit.

"Go Lily!" Kate called out as the final women tried and Lily was officially declared the winner.

Olivia offered Lily the prize basket as Bess announced that lunch would be served. Many of the women hurried into the kitchen—Kate's excuse was that she had to serve a "starving Maddie"—knowing they didn't want to miss a meal cooked by Alexis, but Olivia stayed by Gen's side.

"Do you want me to get you some food?" Olivia asked, but Gen shook her head. She tried to eat as much as she could these days, but baby girl felt like she was taking up too much space, leaving nowhere left for food to go. So Gen would eat, just a little later when her breakfast had finally digested.

"How are you doing?" Gen asked the question that Olivia's demeanor begged to be asked. Gen didn't like Olivia's hunched shoulders or the dip of her chin.

"Fine," Olivia lied.

Gen shook her head. "I do hair, girl. I know when people are lying," she said, and Olivia laughed.

"Is it the girls?" Gen asked.

Olivia shook her head. "I mean, I wish they were creating a relationship with Bart, but Dean has been incredible. He takes them to the beach at least once a week, and he even started coaching Pearl's soccer team when her previous coach had to quit." The wistful smile on Olivia's face told Gen all she needed to know.

"It's Dean," Gen said.

Olivia nodded, looking too weary to try to lie anymore. "He's amazing," Olivia said.

"And he's dating Charlotte." That rumor had been a hot one for a while when the relationship had started a month or so ago, but it was now just a fact of life.

Olivia looked around the room to make sure no one was listening to them. "I think I love him. But I'm not good for him. My baggage," Olivia said.

"Have you stopped to think maybe he loves you too? And if that's the case, he must love your baggage as well. Because, of all people, he's seen it well. He's even carried some of it for you," Gen said.

Olivia stared at Gen with wide eyes. "I'd never thought of it like that," Olivia said. Then she shook her head. "But it doesn't matter anyway. He's with Charlotte. I think I'm going to go grab some food before it's gone."

Gen knew the last thing was said just as a way to escape, and Gen didn't blame Olivia. She was sure Olivia's situation seemed bleak to her, but Gen was quite hopeful that things would still work out for Olivia. Life had a way of doing that for good people. And Olivia was *good people*.

"So is this everything you dreamed of and more?" Bess asked.

Gen grinned. "Yes. Thank you," she said, beaming. "I am loving all of this pink." Gen pointed to the pink balloons, streamers, and confetti Bess had used to decorate the room.

"You're ready to be a two-girl mom," Bess said, and Gen nodded. She was.

Bess sat on the arm of Gen's chair and pulled her little sister into a side hug. "I don't think there are words to express just how thrilled I am for you, Gen. You have been through the worst of it, and you've come out smiling. Not many people could've done that."

Gen wasn't sure about that; Bess had been through some of the worst of it herself, and yet here she was smiling as well. Gen knew Bess was still confused about what to do about Jon. She'd confided in her sister what Jon had said at dinner over a month before and that he'd started texting in recent days. When Gen had found out that Bess was also texting with Dax, she'd teased her sister about juggling two men. Bess had a good sense of humor about it, even though she was struggling to know what to do, and she seemed to be handling this new stage of life well. Better than Gen would've.

"Pretty sure I learned from the best, Sis," Gen said, and Bess gave her a soft smile.

Bess looked around her home. Gen knew her well enough to guess what she was thinking. And Bess wasn't wrong. They'd been through a whole lot. Their lives now looked nothing like what they would've expected a year ago. And yet, here they were, better than ever.

"Somehow we passed through our hells and got our new beginnings. We're the lucky ones," Bess said as she patted Gen's belly.

The lucky ones. Gen mused on that for several seconds as Bess left for the kitchen.

Gen thought about her life, Levi, Maddie, her new baby girl, and even her salon. Without the detours life had thrown her, she might not've had any of these things in her life, much less all of them.

Deb walked in, handing Gen a huge plate of food that she would never finish as other women came back in from the kitchen. Gen gave Deb a smile of thanks that Deb was able to genuinely return.

Without her journey through the fire, Deb would've never found Luke. And, according to Deb, she'd never been more content. She now had two more girls in her life, Luke's daughters, whom she adored. And her newest art, depictions of darkness giving way to light, was selling better than anything Deb had ever done.

Gen's attention turned to Olivia who came back into the living room, laughing with Kate, and Gen remembered the broken woman at the reunion. Not the woman in the bathroom, after Bart had revealed all, but the woman wearing a mask who'd never been able to show the world her real self for lack of repercussions.

Olivia was still very much on her journey, they all were, but she was no longer afraid to be who she truly was. And that was leaps and bounds beyond where she had been.

And then Bess, sweet Bess, juggling two men. Gen knew even with her confusion now, Bess would never want to go back to life the way it had been before Jon cheated. She'd learned too much, come too far, to go back to being that woman who took love for granted and was too scared to dream. Old Bess would've never become a business woman, running her very own food truck. And she would've never juggled two men. Gen wouldn't stop teasing her about that one for a long time.

Gen smiled as she rubbed her belly and watched Maddie run through the crowd of women who loved her.

Bess was right. Because they'd each gotten their own new beginning, they were all the lucky ones.

Made in United States
Orlando, FL
15 November 2023

38978629R00134